HIGH PRAISE FOR JANE CANDIA COLEMAN
AND *TUMBLEWEED*!

"In this well-researched novel about the life of Allie Earp, Coleman successfully brings to life the exciting, unforgettable story of a nearly forgotten woman. With her sharp eye for detail, dialogue and her respect for the people she writes about, it's no wonder she's been nominated for a Pulitzer Prize."

—*Romantic Times BOOKreviews*

"It is a fascinating book, beautifully written, and highly recommended—a must read for Western fans."

—Romance Reviews Today

"Readers see a wider, deeper scope into the Earp legends from a woman who was with them through many of their adventures. Jane Candia Coleman will enthrall her audience with this fine tale."

—*Midwest Book Review*

A HARD ROAD

The trip West was as miserable as our first, but at the worst moments, when the wind that blew night and day scattered our fire and blew our breakfast across the prairie, when Becca was about to drive me mad with complaints there was Lilly to whom everything was new and different—her adventure come to reality.

"Sometimes I feel like such a dolt next to you," Lilly said one afternoon while collecting buffalo chips. "I can't believe you're the same sister who was always sick in bed with a book."

"We do what we have to. I never imagined any of this, either...not the country, not the farm, not what it's like to climb a mountain. Certainly not what it's like to be married."

"Is it wonderful?" Lilly was like Vinnie in her view of romance.

"Sometimes."

"Not always?" Her voice rose and cracked.

"Like life," I said. "You take the good along with the bad and make the best of it. And you learn who and what you are along the way. What else is there?"

Other *Leisure* books by Jane Candia Coleman:

TUMBLEWEED

Jane Candia Coleman

The Silver Queen

LEISURE BOOKS   NEW YORK CITY

A LEISURE BOOK®

January 2009

Published by special arrangement with Golden West Literary Agency.

Dorchester Publishing Co., Inc.
200 Madison Avenue
New York, NY 10016

ISBN 10: 0-8439-6105-8
ISBN 13: 978-0-8439-6105-8

The name "Leisure Books" and the stylized "L" with design are trademarks of Dorchester Publishing Co., Inc.

Printed in the United States of America.

10 9 8 7 6 5 4 3 2 1

Visit us on the web at www.dorchesterpub.com.

The Silver Queen

"When the gods wish to punish us
they answer our prayers."

Oscar Wilde
An Ideal Husband

Prologue

There was so much money! One day we were happily at work—I in the store and Horace as mayor of Leadville with a finger in every political pie—and the next we were rich as Midas. From then on, everything Horace Tabor touched turned to gold, or, rather, to silver, the silver that had been there all along, overlooked in the earlier, maddened rush for gold.

He waltzed me around the aisles of the store, me clutching my skirts so as not to knock things off the shelves. "We can live like kings, Gusta! Like emperors! Anything we want we can have. What do you want? Tell me and it's yours."

I stopped dancing and stared up into my husband's face. It was flushed with excitement and with another emotion I couldn't name.

"Nothing," I said truthfully. "There's nothing I want except what we already have."

He gave me a long, astonished look, and then threw back his head and laughed. At the sound of it, mocking and unfamiliar, my heart sank to my shoes, for it was at that moment that our lives diverged, that I knew I'd lost him, that more than twenty years of hard work and unity would, in the end, be forgotten, renounced as an embarrassment by a man who had or could buy anything in the world.

Chapter One

Maine, 1855

"There will be bloodshed. And it will end in civil war."
My father's words echoed in my head as I stood in the
Augusta station and said good bye to Horace Tabor on
a bitterly cold spring morning.

I clasped my hands together for warmth and to
keep them from trembling. "You'll be careful? Father
was right, you know. The Abolitionists and the pro-
slavers won't ever compromise. You . . . you might be
hurt." *Or even killed some place in Kansas.* Bleeding
Kansas was what they were calling it then, a name that
only increased my anxiety.

But I didn't say those words aloud. To speak them
would be tempting fate. Besides, over the last two
years I'd supported Horace's decision to join the New
England Immigrant Aid Company, a group of Abolitionists whose intent was to populate Kansas and by
sheer numbers defeat those who would vote to bring

another slave state into the Union. Instead, I bit my lip to keep from crying.

Horace was impatient—a young man in search of his fortune, lured by the idea of adventure and conquering the unknown Territory of Kansas. He had no qualms about leaving his future bride behind to wait and worry, and wanted no part of tears or mournful farewell.

"There's not a pro-slavery squatter born who could lick me, Gusta. This is my chance for a place of my own. Our chance, and I'm taking it." He put his big hands on my shoulders and pulled me close.

Actually my entire family approved of his idea. Like the rest of New England, we'd heard and read about the impassioned speeches of Eli Thayer as he toured the North in search of support for his army of immigrants, and we'd applauded when Amos Lawrence, a Pierce distant relative, began pouring huge amounts of money into the Immigrant Aid Company's coffers.

We Pierces were Unitarians, and we believed in the rights of men—and women, believed that slavery was unjust and a crime before God, and that it was our human duty to do all that we could to bring the evil practice to an end. Only a few years before, the publication of Harriet Stowe's *Uncle Tom's Cabin* had roused not only our town but much of the North. Mrs. Stowe was, at that time, living in Brunswick, Maine, in belief and heart one of us, an Abolitionist with a spine of granite and a way with words. And, though it was mentioned only by inference, it was understood that there was a house by the Kennebec River in Augusta with a secret room built solely to harbor runaway slaves.

Everyone we knew, with the exception of our cousin, President Franklin Pierce, was opposed to slavery in any form, but so far, at least in Maine, the opposition had been verbal. In Kansas men were killing each other over the right to own slaves, and, according to Father, Cousin Frank was to blame. The passage of the Kansas-Nebraska Act, which repealed the earlier Missouri Compromise, was, as Father put it: "Frank's way of avoiding his responsibility. No fight in him. None at all, damn his hide!"

In the end, he predicted, only war would solve the slavery problem. War and bloodshed. And the man I'd loved from my first glimpse of him was off to do battle.

Two years before, my father, William Pierce, had been awarded the contract to cut the granite and rebuild the Augusta State Asylum. On the train to Boston to hire more workers, he'd met Horace Tabor and his brother John, both of them master stonecutters in search of jobs, and both of them also fellow Abolitionists and excited by the promise of free land in Kansas and the chance to strike a blow for their belief.

Was it fate? I've often wondered. Is the tapestry of our lives already stitched and in place, so that all we can do is follow the threads that bind us? Whatever the answer, I fell in love at my first sight of Horace as he jumped down from the wagon and stood staring up at our big, white house. He was tall, with broad shoulders and a stonecutter's massive but careful hands, and at dinner that night his dark eyes twinkled whenever he caught me looking at him. Twinkled, as if he knew what I was feeling and felt the same.

That night, and every successive night, the talk at the table was of slavery and abolition, and I can still see Horace's face when he realized we were related, both to our weak President and to Lawrence, the fierce philanthropist.

"You've chosen the right side," he boomed, barely restraining himself from pounding a huge fist on my mother's well-laid table. "By gad, sir, the South, with Pierce's blessing, will split the country in half!"

Father paused in the act of carving the roast. "The country is already split. If and when you go to Kansas, I believe you'll find the war has already begun. On a small scale," he added, "but war, nonetheless."

I folded my hands in my lap and prayed Horace wouldn't go. Surely there was enough to keep him here, safe and well employed, and in no danger. It wouldn't be the last time I uttered such a prayer, only to find it useless in the face of Horace's determination. But I was helpless in the throes of my first adult emotion.

Something of my intensity must have reached him, for he leaned across the table and said: "What do you think of all this, Miss Augusta? Give us a woman's opinion."

He'd picked me out! Me! I unfolded my hands and dropped my napkin on the floor, but when I answered, my voice didn't waver. "It's written that we're all created equal, Mister Tabor. And I believe that's so. Not only men, but women as well. What equality means is not that we're all born with the same strengths, but that we should all have a chance in life to use those strengths, and the freedom to fight for that chance."

This was nothing more than what we all believed and lived by, but Horace was impressed. As he told me later, he'd not met many women who'd been educated or who were even able to express themselves. He reached for his water glass and raised it in a toast.

"Well said. I salute you." Then he swallowed the contents in one gulp.

Father raised his glass, too. "My daughter has spoken for all of us. We believe in the rights of man. And woman," he added with a nod toward Mother and my sisters.

Stunned by the unaccustomed praise, I said nothing, but from that night on Horace sought me out at every opportunity. My sisters teased me about my beau, my mother in her roundabout fashion urged caution, and I ignored them all. At times I believed I'd die, if not from love then from the sheer excitement of being with Horace and listening as he talked about his dreams, wrapping my whole family up in his enthusiasm. That was one of his greatest charms—that boundless, fevered way of dreaming and making the achievement of those dreams sound both practical and assured. Even when he walked, he seemed to be filled with energy, always headed somewhere and sure of what awaited him.

From that first day, my health, which had kept me

bedridden for so much of childhood, began to improve. I willed it to improve, with all the strength I had. From that day my life took on meaning. And it was with my family's blessing that Horace was now leaving Maine in search of a homestead, a place in which he and I could make our home.

"Write me," I whispered. "And . . . and remember your promise not to drink very much."

As soon as the words came out, I regretted them. He frowned at me, his eyes dark. "You worry too much about nothing."

Well, I did. I knew his weaknesses as well as his strengths. He loved the company of men, the adulation of women. He loved politics and the idea that he was striking a blow against slavery. And he never hesitated to speak his mind to anyone who'd listen.

"Take care," I said, my voice drowned out by the whistle of the train.

He bent and kissed me, his lips warm in the cold air, and I clung to him, attempting to memorize the feel of his strong arms and how he towered over me, blocking out the gray sky.

"Stay well." He let me go, and picked up his bag. "I'll write. I'll be back as soon as I can. And . . . ,"— he grinned—"I'll try to be moderate in all my bad habits."

Then he was gone. I stood watching till the train was out of sight, then walked slowly back to where my brother Frank was waiting with the team.

He tucked a robe around me, and we headed back

to the house that would, I knew, feel empty without Horace to bring it to life.

Keep safe, keep safe, keep safe, I prayed all the way home, but there was, of course, no way to know if my prayer had been heard, or if it would be answered.

Chapter Two

Within two days I was back in bed with a cough and a fever, and I lay there aching, miserable, missing Horace, and wishing I'd gone against all the well-meaning advice and boarded the train to "Bleeding" Kansas with him.

From the window of the room I shared with my sisters who still lived at home—Melvina, who we called Vinnie, Vesta, Ruthie, and Lilly—I watched the last of the snow melt from the hay meadow and the first green appear on the trees by the creek that separated our farm from our granite quarry.

With nothing to do but read and sleep, I consoled myself remembering the evening Horace had carved our initials in the trunk of the huge maple just visible through the window. It was the evening he'd asked if I'd marry him. A late-spring twilight, and the lilacs were in bloom, their scent heavy and sweet on the air—like the kiss he gave me when, shy and overcome with the enormity of love, I'd said: "Yes."

"*You mean it?*" Those dark eyes of his registered both amazement and something like the beginning of happiness.

"Yes," I repeated, hardly believing that I, Augusta Pierce, had won this man.

He lifted me clear in the air, hands spanning my waist. "We'll make a life! By God, we will, you and me! You're good for me, Gusta. You've given me something to work for."

I put my arms around his neck. "I hope so," I said, knowing that, left to himself, he was often idle, caught up in momentary pleasures and those dreams that never left him.

"I know it. I've got big plans. You've heard them often enough. All that free land's out there for the taking. I'll make a new start, and nobody to tell me what to do or how to do it."

I smothered a smile. If anyone needed guidance, it was Horace, but that would come later. For the moment, I reveled in his closeness, his physical strength that was more than enough for us both. With him beside me, I knew I'd get well, that my strength would grow to equal his.

I said: "I love you."

Still holding me, he stared into my eyes. I saw myself reflected in his own—oval face, a mass of brown hair, a wide, delighted smile—skinny little Augusta, grown up, with a suitor of her own.

Did he answer? I've never been able to remember. What I see next is Horace, pocket knife in hand, carving two sets of initials into the stubborn maple bark with a heart surrounding them. Well, he was never a poet, never good with the kind of talk I'd read in books. I took the carving as his wordless affirmation.

But how I waited for his letters that were few, slow to reach me, and obviously meant to be shared with—and impress—my family.

Dear Augusta,

I hope this finds you well. The trip to Kansas was tough, thought we'd never get here, but here I am and on a hundred and sixty acres of my own. Looks like good land. I put up a cabin, with help from the others, and have started clearing the field for next year's crop.

We've named our little community Zeandale, and my neighbors have chosen me to represent them at a meeting of the Free State Legislature in Topeka. So now I'm in politics. You never thought you'd be a politician's wife, did you, in spite of all the talk?

Brother John is in Lawrence. That's about eighty miles from me so we don't see each other often, though he has plans to come back East with me and get married, too. When that will be, I can't say yet, as things are heating up here just as expected, especially along the border.

Governor Shannon, another of your cousin's appointees, was called in recently to stop the Missouri crowd from attacking Lawrence. He managed somehow, but it was a tricky time.

I go armed these days, but our homestead is pretty far from the real troubles around Lawrence and the border, so you can rest easy on that. Brother John writes me about another Vermonter named John Brown who's preaching some mighty strong words and is tough enough to back them up. He says Brown was ready to take on the Missourians all by himself in spite of Shannon's treaty.

Your father was right when he said the war had already started, but don't worry about me. I'm holed up in my cabin for what looks like a cold winter. Who can say, though, what will happen in the spring.

I'll close for now. Give my regards to your parents and know I think of you.

Haw

"What's he say?" My sister Vinnie plunked down on the bed beside me.

I handed her the letter.

"He's not very romantic," she said, when she'd read it. "He could have said something about missing you. He didn't even sign it with love."

Although secretly I'd thought the same, I leaped to his defense. "That's not how he is. And, besides, he knew you'd all want to read it. It wouldn't be . . . be correct to say anything else."

Vinnie was two years older than I was and practical about most matters, but at heart she was a confirmed believer in love's magic powers. Several years before, a friend had given us a copy of *Jane Eyre*, which we'd read cover to cover with much weeping over poor, orphaned

Jane. Vinnie had been particularly taken with Mr. Rochester's independent but vulnerable character.

"Don't you wish Horace was a little more like Mr. Rochester?" she asked. "You know? All alone out there on the cold prairie, and desperate. He sounds like he's having fun, war or not."

Oh, we were so very young and innocent! So, for that matter, was the world in which we lived. But that world, and we ourselves would soon be tested, scourged by wars both public and private.

I held out my hand for the letter. "Horace is Horace, and he suits me very well," I said, and that put an end to discussion or soul-searching for nearly twenty years.

The next year was not idle for me or for Horace. I worked on my trousseau, stitching tablecloths, napkins, quilts, and pillow cases, and did it happily as I considered each finished item a contribution to what would be our home be it on the Kansas prairie or anywhere else that life would take us.

Horace's letters came sporadically, usually long after we'd read about the latest violence in the newspaper, but I looked forward to them nonetheless as a link between us, a sign that he truly intended to return for me. Always I wrote back, restraining my own fervor— the letters of a young and untried girl desperately attempting to hint at passion. About the reality of passion, I knew nothing, and there are times when I think I still don't. Blame it on the culture, or on a strict New England upbringing, or simply on my own person—Augusta Pierce, possessed of a loving heart but blind to possibility. In old age, one can look back and realize one's flaws, but in the spring of youth, we lack that ability, a pity I know now, too late, too late.

In any event, as Father had predicted, the bloodshed in Kansas escalated month by month, culminating in the proslavery raid on Lawrence, where John Tabor was in the thick of it, having involved himself with John Brown. Brown, his sons, and possibly "our" John took retribution in the murder of a bunch of pro-slavers in a place named Pottawatomie Creek. "Our" John was imprisoned. Horace, fortunately, was not.

I breathed a sigh of relief when his letter came— the letter I'd been waiting for.

Dear Augusta,

Don't worry about what you may have heard or read in the papers. The reporters always get things wrong, as I've found out. I'll be back in early January, and John will be with me. It took some doing, some mighty swift talking to convince the sheriff he wasn't guilty of treason after the mess with old Brown, but he's out of jail and we're heading home to our brides.

Set the date, and I'll be there.

Yours,
Haw

"Well," Vinnie said, turning sharp-tongued, a trait inherited by all the Pierce women, sometimes to our regret, "at least now he's 'yours'."

* * *

Though it was winter, we cleaned house from attic to root cellar in preparation for the wedding. Mattresses were aired, bedding washed, floors waxed and polished till they were a danger to walk on. The silver shone, the windows sparkled inside and out. My brothers, Ed, Frank, and little Fred, were put into service, carrying mattresses, beating carpets, lugging cans of hot water, and did all without complaint, though I knew they'd rather have been sledding or trying out their new skates.

In spare moments, Mother worked on my dress, a beautiful but practical garment of dove gray wool with sleeves edged with Honiton lace and braid decorating the hem. Although I couldn't know it, in the years to come I'd wear that dress almost threadbare, and at the last cut up what was left for diapers without a qualm. All that remained was the lace, which I saved, it being too beautiful to throw away.

"Stand still, for goodness sake!" Mother was on her knees, tacking the braid to the hem, and I was fidgeting, unable to control my restlessness.

"What if he doesn't get here in time?" I asked.

The wedding had been set for the 31st of January, and already it was the middle of the month with no sign of Horace and no message.

"He'll be here. Don't fret." She hesitated, then went on slowly, searching for words. "After the wedding . . . you must let him do what he wants. It . . . it'll be a shock to you, but that's how married life is."

Amazed, I looked down at her bent head, at her

brown hair, thick and curly as my own but threaded with gray. As far as I knew, she'd never let Father do as he wanted once inside the house that she ran like a ship's captain.

"I don't understand," I said.

She sighed, and sat back on her heels, her face flushed. "He . . . he'll want to do things, and you must let him. You mustn't turn away. It won't last long, and you'll manage."

Her embarrassment was more painful than the lesson she was attempting to teach. I smothered a smile and was relieved of the necessity to answer by the sound of a wagon out front.

"It's him!" I ran to the window, saw my oldest sister climbing down. "It's only Becca," I said, my voice dull with disappointment.

Mother got quickly to her feet. "Stay here. She'll want to see your dress."

There were the usual cries of greeting before Becca climbed the stairs. She was big with her first child, and she sat on a chair and fanned her face with her handkerchief.

"I'll be glad to be thin again," she said, catching her breath. "And from the look of you, Mother's been scaring you with her well-meant advice just like she did when I got married."

"Is that what she was doing?"

Becca chuckled, a sound as deep and rich as melted chocolate. "Yes, but she doesn't have the right words. Did she get to the part where you're supposed to blow out the candle and keep your nightgown on?"

"She didn't say anything about anything," I said.

"Yes, well. They never do. It's a crime what's done to us, Gusta. And by our own mothers. All that whispering and hinting about something perfectly natural. If I'd listened to her, Peter would've divorced me long since."

I think my mouth fell open. "He wouldn't! Becca, nobody gets divorced. It's such a disgrace."

She rested her hands on her belly. "Maybe more people should. But that doesn't concern us. What does is what happens in bed, and not in the dark, either. What happens can be fun, so listen to me because I'm telling the truth. And I'll bet that Horace knows what's to be done, so you don't have to worry."

"He does?"

She laughed again. "I'm assuming that Kansas, like Maine and Massachusetts, has brothels. And your Horace doesn't strike me as a saint. Men, after all, are men, as mother couldn't bring herself to mention."

Shocked, I leaped to his defense. "He wouldn't. . . ."

"He would. He's a man. For heaven's sake, Gusta, listen to me and stop gawking like a schoolgirl."

I sat down at her feet. "All right. Tell me."

She did.

When Horace arrived later that afternoon, when I'd greeted him with a hug and a chaste kiss, Becca's advice was ringing in my head, and I didn't know whether to be glad or sorry at my new-found information. He was taller, broader than I remembered, tanned from his life outdoors, and sure of himself. Beside him I was a blade of grass in the shade of an oak, a pale, skinny woman as unlike those fallen women Becca had attempted to describe as was possible.

Perhaps I'd made a mistake. Perhaps I should have kept to my bed—alone—my head buried in my pillow, my heart full of false but comforting romantic notions. Perhaps I should have listened to my father who, only days before, had taken me into his office at the quarry for a talk.

I sat there in the old, wooden swivel chair, hands folded, wondering why he'd called for me. Dust from the quarry covered everything, papers, the top of his desk, even the sleeves of his coat, and I made up my mind I'd give the place a good cleaning as my last gesture of love.

Oblivious of what was to him commonplace, Father folded his hands together, making a steeple beneath his chin. "You're sure of this?" he asked. "Because if you're not, now's the time to call it off. Nobody's forcing you, least of all me or your mother."

It was the last thing I expected, but I answered truthfully. "I'm sure."

"You're better educated. That could be a problem. And your life's not going to be easy. Think it over again before you answer." He softened his words with a smile, knowing that my tongue often ran away with me, usually to my regret.

But I couldn't bear to hear Horace slighted. "He's not dumb, Father! You've said yourself he's the best stonecutter you ever had. He mightn't know books, but he knows how to take care of himself."

He reached into a pocket, pulled out his old pipe, filled it, tamped it, lit it, then sat back. The scent of the tobacco mingled with the dry smell of rock dust, the fragrance of the logs that burned in the fire, and I thought I'd remember that mixture though I went a thousand miles.

After a few puffs, he said: "I wasn't criticizing, Gusta. Only saying he has his faults. No one's perfect."

I knew Horace's faults—a weakness for gambling, a fondness for liquor. "I'm not perfect, either."

"No. But you're a good daughter, and you'll be a fine wife. For the right man."

"Horace is the right man." I'd set my course, made my decision and wanted no more doubts or criticism from family or friends. "I love him," I added.

"Well, then. I give you my blessing." He put down his pipe and came around to where I sat. "Give me a hug, Gusta. And go with God."

I did, grateful that the interview was over. But as I stood in the parlor, looking at my husband-to-be, it was as if I saw a stranger, a man I'd never met—or kissed.

Horace had been watching me. "Second thoughts?" He put his arm around my waist and pulled me close.

Heavens! He was a mind-reader! I re-arranged my features into a smile. "No," I said. "Not that. I'm glad to see you, is all. It's been so long, and you look so different."

"I am different. You'll see. And you'll be different, too, after a while. There's a whole world out there. It's rough, I won't lie to you, but it's ours for the taking. At least it will be once we get rid of the slavery issue."

"I want to hear," I said.

For the next hour he spoke about Kansas, the vast

prairie, the limitless sky, the kindness of his neighbors, and the difficult slavery question. If he glossed over the depredations of the Border Ruffians, the fanatical actions of the Abolitionists, he had, I knew, his reasons. Regardless of bridal vapors, I was once again caught up in his excitement, his warmth and vitality. Once again, I fell under his spell.

Chapter Three

Horace and I were married in the parlor in the midst of one of the worst blizzards I had ever seen, or that anyone present could remember. The house was filled with happy well-wishers—and stayed that way. As a result, my wedding night and its joys or sorrows were put off, as all the beds were filled with guests unable to get home.

There was a great deal of laughter and joking among the younger crowd, with Horace and me the butt of the merriment, and my face was as red as a holly berry when I kissed my husband good night and turned to climb the stairs to the bed I was to have shared with him.

"We'll have our honeymoon yet, my girl," he whispered into my ear. "Just you wait!"

Was I glad or sorry? Probably a bit of both. I lay awake a long time, listening to the snow beating against the window and Becca's labored breathing in the bed beside me. Although I wasn't superstitious, the storm seemed to be a bad omen, indicative of what married life would be like—filled with dashed hopes and disappointments, and I lay there, attempting to be rational, trying to subdue my fears, while the wind howled around the chimney and the clock on the dresser ticked away the hours.

Morning brought the pale, gray light and silence of deep snow, and there was laughter coming from my brothers' room where the men had been sleeping. Becca pushed herself up in the bed and chuckled. "Saved from your painful duty by a blizzard," she said, then added: "You look awful. You'd better not let him see you like that."

Her words stung. Of course, I looked a mess. I'd had no sleep. "You're no beauty, either," I answered truthfully, for her face was swollen and she was having trouble pulling on her clothes.

"Just wait till it happens to you. It will, sooner or later. Now, come help button me."

The idea of children was a happy one—boys to help Horace on the farm, girls to keep me company in kitchen and garden.

"It probably won't happen till this snow melts," I said, and wasn't sure if I was glad of the reprieve or not.

The truth is that I conceived a few days later when the guests had left and Horace and I finally spent a happy night alone.

On the 15th day of February, 1857, a month before James Buchanan was to be inaugurated President, we left the home that was all I had known for twenty-three years. My family and many of our friends, including

Reverend Ingraham, who had married us, were at the station to see us off. The reverend, I saw, had drawn Horace to one side and was giving him still another sermon on the evils of slavery.

Hiding a grin, I turned to my mother who was clutching her hat with one hand and holding down her skirts with the other. It was a blustery morning, the wind cold off the river, and it whipped tears into her eyes that were already teary.

She let go her hat and embraced me awkwardly, then turned to Horace. "Keep my child well. I entrust her to your care."

She was, of course, worried about my health. All of them were, and the fact that I was traveling halfway across the country to a dangerous place didn't make her very happy.

"Write," Vinnie said when it was her turn to say good bye. "Tell me everything. And take care not to lose the book."

The book was Vinnie's farewell gift, our battered copy of *Jane Eyre*, packed in my trunk along with a Bible, a Shakespeare, a handwritten collection of Mother's best recipes, my silver, linens, and clothing. What none of them knew was that at the bottom of Horace's trunk, ready to be re-assembled, were two new Sharps rifles—weapons much in demand in Kansas—that were now having to be smuggled in by Northern Abolitionists, this in spite of the fact that, for the moment, an uneasy peace had been imposed on Kansas Territory.

Safe! I thought, shuddering as the enormity of what

I'd done came home to me. I might never be safe again, might have to learn to shoot one of those rifles in self-defense. Though in many ways all was a grand adventure, there were times when my spirits sank and my small store of courage faltered. Ruffians, murderers, and even the thought of Indians were enough to shake my confidence, but when I brought up the subject, Horace had only laughed.

"It's not women they're after, and it's not women who're fighting in old Jim Lane's free-state army. Things might be different now that your cousin's out of office and we've got a new governor, but you'll be safe enough at the farm. We're nowhere near the worst of it." As he spoke, he got the gleam in his eye that was so much a part of him—as if he thought himself impervious to danger. I thought perhaps he was. If so, then I need have no fear.

Father was the last to say good bye, and, as he did, he slipped a purse into my pocket. "For you, child. Money of your own. A woman always needs something to fall back on. Keep it to yourself."

I looked up at his kindly face, astonished. He'd already given Horace a hundred-dollar wedding present with the admonishment to spend it wisely. "Why?" I asked.

"As I said, it's there if you should need it. You be the judge of how it's spent."

I threw my arms around him, knowing I'd miss him even more than I would miss my sisters, my mother. He was, and would remain, the solid core of what I, for the rest of my life, called home.

Horace and I boarded the train, I next to the window, and I waved till all that was familiar had vanished from sight.

"Now," he said, slipping his arm around my shoulders, "now it begins. Now you're mine, and I'm yours, so do with me what you will."

I gave a chuckle at that, and leaned against his warmth. "I don't think it'd be proper here."

He laughed, too. "Then sleep if you can. There's nothing to see but snow from here to Vermont. And there won't be much comfort or sleep when we get there. My family's not like yours. If I wasn't standing up for John, I'd take you some place for a real honeymoon and a little fun."

"Fun is expensive," I reminded him. "We have to watch what we spend."

"Penny-pincher," he retorted. "How many times does a man or a woman get married?"

"Once. But I thought. . . ."

"I know what you thought. Now, close your eyes and no more talk about money. There's nothing worse unless you're filthy rich and talking about how to spend it."

I did as I was told, and was glad later. Gladder still that we spent only two nights and a day at his parents' home. It was easy to see how his stepmother, with her dour outlook and hatchet face, had alienated her adopted children. Instead of the warm greeting I had expected, what I got from my mother-in-law was a nod and a few uncomplimentary words concerning my appearance and ending with: "Well, he's your problem now."

Oh, I wanted to throttle the woman! Scourge her with my opinion of her shoddy housekeeping, her attitude toward the children she'd consented to mother but had driven away. But though I've always had a sharp tongue, manners were bred into me. Without a smile I answered her. "And I'm glad of it!"

I was glad, too, that Emily, Haw's youngest sister, announced her decision to accompany us to Kansas. The poor child! She had no place in that forbidding house except as a servant, and she was young and eager, with eyes that pleaded for acceptance. For me, she took the place of a younger sister, and I welcomed her with pleasure.

"Will there be Indians?" she asked me the evening before our departure.

Like most women, myself included, she'd read the horrible stories of captured white women forced to live in degradation and disgrace. Privately I thought even that might be better than living under the same roof with her stepmother, but I attempted to reassure her, using Haw's arguments.

"Probably. But both Horace and John say there's nothing to be afraid of. Most of them are poor and come to beg, or out of curiosity. And you won't be alone, after all."

She looked out the window at the snow-covered earth. "I'm used to being alone," she said.

How to answer that? How put into words that one glimpse was enough to tell me why Horace had left and why he'd been moody and uncommonly silent since we'd arrived? In my best big-sister voice, I told her that there would probably be parties, dances, young people even on the frontier and even if there was a war, and was pleased to see anticipation light her eyes.

"I'm so glad Haw found you," she said.

He came into the room in time to hear her and laughed for the first time since our arrival. "And Haw's glad, too."

By then I'd adopted the practice of calling my husband Haw after the initials of his given names—Horace Austin Warner. It was a nickname that, in less than twenty years, would be known across America. Haw Tabor. As for little Augusta Pierce Tabor, there would be small recognition.

Both Haw and John were eager to return to Kansas, and we women—John's bride, Hannah, Emily, and I—were not less eager to leave the bleak and depressing farm that had been Haw's home. The day after the wedding we headed West—"All one family," as Hannah put it. She was a competent and happy woman, and I was more than grateful for her presence when, at Niagara Falls, I fainted for the first—and last—time in my life.

It was the journey, I thought as I came to, the excitement, the dreadful food I'd been unable to eat, and the sight of the falls themselves. The tremendous force of them made the earth tremble under my feet. Even though still half-frozen, acres of water thundered down and down, and then sprayed upward in clouds of mist till, watching, I became dizzy and my breath stopped in my throat.

I saw Haw's face filled with concern. Hannah and Emily were rubbing my hands, and John stood by, frowning, as if he thought my frailty would halt our journey.

"I'm all right! Those falls! They're just so . . . so big!" I struggled to sit up, ashamed of my own weakness.

"We'll stop over here tonight. No argument." Haw was worried, and I was more frightened than I wanted to admit.

"Only one night. I'll be fine in the morning."

Hannah gave me a look but said nothing till later when I was lying on a small, not particularly clean bed in a room that smelled of mold and damp. She was a plump, pleasant woman, far more conversant than I with life, and she didn't mince words. "You're breeding," she said without preamble.

I stared at her. "It can't be."

"Well, it is. Think. How long since your last time?"

Because of bad health, I'd always been irregular and could only shake my head. "I can't remember."

"Well, it's not important. What's important is that you're carrying a child. Does Haw know?"

"I didn't myself." The horrible thought struck me that I might be sent home if the truth came out, and I sat up. "Don't tell! Promise you won't! If you do, he'll send me back."

Though I missed my family, it would be far worse to be separated from the man I loved, to give birth with him far away.

She sat down on the edge of the bed. "You haven't been eating. God knows, we'd all kill for a decent meal, but if you're going on, you'd better start taking care of yourself."

I grabbed her hands. They were big and solid like the rest of her. "But you won't say anything?"

"Not my place. That's between you and him. But it's not going to get easier, and who knows where you'll be when your time comes?"

"I'll be where I belong." Brave words, spoken to blot out nightmarish scenes of childbirth on some empty prairie. "I'll be with Haw."

Hannah nodded. "I'll see if I can't get them to send you some soup. If not, I'll take over the kitchen and make it myself!"

In the next weeks, she nurtured me, forced food into me with the determination of one born to motherhood. For that alone I loved her, and wept when, at the last, we parted company.

At St. Louis we boarded a river boat to take us upstream to Westport, the last leg of a journey that already seemed endless. Maine was so very far away and so civilized compared to this raw, waterfront town where the outlook was always to the West and where the streets were crowded with traders, trappers, gamblers, and men of business as well as a stream of immigrants impatient to continue their trek across the plains. Wagons and drays rumbled up to the docks where the boats lay at ease upon the water, and more slaves than I'd ever seen in my life labored to load each with barrels, crates, bales, cattle and horses and cages of chickens, the trunks of passengers, anything that anyone wanted shipped up the Missouri to Kansas.

Here, the river was wide, its waters churning with the spring run-off, and muddy, filled with chunks of still-melting ice and all the shameful refuse of humanity. I stood at the railing as the boat shoved off, hoping the freshening breeze would quell the nausea that threatened to betray my still-kept secret. If only we could get to Kansas before Haw found out! He wouldn't think of sending me back from there! Even if he did, I wouldn't go. I squared my shoulders and swallowed hard.

"Won't be long now." He had come to stand beside me and was sniffing the wind as if he could already smell the Kansas prairie. "At least we won't have to worry about the blockade any more. Just sandbars."

I looked a question at him.

"The slavery crowd tried to close off the territory last year," he explained. "I didn't write about half of what was going on. Didn't want to scare you. But they had gunboats on the river and armies at the border. Your father was right. It was war even if it was a bunch of ragtag squatters, shooting at each other. If the river had still been blocked, I'd have figured some other way to get back, maybe through Nebraska with Jim Lane and Hickok. They got a lot of immigrants through. Or maybe I'd have left you here till it was safe."

"You'd have tried . . . and lost," I said.

He looked at me with a new respect, then laughed. "Guess I would have at that. God help me or anybody when your mind's made up. You're like a little bull-dog. I don't stand a chance."

He didn't, either. Although I was young and in many ways naïve, I'd always been strong-willed. I hated losing—anything from a card game to an argument—and that's what got me through sickness and childhood to the deck of a boat rocking on the current of the Missouri. It was what had got me through nausea and the light-headedness that struck without warning. With my marriage vows I'd accepted duty, responsibility, and loving, and the only way to achieve those things was at my husband's side.

I swallowed again, watched as a large tree swept past, one branch reaching skyward as if pleading for help. It disappeared in our wake, possibly chopped to pieces by the massive wheel that was pushing us upstream.

When I spoke, it was slowly, in search of words, for I was unaccustomed to making frank declarations. "You're my life," I said. "I have no other."

"For better or worse. Richer or poorer." He took my hand, and as always I felt the vitality, the heat that seemed to come from his very center. "I'll tell you this, Gusta. I'll make you a promise. We'll end up rich, or my name's not Tabor."

There were times on that trip when I thought I'd end up not rich but dead, buried in the muck of the river-bank, if not in the river itself. Our way twisted and turned, the boat stopped and started, ran aground on unmarked snags, nearly shook itself to pieces when it encountered hidden boulders, uprooted trees, and once the bloated carcass of a mule that got caught in the wheel, swept under, and never reappeared—not that I looked to see.

It was a small boat, and overloaded with passengers, most of them headed for Kansas and the fighting. Quarrels broke out daily between Free-Staters and Southerners. There were fist fights and several times shots were fired, which caused the captain, armed with a shotgun, to leave those involved off at a sagging wharf that jutted out from the bank, while the rest of us watched in silence. What happened to the men put off in that manner, I couldn't imagine. We seemed so far from everything I understood.

Haw had been delighted to find two friends of his on board—Nathaniel Maxcy and Sam Kellogg, both of whom decided to throw in with us and make their way to Zeandale. There was, the men decided, safety in numbers, particularly in Kansas. I liked both men from the start, especially Nat Maxcy, who had brown, honest eyes and the broad shoulders of a man used to hard work. By contrast, Kellogg was thin, wiry, quick in his movements, and together the pair of them reminded me of an old nursery rhyme about the lean and the fat—though Maxcy was far from overweight. It was he who took pity on me the afternoon we ran aground and all passengers were forced to disembark to lighten the boat's load.

The weather was cold, with the scent of snow on the wind. It had been a long winter and the trees and brush that lined the river were still dark, leafless, rooted in the foul-smelling mud that sucked at our boots and made walking even a few yards a torment.

Still, I did the best I could, guarded by the faithful Hannah. Haw, as was his way, had gone off to explore, leaving me to slog along, thinking not thoughts of love but of bitter accusation. Was this what Father had meant—a warning—that I'd be left alone by a husband who had no idea what I needed or wanted? Was this to be my future? I swallowed a sob and kept on.

I was so deeply immersed in what I'd say when Haw came back—at his usual high-spirited gallop—that I failed to see the log, half buried, covered in moss. I tripped and fell face down, lay still, testing arms, legs, the slight roundness of my belly. Was the baby safe?

"You all right, Miz Tabor?" Nat Maxcy lifted me up as easily as if I were a twig.

"I think so." The taste of dirt in my mouth was so strong I wanted to spit, but spitting was something ladies did not do—either in public or private. Instead, I dabbed at my face, smearing the filth around.

One-handedly he reached in his pocket and pulled out a bandanna that had, I must say, seen hard use. Beggars, however, can't be choosers, as the saying goes.

"I'll just carry you a ways," he said.

Carry me? I should say not! How would that look? As if Augusta Tabor was a quitter—or worse. "Put me down," I said.

He kept walking, each step accompanied by the sound of his big boots coming reluctantly out of the mud. "You'll pardon me for stickin' my nose in, ma'am, but you need to take care." His honest eyes met mine, and I read in them concern, kindness, and compassion as well as the knowledge of my condition.

Oh, I was mortified! To be discussing this with a man I hardly knew, a man in whose arms I was being carried effortlessly! I looked away. "Does everybody know?" I whispered.

"No, ma'am." He gave a quick smile. "But Ma had twelve children, and I was oldest. I reckon I just learned without knowin' it."

In the years to come, I would give thanks for the things that Nat Maxcy had learned without "knowin' it", but that day I simply gave in to another facet of his character. Nothing budged him once his mind was made up.

That night, back on board, I told Haw about the baby. His happy reaction blotted out all the bitter words I'd been saving up to tell him.

Chapter Four

At Westport, John, Hannah, and Emily left us, headed south toward Lawrence. I was sorry to see them go— the faithful Hannah, and Emily with her wide-eyed wonder at everything from the scenery to the patterns of the clouds. John? Well, John was almost as fanatical about abolition as John Brown. There were times when his eyes blazed as if he'd been struck by a lightning bolt, and it was easy to see how he'd gotten into the trouble that had sent him to jail. More than once, Hannah had come between him and a passenger on the boat, putting an end to argument before it escalated into violence, and doing it all with that firm but gentle way she had and that I so admired.

Like St. Louis, Westport was thriving, not only because of the immigrants determined to settle in Kansas. Every day it seemed, a train of wagons departed headed for Oregon, California, Santa Fé. From the window of our hotel I watched those awkward-seeming prairie schooners pulled by teams of mules or yokes of oxen move slowly across the immensity of the land and gradually vanish over a horizon that was, as I came to know, an illusion. For the land never ended. It went on— toward the setting sun, toward mountains that, to me then, were only mythical ramparts that cut the world in two, toward another, different ocean from the Atlantic that I knew.

While I watched, while I took in the noise, the dust, the excitement of a town that was bursting at its seams, Haw, Nat, and Sam were busy purchasing our own oxen and wagon, a pair of mules, sacks of seed, flour, beans, coffee, sugar, and salt in preparation for our journey to the place that would be home.

A wind was blowing straight out of the west on the day we departed for Zeandale. Without consulting me, the men had decided that I was to drive the oxen while they walked or rode alongside.

"You'll be safer this way," Haw said as he helped me up on the rough wagon seat. "We'll be free to fight off anybody who tries to stop us."

"Do you think they will?" In my imagination I saw a horde of Missourians armed to the teeth riding after us, mounted Indians, faces painted in hideous colors, their war cry terrifying.

He shrugged. "This is Kansas. You never know when the Missouri crowd might try something. But don't you worry. There's three of us, and we're all armed." By then he'd reassembled his Sharps rifles, and Nat and Sam had brought their own.

I looked out over the bony rumps of the oxen to their huge heads and curving horns. Certainly they'd never outrun an attack, even if I could manage to control them. Still, if all those women in the wagon trains could drive oxen, I supposed I could, too, and I'd say nothing about my fears.

I'd watched them—sunbonneted women perched on the wagon seats, reins or ox goads in hand, learning to drive out of necessity, I was sure, just as I was sure that I looked no more ridiculous than they in my own new sunbonnet and the heavy boots Haw had insisted I wear.

"Drivin' oxen ain't hard, ma'am," Nat said in his easy way. "Once you get 'em started, they go on their own. You jist use the goad to keep 'em straight. And remember . . . 'gee' means right and 'haw' is left, and they'll stop when you tell 'em 'whoa' . . . jist like horses."

"And does Haw respond to his name by going left?" I asked with a grin.

Haw was astride one of the mules, a slick, mouse-colored fellow with a knowing eye. "Only when you goad me," he answered, and his teeth flashed white beneath the sweep of his brown mustache.

I thought he looked like a pirate, and once again marveled that I was the woman he'd chosen. Well, I wasn't about to disappoint. I gripped the goad firmly, gave the oxen a smart rap, and they moved off slowly, their big, cloven hoofs raising a cloud of dust that the wind stole and whirled away.

And so, with much laughter, we began our trek west, always west toward the horizon, toward a life filled with who knew what sorrows or joys? If I had known, what then? Would I have turned back, run home, borne my child safely in my childhood bed? Even now I can't say, for there was something glorious in our adventure, something that defined us, all of us, once and for all, and around us the land rising, falling, stretching away like a vast and undulant sea.

I shall never forget the morning of my arrival. To add to the desolation of the place, one of the Kansas winds was blowing furiously. Setting upon an open prairie was my future home—a log cabin 12 × 16 feet, not an outhouse, or a stone, or a stick in sight. I was ushered in, and the only piece of furniture in the room was a No. 7 cook stove that was confiscated from the Border Ruffians' brotherhood. I sat down upon an old trunk, the only thing to sit on, and the tears began to flow copiously. After a few hours, I dried my tears, cleaned up the cabin, and prepared the first meal that I had ever tried to cook.

Oh, why had I let my family indulge and spoil me so? Why had I taken advantage of ill health and avoided all the tasks that might have prepared me for this new life? Instead of cooking, I'd buried myself in books, never realizing what I needed to know simply in order to survive—here or anywhere.

On that April day, with the wind blowing, the cloud-streaked sky covering us like a cup turned upside down, and everywhere nothing but empty, scrub-covered prairie, I made a vow. *Never again will I be helpless! Never again will I give in to tears, loneliness, my own lack of courage or spirit, and be damned to weakness of my own making!*

Sam came with a bucket of water from the creek and the advice: "Better let it sit a while, ma'am. It needs to settle."

Nat brought in wood and explained the workings of the old stove. "Not so hard once you get the hang of it."

Haw was busy hammering three-legged stools together, cursing now and again as the wind stole his hat and he had to chase it across what, pathetically, he called "the yard".

"Bring in my trunk," I said to Nat, hoping to find among Mother's recipes an easy meal, one I could make without disastrous results.

In spite of my determination, I almost wept again as I sifted through reminders of home. There was my linen tablecloth, my silverware, the quilt I'd stitched at till I'd nearly ruined my eyes. And there was my wedding dress, as out of place here as were the little gray kid shoes that matched it. All of it folly. All of it useless in this place I now called home.

Haw came in, carrying a pair of saw horses, went back out for a plank, and within minutes had constructed a table in the middle of the room. "It won't always be like this," he said, and there was a plea in his voice, in his eyes as if he were ashamed. "I'm sorry you're unhappy. I didn't think how it would look to you."

Of course, he hadn't. He was a man, and one accustomed to hardship. I forgave him with a smile and the glimmering of an idea.

"We're in it together," I told him. "And I'm sorry,

too. Just for a minute, I couldn't help it. All that space out there and nobody in it. I felt so lost, so helpless. Like we'd come to the end of the world."

He put his arms around me and, as always, strength seemed to flow out of him and into me. "Once we get a crop raised, I'll build us a house. A real one. That's a promise. We'll not raise a baby in this cabin."

"If we have to, we will." I stepped back, and bent over my trunk. "Now go see to the animals. I'll start supper."

While the men were gone, I laid the plank table with the heavy linen cloth, arranged my pieces of china, set out the still-bright silver, then turned to my enemy, the stove. I sliced bacon into the big cast-iron skillet we'd bought in Westport without cutting off any fingers. I set out a round of cheese, a bowl of withered apples. Bread and biscuits would have to wait till the cook gained expertise, which, out of necessity, would be soon. I ground coffee, dipped the enamel pot full of creek water, and set it to boil. I lit the lantern and hung it from its hook over the table, washed the tears that had dried on my cheeks, and tidied my hair.

Then I went to the door. "Gentlemen," I said. "Dinner is served."

Chapter Five

The snake crawled under our bed and disappeared. It was a big one, wide around as my arm. There were times when I thought Kansas had more rattlesnakes than people, and most of them were in my house. There was no point screaming. Haw was in the cornfield. Nat and Sam gone to another farm as day workers. I reached for the shovel kept beside the door and then screamed, loud as I could.

An Indian stood there, nearly naked, and he was watching me without expression except for what might have been amusement in his black eyes. Trapped between a rattler and a naked man who was laughing at me, I froze, one hand stretched out for the shovel. "What do you want?" I whispered, not especially eager to hear his answer.

He was silent, unblinking, a dark shape blotting out the sunlight. Haw had told me most of the Indians came to beg, could be gotten rid of with a gift of food, a cup of sweetened coffee, but I'd heard too many stories, imagined too many terrors. I was a woman alone, awkward, and big with child. It was the thought of that child that gave me strength, the not-yet-fully-formed instinct of a mother protecting her young.

"You get out!" I thrust my face close to his and my words rang like a church bell. "You get out of here right now!"

Then I went for the shovel, the only weapon I had. But he was quick. In an instant he grabbed the handle and advanced toward me, and I knew he'd come driven by a motive I'd never understand. I closed my eyes and prayed.

When he moved, it was without a sound, but I felt him pass me by, a breath of air, a smell of something wild. He grunted once, and, when I looked, the snake was writhing on the floor, its head cut off, its gaping mouth still lethal. I shuddered, then began to laugh, a laughter born of hysteria that refused to be controlled.

Ignoring me, he carried the still-moving reptile out the door and around the side of the house. Perhaps he wouldn't come back. Perhaps he'd take the shovel and go to wherever he came from. But I needed that shovel! Without it I was helpless. So I went out, determined to fight for what was a necessity.

Hunger can be a powerful deterrent to theft. He gave over the shovel without a struggle and pantomimed food. Seen up close, he wasn't at all the formidable creature I'd thought at first. He was simply a human with an empty stomach.

I gave him coffee with plenty of molasses, and a plate of the soda biscuits that I'd recently learned to bake. He ate them all, pouring the molasses like water and cramming them into his mouth. I saw that his blanket was ragged, and beneath it he was thin to emaciation, and compassion overrode my fears. He was only a man like many—ill-clothed, close to starvation.

"You poor thing!" The words burst out, but he paid no attention, just kept chewing and slurping, possibly aware of my feelings but unmoved by them.

When he finished, he stood, wrapped his poor blanket tightly around him, and went out without a sign of thanks or recognition of me as a person. It was only then that my legs gave way and I sat down, hard, on one of the stools. Something had to be done. I wasn't going to bring a baby to a place crawling with snakes and strange visitors.

"I want you to teach me to shoot," I said to Haw that night. "And I want a cat or a dog for company and protection."

"There's not a cat for five hundred miles," he said. "Coyotes get them soon as they're out the door."

He was right about that. Years later I heard of a man who made good money bringing carloads of cats to the West. But then I was desperate.

"A dog, then. A good-sized one that won't run off and won't get killed by coyotes."

He nodded. "Not a bad idea. When I'm in town, I'll see what I can find. In the meantime, I'll teach you to shoot the pistol. The Sharps would knock you flat with its recoil."

"As long as it shoots," I said, and meant it. Augusta Tabor was learning to take care of herself!

* * *

I killed plenty of snakes that summer, mostly with the shovel because I hated shooting the pistol in the house for fear I'd shatter something—a lamp, a dish, a glass jar—things that would cost money to replace. The fact is, our money was almost gone, and, although our corn came up green and healthy, no rain came to nourish it. Every evening Haw and I walked out to look over our crop, and every evening our expectations grew less. The soil was dry. It crumbled in our fingers and turned to dust, and the green stalks drooped and grew brittle. Even the weeds were struggling for life.

"A man can't farm without water, and I'm damned if I'll haul water from the creek to wet down sixty acres." Haw's shoulders were slumped.

I took his hand. It was rough, callused, with dirt caked under the nails, the hand of a farmer. My own hands weren't much better. "Maybe next year," I said.

"There won't be a next year if I don't make some money. Christ, whoever said this was farm land never thought about the damned weather!" He looked up at the sky as if cursing it.

"Don't," I said.

"Don't what? Cuss? Give up? Wish to hell I'd never dragged you out here? It would've been better for us to stay back in Maine where at least you'd have a decent roof over your head."

I'd never seen him so angry, or so depressed. "What can I do?"

"Nothing. We've already spent your money. Without Nat and Sam we'd be broke. If you can manage,

I'm going to Fort Riley and get a job. They need stonecutters for the new buildings. At least I can do that. Nat and Sam'll see to things here, and I'll come home on weekends."

What he was saying was that I'd be alone for weeks at a stretch, just me, and the wind, and the child that at that moment moved as if it was beating with its fists, crying out unheard. Of course, I wasn't the only woman on the frontier whose husband left to find work, earn enough money to keep going. In that, at least, I wasn't alone. I squared my shoulders. "Don't worry about me. I'll make out," was all I said before turning back to the house.

In the long summer twilight the little cabin seemed insubstantial—frail and lost in the light mist that rose out of the ruined corn, wrapped around the willow switches I'd brought up from the creek in an attempt to grow trees for shade. Even with regular applications of dishwater they were pathetic, thin as lines drawn with a pen, leaves drooping.

In spite of all, though, there was a loveliness to those prairie evenings, a magic I've found nowhere else—the wind sweet-scented, the crickets scraping in the grass, night birds crying, the sun like a golden trumpet on the horizon, its music not sound but color: red, orange, apricot, and the purple drumbeat of night waiting its moment. There was, I thought, a balance to everything if we could but find it, and I sighed, seeking my own precarious balance in this strange and difficult place.

"I'll make out," I repeated. "But don't forget to find me a dog."

Haw's answer was cut off by the sight of a rider coming toward us at a full gallop. He was shouting like a madman.

"Get over to Tynan's! There's a bunch of the bastards tryin' to burn him out!" He galloped on without slowing down, and Haw broke into a run.

"Get in the house, Gusta! And bar the door. No telling what'll happen."

Of course, I couldn't run but followed as best I could, watching for snakes underfoot and looking back over my shoulder for the appearance of the Border Ruffians who might, at any moment, come over the rise. We could be next. We could lose our land, our cabin, our lives.

Sam was bridling the mules when I trundled into the yard. Nat and Haw came out, carrying their rifles.

"Stay inside," Haw repeated. "And don't open the door for anybody but us unless you know them. The pistol's on the table. Use it."

Then they were gone over the darkening plain, a darkness splintered by a distant light that I knew spelled disaster for the Tynans, and possibly for us if the dry prairie caught fire. I didn't light the lantern that night but kept watch in the dark. If I couldn't see, neither could anyone else, and my hearing was sharp. Let them try sneaking up on me! On this place I'd labored to make into a home! The walls were papered with newspapers, true, but better that than logs and dirt chinking that dried and fell out on the bed, the table, the floor. There were curtains at the window made from a petticoat I no longer needed and my quilt lay on the bed, covering the mattress filled with fresh straw and sweet grasses. Let them try! Try and be damned!

The silence wrapped around me, a dark cloak. There is nothing like the silence of the plains, nothing to equal the perfect stillness, as if time has stopped and the land holds its breath, waiting, waiting. In that silence the moon rose, a rough diamond on a black cloth. I listened and heard no sound, not even a mouse rooting in my shelves, not a snake moving across the floor. Well, I thanked God for that! What I'd have done if a snake had touched my feet, I don't know.

I cannot tell how long I sat, the pistol in my lap. The hours passed. I closed my eyes but did not sleep. Once I heard riders pass close by, too close, and I started up, frightened, angry, ready to defend self, child, place of belonging. But they rode on, possibly not even realizing that a woman was waiting with murder in her heart. They passed by, and I sat again and waited.

The moon moved to the west, and I was nodding, exhausted, when Haw's shout alerted me.

"Gusta! It's us. We're all right!"

I thanked God, and later prayed for Sibbie Tynan who'd lost her house, her barn, and her husband in yet another example of man's ruthlessness toward his own.

Chapter Six

"Hello the house! Horace! Horace Tabor!"

The shout awakened me, and I grabbed the pistol I now slept with—a poor substitute for a husband, I must say—and went to the door.

"Who are you? What do you want?" My heart was pounding, my hand shaking so hard I couldn't hold the pistol steady.

The strange-looking man on the dun horse stared at me, then gave what I assumed was a smile and a nod.

"James Lane, ma'am. No need to wave that at me, I assure you."

It was the Grim Chieftain of Kansas himself, and behind him, in the remnants of our cornfield, his antislavery army.

I let the pistol drop. "My husband's not here, Mister Lane. Is there anything I can do? Or Nat or Sam," I added, as the two men came at a run.

Lane removed his hat that had a turkey feather

stuck jauntily in its band, and banged it on his knee. "I'd be glad of some water. My men, too."

"Take Mister Lane's horse, Nat," I said, "and you and Sam see to the men. Mister Lane, you're welcome to come inside and rest a while."

Of course, I'd heard the stories about Lane and his army of anti-slavery volunteers. He was on his way to becoming a legend. He'd fought hard against the Missouri crowd, and with the assistance of Wild Bill Hickok and a few others like him had led thousands of immigrants around the blockades and into Kansas.

Inside the house, I dipped some water into a cup, put a plate of day-old cornbread and a bowl of beans on the table, and waited for the man to speak.

"Bad business, Missus Tabor," he began, wiping his mouth on a tattered sleeve, "Everybody's talking peace, but there is no peace and won't be until this slave business is settled. Buchanan's no better than Pierce, whatever anybody says. He hasn't made up his mind how to manage us out here, probably doesn't want to. And I'm hoping to distract him and his damned toadies further." He took another swallow of water and scooped up the beans. "I figured your husband might join me and go after the bunch that's been raiding all the way from the border. Looks like they've been busy right around here from what I saw. What've you heard?"

I recalled the horses that had passed by the night Tynans' was burned and told him.

He nodded. "That's them. They've been raiding,

hit or miss, but don't you worry. We'll find 'em. Every last one, or my name's not Jim Lane."

From an uneventful existence in Maine, I'd come to a battlefield, was sitting in my house, hoping, praying that this grizzled old fighter would take his revenge. Life does, indeed, lead us down a strange and twisted path.

"I wish you luck," I said. "The Tynans were fine people. And now Sibbie's alone. She's gone back East, or so I heard."

"And left a good piece of land for some Missouri bas— . . . murderer," he amended with something like humor in his eye. Then he pushed back from the table. "I'll be on my way, Missus Tabor. Tell your husband I can use his help if he gets back soon, and my thanks for the meal." He helped himself to the rest of the cornbread, shoving it into his pocket, and then was gone, spurring his horse across the yard and into the field as if the devil was after him.

Perhaps he was. Or more likely, perhaps Lane himself was chasing the devil and wouldn't quit till he found him.

Haw was as good as his word. On his first trip home from Fort Riley, he brought a dog, a quick-moving, slick hound that immediately made himself at home. I named him Petty after a dog I'd had as a child, and in the weeks that followed he became companion, shadow, guardian of me, the house, the yard. Whether it was his presence, or the fact that cooler temperatures had come, I couldn't say, but quite soon the snakes relinquished their claim on the house, and I breathed a sigh of relief. At least, I wouldn't be finding one of the odious creatures curled up in my baby's basket.

In those last days of September all I thought about was the baby. It was hard to think about anything else in my condition—swollen, ungainly, short of breath, and short of temper, too. How had Mother managed? I often wondered—bearing ten of us without complaint and still keeping the house running smoothly, the meals on time, the washing done. She, of course, had had help. I had my two hands and Nat and Sam who did their best but who were men and not the feminine companionship I longed for.

"Is there any way to tell when?" Haw asked. "I could stay home, if you want, though I won't be much help."

I laughed. Like most men, the very idea of childbirth terrified him. "You do what you have to. Leave baby to me."

Brave words, but I wasn't sure I'd be at all brave when the time came, though Nat had promised Haw he'd call Lucy Porter, Zeandale's midwife, at the first sign of the baby. I'd met Lucy at the town's 4th of July celebration and, though I liked her, doubted she knew much more than I. She was young, pretty in a scrawny way, and she'd eyed me out of eyes black as sloes.

"Three months?"

I nodded.

"Send for me when it's near time. You're such a little bit of a thing, you might have some trouble." At my sound of distress, she waved a hand. *"Oh, I didn't mean*

*to scare you, but it's best to be prepared. For now, keep off
your feet. Start makin' clothes and diapers. Plenty of
those. Babies are always makin' a mess, and you tryin' to
do a wash with a blizzard outside. Be prepared, I always
says."*

Though I'd tried to forget her well-meant advice,
I was haunted by the thought that something could
go wrong, that I'd die, or the child would be stillborn,
or, even worse, deformed. I started having nightmares,
horrid ones, about monstrous babies, sickly ones who
died in my arms. On those nights when I woke up
alone and in a sweat, Petty kept me company, and
his knowing eyes seemed to say that all would be
well.

The pain struck without warning. I crouched in the
kitchen garden, wondering if I'd make it to the house
before another blow came. I was a tree being felled by
the bite of an unseen axe, I was wheat cut in two by
the curving scythe. I was every woman, every living
thing that had ever been sliced, battered, broken by
whatever means, by the mercilessness of life.

Beside me, Petty whined. *What?* he seemed to be
asking. *What?*

I grabbed his neck, and half crawling got inside
where I managed to set the kettle to boil. Then I fell
on the bed, not knowing what else to do.

It was late morning. It would be hours before Nat
and Sam came in for supper. But there would be no
supper tonight, only cold beans and stale cornbread
and pain that stabbed without remorse.

Lying there, I prayed—for strength, for courage, for the child that was so determined to be born. I prayed, unlaced my boots—a process that took what seemed like an hour—pulled off the old cotton stockings that I'd darned so often they bore no relation to their purpose. Undergarments next. Why did women put up with so many foolish items of clothing, each of them a struggle? I prayed, and lay back in a sweat.

"Please won't somebody come?" I'd have welcomed the devil himself.

With a grunt, the dog lay down by the bed and watched me without blinking.

The day moved in a fog. I believe I must have been unconscious part of the time, for there are things I can't remember. It was Petty's bark that brought me awake, and I heard the men come into the yard. They were laughing, those cheerful, hard-working souls. I struggled to push myself up on one elbow.

"We're back, ma'am!" Nat stopped in the door and stared. "Is it . . . ?"

"Yes," I summoned a whisper.

"My God! Sam!" he called over his shoulder. "Go get Lucy. And be quick! It's Miz Tabor!"

"You stay." I didn't want to be alone, and I didn't care that he was a man.

"I will." He walked to the stove, checked the kettle that had boiled nearly dry. "We'll need more water. Some wood, too. You lay still, ma'am. I'll see to things."

When he came back, he bathed my face with water from the basin, then knotted a towel, and handed one end to me. "Use this, ma'am. When it gets to hurtin'. Bite down, yank on it. It might help a little."

I took the towel, closed my eyes, and did as I was told. There seemed nothing else that I could do. My body, my mind, my life had been taken over by others, and all that was left was to obey.

Nathaniel Maxcy Tabor was born before Sam and Lucy returned. It was his namesake's cool head and gentle hands that had helped him into this world—a debt I could never repay, an act I could never speak about. Who, in those days, would have understood?

Little Maxcy lay, finally, squalling in my arms. He looked like a baby bird, all gaping mouth and hairless head.

"I'm naming him after you, Nat," I said. "And while we're talking about names, it's time you stopped calling me 'ma'am'. It makes me feel old."

He stood there bewildered, staring at little Maxcy. After a minute, he shook his head. "No, ma'am. I can't do that. It wouldn't look right. Folks'd think I was bein' familiar, and think badly of you."

He was right, of course, but there were times, and this was one, when the rules of society were irksome. "Oh, stuff!" I said. "People think what they think without any reason or prompting. But . . . all right, you call me what you think is best. I'm grateful, Nat. There's no words to tell you."

"No need for thanks." He spoke in his slow, honest way. "I reckon, though, that I learned more than I thought from my ma."

"Reckon you did," I said with a chuckle. "And thank God for it." A noise from the yard caught my attention. "Here's Sam and Lucy. A little late. You can tell her you're taking over her job."

"That wouldn't be right, either, ma'am." Nat put on his hat and went out, leaving me to give thanks for the beautiful child who lay so trustingly in my arms.

Chapter Seven

"Come meet your son."

Haw was back from Fort Riley, and I wished I could have photographed the astonishment, joy, eagerness on his face. He held out his arms, and I put little Maxcy into them.

"When?" he asked, his voice hoarse with emotion.

"Five days now."

"You're all right?"

"As you see."

"My God. He's so little." Haw stared at the sleeping child.

"He'll grow." I took a breath. "I named him after Nat. Nathaniel Maxcy."

That got me a hard look. "I thought we'd decided to name him after his grandfathers."

I'd known Haw would be disturbed, but right was right. Our parents had nothing to do with this child. "I'd not have made it without Nat," I said.

"And where in hell was Lucy?" He was shouting, and Maxcy woke with a cry.

I took him back and rocked him. "She came at the end. Nat stayed with me. Don't be angry, Haw. He was good and kind, and he got me through. I think I'd have died otherwise."

"And I wasn't here." His anger had turned on himself.

"You weren't. There wasn't anybody for a long time."

"Damn this life! Damn this always having to grub for a dollar! There's got to be better ways to make a living." When he looked at me, his eyes were intent and focused. "There's talk about gold around Pike's Peak. Gold just lying on the ground waiting to be picked up. What would you say if we went to Colorado? Took a chance? We could always come back here if it didn't pan out."

His words took me by surprise. To my astonishment, I found I'd come to love our little house, the ruined cornfield, the long view in every direction across empty prairie. I'd even come to terms with the constant wind. "Leave here? But . . . but we haven't given ourselves a chance. One summer isn't enough. We knew that when we came."

He paced the small boundaries of the cabin, his boots thudding on the hard dirt floor. "I know all that. But life's about chances. We took one, and look at us. What've we got?"

"And who's to say we'll be better off chasing after gold? Fool's gold is more likely, and it won't be lying there in plain sight. If you believe that you are a fool." My anger was rising, and I tried my best to keep it under control.

I knew him, you see. Though he was a hard worker, his heart was never in it. He wanted instant results, and, when they didn't occur, he'd be off, gambling on another rainbow. Standing there, I envisioned us—always on the move, always chasing an elusive pot of gold, and the thought made me more exhausted than I already was.

"I won't go." The three words rang out, tough and bitter.

He turned on his heel. "You won't? What happened to your notion that you'd follow me anywhere? I'm your husband. I know what's best for us. You want to live in this . . . this hole forever? Both of us working ourselves to death, and me gone just when you need me so you turn to a stranger?"

That was it, of course. The reason for his anger. I laid Maxcy in his basket and, worn out as I was, prepared to do battle.

"We came here with high hopes," I began. "And nothing worthwhile comes easily. I came prepared to work as hard as you, and I will. We have ourselves, and we have a child. Think about him. He deserves a settled place. The house you promised to build. *I want that house, Haw.* I want us in it together. Nat's being here, helping me when there wasn't anybody else to help, has nothing to do with us, no matter what you think, and quitting isn't a word I understand."

His face twisted in rage, and for a moment I was afraid. Then he said: "You call me a quitter?"

"I'm giving you the chance not to be one. I'm gambling our life, like you'd like to do."

"It's not gambling!"

"Call it what you want."

At Maxcy's wail, I picked him up, unbuttoned my dress, and sat down on the bed. "He's hungry, poor babe. And us arguing won't do him any good, either."

I've never been one to use feminine wiles to manipulate for my own purpose, but somehow I realized the picture I made in the lamplight with our child at my breast. Maxcy and I were half of the picture, and Haw was outside, looking in. He had only to choose, to step across an imagined threshold to become part of it. Looking at him, my heart twisted. He was so lost, so confused, as helpless as the infant I held, and all because I'd spoken my mind. But if, indeed, I was gambling, I held the high card.

The fight went out of him as if he'd been punched. "All right! All right! You win. You'll have your damn' house and me in it. Only if we starve, it'll be on your head."

"If there's danger of that," I said, "we'll go to Colorado. But let's at least try. Let's at least wait till the baby is stronger."

"You mean that?" The gleam was back in his eyes. Gold fever. I was to see it many more times in my life.

"Yes," I said, "I do."

With our bargain struck, I sealed my own fate.

Haw was good as his word. That fall and winter, he, Nat, and Sam went out every day to gather stone for the new house. Not the tough, resistant granite that was the backbone of Maine, but the stone of the Kansas prairies and riverbeds, already shaped by wind and water and there for the taking. A good thing, too, for we couldn't afford lumber and what trees grew along the streams and rivers were soft and unsuitable.

That was my first experience with winter in Kansas, with the blizzards that swept out of the north and isolated us even more than we already were. The wind howled around the corners of the cabin and blew down the chimney, scattering smoke and soot. It came through every chink and crack, and froze the water in the pitcher. And it brought sickness to little Maxcy when I was the only one home to doctor him.

All three men had taken the sledge and gone to Zeandale for supplies. When they left, the sun had been bright, but in only a few hours the sky turned dark, and the scent of snow was sharp on the wind.

I went out and brought in more wood, knowing, as anyone born in Maine knows, that a storm was coming. I prayed Haw wouldn't be caught in it, become disoriented, lost, without a sense of direction. And then Maxcy began to fuss and cough and tear at his blanket so that all thoughts of storm were driven from my head. When I picked him up, he was burning with fever.

I tried every remedy I knew to ease his obvious pain—plasters, mixtures of sassafras, horehound, chamomile, even the poor thread of steam I was able to coax from the spout of the kettle, but his coughing grew steadily worse, and his cries were louder than the sound of the wind, the spitting of snow and sleet against the window.

At last I took him in my arms and lay with him on the bed where I prayed all the prayers that I knew. Perhaps it was that, or perhaps the simple closeness of our bodies, but in the darkest part of night he sighed once, curled against me, and closed his eyes.

Had he died in my arms, his little heart unable to stand the strain? Terror seized me, and an anguish so deep I thought I would die, too. And then I felt his breath on my cheek, a cool breath, free of fever.

I wept then, silently, alone in that small room with the snow-covered plains stretching around us and the silence so deep it was, in itself, a presence. I wept, gave thanks, and fell into my own exhausted sleep.

When the men arrived late the next day, they found me fevered, my lungs on fire. How illness travels is a mystery. How there, so far from the world, both baby and I were stricken, I couldn't explain. I lay shivering under the quilt—as I'd done so many times as a girl—hating my own weakness, hating my body that so often betrayed me.

It was Haw who comforted Maxcy, put him to my sore breasts when he cried from hunger, changed his diapers without complaint. Nat and Sam hovered around the stove, coaxing the fire to brew a tea I was too weak to drink.

Night came early, with the finality of winter, and the two men went to their own cabin. Haw put the sleeping Maxcy in his basket and came to the bed.

He took my hand, and, as always, I felt the pulse of life in him, a strength derived from what I thought was his total belief in himself. "Can you sleep?" he whispered, his eyes filled with concern.

I shook my head. Every time my eyes closed, the coughing began. Staying awake was the only way I knew to keep it at bay.

"Try," he said. "You have to get well. And don't worry about Maxcy. I'll be here and awake."

Didn't I know I'd have to get well! Without me, they'd all be as helpless as I felt. And Maxcy, dear God, what would happen to him if I died?

"Tea," I muttered with an effort.

Haw helped me sit up, held the cup while I took a sip, then another. I was too weak to swallow more, but the brew was soothing, sweet, and made me long for sleep. Once again, I reached for Haw's hand.

When I awoke, it was bitter cold. My breath frosted the air, and Haw lay asleep beside me. In his basket, Maxcy squeaked once, and then was quiet again.

The wind had dropped, and a nearly full moon poured a miracle of light over the deep snow. Miraculously, my fever had gone as quickly as it had come, and, although my chest was heavy and each breath still pained me, I knew I'd pulled through.

Beside me Haw stirred. I pulled the buffalo robe over us both and lay down again, savoring his strength, his warmth.

Chapter Eight

Spring came. Work on the house stopped, and all of us labored to get the corn planted, even Maxcy who I pulled along the rows in the small wagon Haw had made for his first Christmas.

That had been a happy time, that Christmas—a day we had gathered and counted our blessings, the greatest of which was my return to health. In addition to a large package from home that contained books, magazines, clothes, toys for Maxcy, and a much-needed draft for fifty dollars, I'd sewed a new shirt for Haw and had knitted warm socks for all the men in what I called "my family". Haw had bought me a fringed wool shawl with part of his earnings from Fort Riley.

"You shouldn't have spent the money," I'd told him, even as I wrapped it around my shoulders and took pleasure in its warmth and weave. "My old one is good enough."

"Yes, I should have. You deserve more. If I could,

I'd buy you diamonds, silks, velvets, have a decent bed for Maxcy, and all the toys he wanted."

"And I'd wear velvet in the field, I suppose." Harsh words, but to soften them I hugged him close. It wasn't a moment to be ungrateful.

Nat and Sam had the biggest surprise of all—in addition to the partridges they'd shot for the Christmas feast. Tied outside the door was a cow. A large, placid creature, her belly swollen with the calf that would assure us all fresh milk—and butter.

"Wherever did you get her?" I'd asked, stroking her soft nose.

They'd looked embarrassed. "Found her," Sam had muttered at last. "And she don't seem to belong to nobody. We asked."

"Prob'ly somebody got burned out and she got left behind," Nat had added. "But don't worry, ma'am. We didn't rustle the neighbors!"

"Well, thank heaven for that! Now come and let's eat."

Poor as we were, it was a splendid feast, and, as I followed the plow, my pockets filled with corn, I was remembering that day and smiling. How could I not?

The weather had turned mild. The soil was damp and newly plowed, and we were going to succeed—or else!

That spring, though, all the talk was of the gold strikes in Colorado. The newspapers Haw brought back were full of glorious tales, and the strangers who passed through on their way to seek their fortunes spun yarns that even I found fascinating. And there were plenty of travelers that year—men and families who'd grown weary of the constant fighting, the necessity to be always on guard, of wresting a meager living out of the often unco-operative land.

Haw listened and watched them go with the restlessness of a horse restrained, and though I said nothing, though I went about my chores with all the determination of a woman making a home, I wondered how long it would be before we were following those travelers, the dust of the trail in our throats, the west wind in our faces. As it turned out, in less than a year we were on our way.

Though our crop was bountiful, it was a year of plenty everywhere, and as a result the price of corn dropped to a pittance. We made only enough to pay what we owed, precious little left.

I finished moving into our new house came in with maps and newspapers under I've mortgaged the farm," he announced. got enough money for a new wagon and a pair xtra oxen, and I've decided on a route to Denver."

I opened my mouth, but no words came. After all, I had agreed to this if all else failed.

"You and Maxcy can go back to Maine," he went on. "Nat and Sam and I will go on ahead. If I make a strike, I'll come for you."

Just like that! Just like that he'd made a decision that affected us all, and I was to be packed off home! The words came then, plenty of them.

"Oh, no, Haw Tabor. You may have mortgaged the place without so much as a by your leave, but you aren't deciding the rest of my life for me. I have as much a say in our future as you, and I won't be sent home like I'm a burden or a failed wife no matter what! Where you go, I go, and there's an end to it. Now, it might be nice if you'd tell me how soon you intend us to leave."

He laughed. Laughed and pulled me close. "What a little spitfire I married. And who'd have guessed from the look of you?"

"Looks are deceiving," I replied. "And just how much is the mortgage?"

"As much as we needed. Stop fussing."

"I'll fuss if I want. You've got us into debt, and who knows if we'll ever pay it off." I hated debt, hated thinking we might lose the farm and my lovely new house for what could turn out to be a grand mirage.

He placed his hands on my shoulders and bent down, face close to mine. "Listen to me, Gusta. I've talked to men who've been out there. Who've seen the gold. It's a fortune waiting for us. Trust me in this."

Well, there wasn't much else I could do. I looked him straight in the eye. "I guess I'll have to," I said. "And I think I'll also put some trust in the Lord. They say He looks out for fools."

It was April, 1859 when we headed West—four of us and Maxcy who was now an alert and active little boy. It wasn't easy keeping track of him, making sure he didn't fall out of the wagon and under the wheels, or toddle off across the prairie when we stopped for the night. Fortunately Petty had taken him in charge, and Maxcy was rarely out of the faithful dog's sight.

None of that trip was easy. We followed the trail along the Republican River going north before turning west, moving slowly over a sweep of country so empty and so magnificent in its scope that, at times, I wanted to weep.

Who was I, Augusta Tabor, in the face of such a country? Who was any of us—man or woman—to attempt such a journey, to believe we could conquer what had never been conquered, the wind always in our faces, the land shaping itself like waves in a sea that could swallow us up without a trace?

The men, of course, had no such fears. They rode alongside the wagon, or scouted ahead, or hunted for meat with a joyful sense of adventure, and, when one of them came in with a deer, a rabbit, a brace of birds, he strutted around my poor cooking fire like a young rooster expecting praise or, at the very least, an extra portion from the cook. But the cook was lost in a world not of her making, a treeless world where the only source of fire was dried buffalo chips—chewed-up grass, nothing more—that produced a short, hot flame, and that had to be gathered every evening. The cook was a pair of hands and trembling legs, a wind-and-sun-blasted wraith who scoured the prairie with a pail, ever on guard for snakes, Indians, whatever dangers might lie behind the next rise, be hidden in the folds of dry streambeds—a woman followed by a child to whom every stick, stone, flower was marvel, distraction, possible danger.

It was a journey that took me to the limits of my endurance, but there were times, brief flashes of something greater than our trials, that have stayed with me all my life, that I remember as moments of unity with what I, lacking words, can only call the universe. Moments that came, not often, but often enough to give me the hope and the courage to endure. We had been on the trail two weeks and perhaps a few days more. I was still getting used to the sameness of days, the never-ending chores, the dust, the fears that came and went more often than I ever let on.

It had been a day of drizzle and mist rising from the low places. The sky was gray, the wind chill and damp. I poked at my poor fire, cursing it silently. How could one make anything edible on its slight warmth, its chips that turned to instant flame and then immediate ash? Maxcy had followed Haw and the men as they saw to the animals, and was watching with interest as Sam began to milk the cow.

At least there's that. At least we have milk. My thought was bitter, and I was filled with longing for the farm. *At least there we had walls and a roof over us.* Then I heard it—what sounded like the baying of a thousand hounds, far away but coming closer. There was a rhythm to the wild chorus, a music never written by man, and I stood motionless, some part of me—soul, mind, the place where being lives—rising up in wonder.

They came out of the south, great wings beating the sky, necks outstretched, more cranes than I had ever seen, each a voice, a trumpet calling, calling, one to the other and to us who stood transfixed below. I wanted—what was it I wanted, standing there, my face to the miracle of migration? Freedom? Release? The swiftness and seeming ease of flight? Or was it simply the desire to capture what was beautiful, a talisman to treasure, a charm to ease my way through life? Even now I cannot say. I have no tangible proof to hold tightly, to take out and examine. What I do have is the brilliance of an evening recalled—the sight of the cranes like a tattered shawl across the darkening sky, the perfection of their wild music, the utter silence of the plains when the last one had flown.

Chapter Nine

"There ain't no gold out there, mister. I been and seen for myself. You'll dig till yer hands stick to the shovel, 'n' all you'll get's black sand 'n' dirt. Mark me. I'm sorry I ever left home, 'n' so will you be. Your missus, too. It's no place for a woman. When winter comes, she'll be lucky to make it to spring. Same with yer young 'un."

Our visitor, if that's what he could be called, had arrived at our camp footsore and half starved, and the mule he led was no better, its hip bones so sharp I could have used them for clothes pegs.

I said nothing in reply to his litany of woes, but Haw was annoyed. "You're frightening my wife."

The man cackled. "But not you. You got the fever in you but no sense. Well, I've had my say. What you do is up to you."

"I've talked to others," Haw said. "Their stories are different from yours. And I've seen the gold they brought back for myself."

A snort came from our guest. "Prob'ly salted. You got

to watch out for that. There's thieves and con men run-
nin' wild, and they ain't above droppin' a few nuggets
somewheres and then sellin' out fer a price. Oh, there's
gold somewhere, but it's a lucky man lasts long enough
to find it. Me . . . I'm for home where I belong."

In the faint light of the fire, he was an apparition, a
prophet arisen from the pages of the Old Testament,
but oddly neither his appearance nor his message frightened me. He was, I thought, more than half crazed, and
besides his doom-saying had given me an idea.

"Mister . . . Payne is it?" I asked.

"Yes'm. Eli Payne."

"From what you say, there's need of people who are
neither miners nor crooks. Regular folks doing regular
work. Am I right?"

Another snort issued from behind his beard that
seemed not to have been washed or trimmed since it
sprouted. "Yer right there, missus. All you'll find's men
diggin' up the gulches, goin' hungry, drinkin' up what
little gold they dig. Anybody who'd cook or haul in
supplies could make more than the poor fools with
their hands in the dirt."

"I see."

I sat back and kept on with my sewing, a chore that
never ended, like all the other chores that fell to
women—laundry, meals, clothing, searching the prairie
for buffalo chips and kindling—enough work for ten
pairs of hands and an equal amount of strength. Men,
as I'd had plenty of time to observe, were helpless when
it came to caring for themselves. Perhaps that's why
they married in the first place. Perhaps love, passion,

companionship were secondary to food in the belly, clean clothes, and a bath on Saturday night. It was then that I formed the outline of a plan that I hoped might keep us solvent, whether or not Haw struck it rich. But for the moment, I kept my thoughts to myself.

In the morning Eli Payne left us, trudging alongside his gaunt mule and whistling. I watched till they disappeared, two black stick figures swallowed up by the rising sun, and for no reason, except that our odyssey seemed similar, I remembered the tale of Don Quixote.

"Tilting at windmills," I said, more to myself than to Haw, who missed my reference.

"Everybody's fate's different," he answered. "Payne's a loser."

"And we're not? What else are we doing here?"

He stiffened. "Don't start on that. We haven't lost the farm. We haven't lost anything yet, and we won't. The gold's out there, waiting for us. For you, me, and Maxcy. Don't doubt it for a minute. Or if you do, don't tell me. I don't want to hear."

Well, he never did, but if it pleased him to believe in his dream, then I'd do my best to support his effort and see us through. I picked Maxcy up and placed him on the wagon seat, then crawled up beside him, and reached for the goad.

As the oxen moved ahead, Maxcy gave a delighted chuckle. "Go!" he said. "Go!"

And westward we went.

Of course we weren't the only hopefuls traveling the Republican River route. Often we camped for safety with other parties, most of them as poorly equipped as we, and there were days when the trail was crowded with wagons, mules, men on horseback like an army of ants stretched out as far as I could see.

Pity us! Pity them! The homeless, the optimists, the down and out with nothing to lose but their lives, and the lure of gold calling like a siren. There was even a woman, Jane Gault. I remember her ruined face, her shattered life, her determination. She had buried her husband and son some place far behind, and had kept on, for nothing was left back in Iowa for her or her remaining children, a boy and a girl who looked close to starvation.

We shared our evening meal with them, and, after they'd returned to their poor wagon, Haw came to me, his face distorted by a worried frown.

"Do we have any food to spare?"

I sighed. "A little meal. Some milk in the morning. It won't help them much."

"Damn it! I hate this . . . this poverty! The way those kids look . . . like they've been to hell and back. And that poor woman. . . ."

"I'll see what I can find," I said. If it was up to Haw, we'd give everything away and have nothing left for ourselves, but Jane's face haunted me that night and for many a night thereafter, and, when I looked at Maxcy, bursting with health, I saw the hunger and the terror in the eyes of those children. We never saw them again, and I have often wondered whether they made it through, whether some kind man took them in and cared for them. I hope it was so.

* * *

From far out on the plains the mountains were visible, a barrier that took my breath. To climb those formidable peaks! To live within their confines! I, who'd become accustomed to a world unbounded, faced the fact that my life as it was and had been had changed forever.

We had met many like Eli Payne on our journey, but I'd refused to let their tales dim my optimism. Now, brought up against the utter reality of these mountains, I was even more daunted than I'd been at first glimpse of our little prairie cabin.

Haw caught me staring open-mouthed, attempting to hide my sudden, fearful insight. "The gateway to a fortune. What do you think? Glad you came?"

"Gateway?" Strain my eyes, though I did, I found nothing that resembled a door, a trail, an entrance into the interior. "There's not even a road!" I exclaimed.

"We'll build our own! We'll do what we have to. Blast, tunnel, whatever. We've come this far, we'll go all the way to the treasure. It's there, waiting."

"If we live that long."

He turned on me. "That's you. Never any encouragement, just a long face. I didn't ask you to do this, if you remember. You could be back in Maine right now."

His words stung. I'd never learned not to speak my mind. In fact, my family had always been forthright and sharp-tongued. "You knew how I was when you married me," I retorted. "It didn't bother you then."

"People change."

"To me, you're still the man I married." I looked

down at myself, scrawny from illness and the long trek, my boots cracked, one sole flapping, and imagined what my face must look like—thin, lined, brown, unattractive. Somewhere I'd lost myself, and, standing in Denver that June day in 1859, I wondered if I'd ever find me again. "Don't let's fight," I said, holding back tears. "I'm still me even if I've gotten ugly."

That startled him. "Ugly? Tears? No place for tears here, my girl. And I'm not fighting. You are." Then as I sniffed, he grabbed me around the waist. "And I didn't use the word 'ugly'. You did. Come on. Smile your pretty smile. The world's ours for the taking."

I smiled, having no choice. For better or worse, we were bound together, and I loved him. In spite of my efforts, the tears fell. "I'm so tired. Can't we stay here a while?"

"We're all of us done in. The animals, too. We'll stay and get our bearings. Rest up before we tackle the mountains. No sense going off half-cocked. Come on, let's look for a place to set up camp. Maybe by the creek. And tonight I'll find a restaurant. How'd you like a night out, Missus Tabor?"

A night out! No cooking! No chores or buffalo chips! It sounded like heaven. I said: "We can't afford it. And I'd rather have a bath."

All the pleasure vanished from his face. "Then I'll go by myself," he said, and left me.

If the travelers on the trail had seemed like ants, the banks of the Platte River were the ant hill toward which all were headed. There wasn't a square foot of ground anywhere for a mile, only row upon row of wagons with more arriving each hour. You could see them coming, see the dust they raised far to the east, and it never stopped, not once in the weeks we were there. At night the smoke from the campfires mingled with the dust so that often I thought I'd choke on a breath. The lights of the fires, the lanterns that glowed from wagons and from the doorways of the saloons, were visible for miles.

Haw took the oxen and mules to the Elephant Corral and was paying handsomely for their feed, a necessary expense for we needed strong animals to get into the mountains. He'd also discovered that Denver was a town of saloons, dozens of them lining the streets and offering everything from drink to gambling to lodging, even if that lodging was a bed atop a billiard table after the place closed in the early morning hours.

When he came back, I suspected he'd sampled the beer, but he was once again in a good mood and took my hand. "I've found you a bathhouse. It's not fancy, but you can get clean."

"How about you?" He smelled at least as bad as I did and looked worse, if that was possible.

"The river will do for me."

I'd observed what floated past on the current and had sent Nat off to find us some decent drinking water. "The river's filthy," I told him. "Everybody empties their slops in it."

"Then I won't hurt it a bit!" He roared with laughter, tugged at my hand. "Come on."

He was right about the bathhouse. It wasn't fancy,

the tub was dirty, and the towel just as bad, but the warm water felt like heaven on my skin that had dried out like a cornhusk, and the soap was several cuts above my own strong lye soap. I never asked the cost of that brief indulgence, being too weary, too grateful to care.

We stayed for several weeks in that town at the base of the mountains, that town swarming with those who had only one purpose—gold! And though my first glimpse of those mountains had been frightening, I was relieved when, on the first day of July, we left Denver, its noise, dust, smoke, smells, and headed up Clear Creek.

The high, clean air was invigorating, and the farther we went, the better I felt. Even Maxcy, who'd been teething and cranky, seemed to appreciate the freshness, the scents of pine and grass that drifted around us.

After two nights on the trail, we stopped and Haw and the men pitched our tent.

"Is this where we'll dig?" I asked, innocently enough, for though I'd listened to a hundred conversations about possible sites, I actually had no idea where we'd settle. "There's nobody here," I added, taking a good look around.

Haw finished pounding the last stake and straightened. "Tomorrow Nat, Sam, and I are going ahead to check out the Gregory Diggings. See if the trail's fit for a wagon. You and Maxcy'll be all right here."

"Alone? You're leaving me alone?" I couldn't believe what I'd heard.

"Not for long. You'll be better off here than in town, and you have the pistol and Petty."

I'd come this far only to be abandoned! "What if . . . what if you don't get back?"

"I'll always be back," he said.

There are some who say I was a fool, and some who find me an object of pity, but no one ever pitied me more than I did as I stood holding Maxcy and watching the three men trudge up the creek, Haw in that funny, almost lop-sided walk as if one leg was shorter than the other. Maybe it was. For a reason that eludes me, I never checked to see.

It was late afternoon of my second day. Maxcy was asleep in the tent. The cow and oxen were grazing happily, moving from one clump of grass to another. Wind hummed in the pines. The creek splashed and murmured to itself. Overhead, a hawk cried harshly.

"Keep us all safe," I prayed aloud, and the sound of my own voice was a comfort. That's when a lifelong habit got its start. To pass the time, to break the silence, I talked to myself and to Maxcy who was picking up words faster than I could say them.

"Best clean out the wagon," I told myself, "get a start on supper, too," and with the chores laid out for me, I set to work with a will.

When it came time for me to bring in the cow and oxen for the night, I discovered that, while I'd been busy, they had climbed halfway up a rocky hill and wouldn't come down, although I climbed after them and shooed them with my apron while Petty snapped at their heels.

Nearly reduced to tears of frustration, I yelled at them: "Damn', dumb critters! Move! Move!"

They swished their tails, went on eating, ignored me. And then a voice came out of the brush, scaring me nearly to death.

"I'll get 'em down, ma'am. You go on back."

A bearded stranger stepped out, laid down his pack, and came toward me. I felt in my pocket for the pistol, and he read my intent.

"Didn't mean to scare you. But if you'll go down, I'll bring 'em in. If there's one thing I know, it's cattle."

Petty laid back his ears, sniffed at the hand the man held out, then wagged his tail.

"I'd be grateful," I said. "They don't seem to want to listen to me."

"And I'd be grateful for a bit of whatever it is you got cooking, if there's any to spare." He gave a grin. "It smelled so good I followed my nose to here."

I smiled back. "One good turn deserves another, Mister . . . ?"

"Packard. Hank Packard from Columbus, Ohio," he said, and then moved off after the recalcitrant cattle.

Over a bowl of stew and biscuits, Hank said: "If I can ask . . . what's a lady doin' out here alone?"

"I'm not alone," I said with a smile. "And my husband and his partners will be back soon. They went ahead to look for the best place to prospect."

He wiped his beard with a huge hand. "For a meal

like this, I'd come back quick myself. It's a long way from Ohio, eatin' my own grub."

I sighed. "It's a long way from Maine, too, but I can't say it hasn't been an education."

"You're right about that. I never figured the country was this big. Or that I'd join up with a bunch of fools as big as myself. One thing I know, I ain't ever goin' to go back to farming. Drivin' your cattle reminded me of that. What're you goin' to do when I've left? You might break your leg, crawlin' after 'em."

"It's a risk," I said. "Like all the rest of it. More coffee, Mister Packard?"

He shook his head. "Thanks, but no. If it's all right with you, I'll camp over yonder for the night."

I studied him, wondering if he had more in mind than a night's sleep. How was I to know? Finally I nodded. "I . . . I guess."

"No need to worry, ma'am. I'll be off first thing. And thanks for the grub."

That decided me. "I'll have coffee on early, Mister Packard. Maybe even more biscuits."

"That'd be good of you. And if you want, I'll fix some hobbles for your livestock before I go."

As it turned out, a steady stream of gold-seekers came up that creek, many of them exhausted from the altitude, all of them hungry. They paid me in coin or in services—cutting wood, sharing their provisions—and I hardly had time to notice that Haw had been gone almost three weeks.

Each night I counted my little hoard of well-earned

coins and laughed to myself. Let others go out and dig. I'd stay home, do what I'd always done, and bank the money for when it was needed.

Men had to eat. I'd see to it that they did. Over the past two years I'd learned to bake, to boil, to roast, to fry—over buffalo chips on the prairie or a wood or corncob fire in a cast-iron stove. If, as I'd thought, I'd lost a part of who I was, I'd replaced it with another, competent self, a self I'd come to like, a woman of independence who faced down her fears and came out with money in her pocket.

Chapter Ten

"Pappy! Pappy!" Maxcy's cry of delight split the air.

"It's Pappy all right. Back from the digging." Haw strode down the trail, and lifted the shrieking child to his shoulder.

I was happy to see him. The three weeks had been endless, even though I'd been busy with my new job. I threw my arms around husband and child.

"What did you find? How far did you go? I'm so glad you're back! Tell me, quick!" I was babbling and didn't care that the man striding beside me bore no resemblance to the man I'd married.

He was ragged, bearded, burned black by the midsummer sun. But there was an unusual exuberance about him, an electricity, as if he'd touched the mother lode, found his reason for being. That I wasn't the reason didn't bother me in the least. Not then.

"We're leaving in the morning. There's gold not forty miles from here. We saw it. We talked to the men mining it. It's money in the bank, my girl."

"Not yet."

"But soon. What's for supper?"

"Venison stew."

He cocked an eyebrow. "Don't tell me you shot a deer with that pistol."

I giggled. "Some men came through. They gave me the meat in exchange for supper. I saved some for you." About the money, I said nothing. My secret.

"Clever girl. And clever boy," he said to Maxcy. "Who taught him to call me Pappy?"

"I did. He learned a lot while you were gone."

"Nat! Sam! Cow! Dog!" Maxcy shouted. "Pappy!"

Haw's laughed echoed around us. "By gad! A real chatterbox! It's good to be home."

I thought he had a strange picture of home but said nothing, being happy to have him back alive and well. That night he showed me just how glad he was to be with me. That night, with the moon high up and turning the land to silver, he took me with a surge of passion I won't ever forget, and I met him with an eagerness of my own.

Up and up, all the way to the sky, the mountain rose almost vertically out of the gulch, its sheer, black rock slopes dense with pine and brush.

"We'll never get the wagon up there!" I was panting already, and I'd only climbed what seemed like a few feet with Maxcy clutched in my arms.

The oxen groaned as they trudged on, their heavy necks and shoulders leaning into the yoke, their legs at an impossible angle. Up and up, till at last they stopped and refused to go farther, but the weight of the wagon pulled them slowly back down even with the brakes set.

Haw put his shoulder to one wheel. "Get me a rock, for Christ's sake! Quick!"

The cords of his neck stood out with his effort, and I envisioned him broken and bleeding beneath wagon and hoofs. Still clutching Maxcy and helpless, I watched the scene with horror—Haw straining against gravity, Sam holding the oxen as best he could, and Nat staggering toward us, a large rock in his hands.

I heard the grunt Nat made with each step, prayed that his feet wouldn't shoot out from under him. "Hurry, hurry." My lips formed the words, but no sound came except Maxcy's sudden cry.

"Pappy!" It was as if he, too, recognized danger, squirmed in my arms, and reached out to his father.

"Hush! Not now!" It was a thought only, like a prayer.

How long we stood, balanced like rope-walkers on the edge of death, is hard to say. Minutes became hours, hours, days, and my lungs ached from holding back a scream.

At last, Nat came sliding down, a clumsy business made worse by the incline and his own inability to gain purchase while he wrestled the small boulder behind the rear wheels.

"Get out of the way!" he shouted to Haw. "And hope to God it holds!"

I shut my eyes, not wanting to see. If the wagon went, all that we owned would go with it.

From what seemed far away, I heard Sam, steadying the oxen, the sound of boots scraping rock.

"It'll do." That was Haw, voice rasping in his throat. "Let's drive in a couple stakes to make sure. Gusta! You all right?"

I only nodded.

"Stay there, then. We'll get this done, then go ahead. Try to clear the trail."

Another nod. I was beyond speech. All my own fault. If I'd listened to him, I'd be back in Maine, sitting on the secure and level porch with all the sounds of summer a sweet serenade around me.

Fool! See where it's got you, that stubborn streak you're so proud of! But scolding myself made not the slightest difference. It was, obviously, too late.

Up and up, a few feet at a time, the wagon unloaded, the goods hauled up by straining bodies, everyone for himself. Darkness comes early in those mountains. The sun slipped behind them, leaving all but the heights in shadow. Ahead, too far to reach in the hours remaining, the crest glowed golden in the late afternoon light, tantalizing, taunting, secure in its might.

"We'll stop here."

I stared at Haw. "Here?"

"It's level, at least, and we got to give them oxen time to rest," Sam said. "Us, too. Accidents happen when you're too tired to think right."

A glance up. A glance down the impossible slope. "How will I cook?"

The men looked at each other, perhaps too exhausted

to answer. What food we had was still inside the wagon that rested against another rock.

At last Nat said: "I reckon we'll do without. Sorry, ma'am."

"At least we can get to the water," Haw said.

Fortunately the water barrels were lashed to the sides of the wagon, but I thought with longing of the bread in its tin box, the strips of jerky I'd made from the last of the venison—both out of reach.

Just then Maxcy whimpered: "Hungwy."

That settled it as far as I was concerned. "Maybe I can crawl in and at least get the bread. I don't weigh very much." At that time, I weighed hardly ninety pounds, mostly skin over bone.

"We can't risk it. Or you." That was Haw.

Nat looked at me, then at the wagon.

"She might do it. She could get through the back if we make sure that log'll hold."

"Hungwy!"

It was his son's misery that decided Haw. "Try it, then. But you'd better be ready to jump. Nat and I'll stay back here. Give Maxcy to me. I'll keep a hand on him."

"Keep your hands free," Nat said. "Put a rope on him so he don't slide."

When they were all in place, when Maxcy was firmly tied and set to one side, I approached the rear of the wagon. Slowly, slowly I rested myself on the tailgate. Had the wagon moved? I froze, dangling half in and half out.

"Go on," Haw muttered. "But go easy."

Inside it was dark. I groped for the food box, and the wagon shifted, groaning as something rubbed against something else I couldn't see. I froze again, knowing neither the oxen nor the men could hold long at that precarious angle.

With the box finally in both hands, I discovered I hadn't the strength to lift it out over the gate. God! Why did I have to be so weak, so helpless!

"What's taking so long?" Haw asked, and suddenly I was angry—at him, at my own physical defects. But it was an anger I dared not let loose.

Instead, my fingers found the hasp, lifted the lid, closed around a loaf and the sack of jerky. I prayed then as I let myself slide out, inch by slow inch, hands grasping nothing but the precious food.

At last my feet touched the ground, but rather than steady me, they twisted and went out from under me, and I was sliding down the rocky and uneven slope unable to stop, still clutching our meal.

It was Nat who, hooking one arm around a sapling, reached out and grabbed my wrist, held on while I struggled to my knees.

I was scraped raw, my dress ripped, but I'd provided for us. Once again, I thanked Nat for my life.

That night we hobbled the oxen and slept on bare ground. That night, following Haw's lead, I tied a rope around my waist and secured the other end around Maxcy. That way, I figured I'd awaken if he took a mind to explore. But I needn't have worried. I never slept a wink. The snores of the men, the bellowing of the cattle, the wind roaring in the tops of the pines kept me awake till a faint, pink light told me morning had come.

Somewhere off in the distance, Petty was barking.

We reached the crest around noon. Beyond us stretched mile after mile of untouched wilderness, of mountains that speared the sky, some of them still snow-covered, though it was the middle of summer. I had seen the Atlantic in a storm, the gray waves breaking, crashing, flinging white spume high in the air, and something in that expanse of water had called a challenge that, young as I was, I recognized. We fight the elements—wind, water, weather, rock. We go on—and on—winning or losing, but with a determination born in us.

So I felt looking out over the frozen waves of the mountains whose very presence was a dare. *Take us if you can!* I squared my shoulders and responded. *Try me!* To Haw I said: "Now we have to go down."

"And it's worse than climbing up. You'll find out."

He spoke the truth. Even using the wagon brakes, we had to cut and chain huge logs to the rear to keep from running over the poor oxen. The logs acted like a second pair of brakes—most of the time—and most of the time I walked behind, slipping, sliding, protecting Maxcy as best I could, heart in my mouth, terror in my bones, fighting the mountain with all my strength. But what is a mountain in the face of a woman's will? Perhaps a better question would be: what amount of gold is worth a life?

* * *

Our journey to Payne's Bar took three weeks, and to my surprise one of the first prospectors to welcome us was Hank Packard, hardly recognizable behind a bushy beard and uncut hair that fell into his eyes.

"Why . . . it's Missus Tabor!" he exclaimed. Then, turning to the others who'd come to greet the new-comers: "This here lady's the best cook west of the Missouri. I'll bet my claim on it!"

So, without uttering a word in my own behalf, I be-came cook, laundress, mother confessor for the prospectors at Payne's Bar—the first woman in any Colorado mining camp—a fact which filled me with a kind of pride. Hard work, work that kept me on my feet from first light till long after the sun had gone, but I loved every second of it, and I loved my steadily growing stack of coins, almost as much as I loved the cabin those men built for me. It had log walls, our tent for a roof, and within days the dirt floor was hard-packed from constant use.

"Missus, d'ye think ye kin mend my shirt? It's the last I've got."

"Would it be too much to ask if you could launder this along with your own wash? I'll be glad to pay."

"It's been a year since I had fresh milk. How much for a cup?"

"A lucky shot, ma'am. Reckon you can use some venison."

"I'll mind the boy, missus. He's no trouble. He kin pan fer his own gold right alongside of me."

"Missus, Pete here got himself shot. Kin you help?"

"How did it happen?" There was, it seemed, always a shooting or two in a mining camp; tempers were lost over a card game, a claim site, and aggravated by the cheap whiskey most of the men brought in.

"Him and another fella was arguin'. Nothing to worry about, but that ball's got to come out."

So I'd learn to be a doctor as well! "Lay him on the table."

The table was where I served meals, but there wasn't another place and I wasn't about to have him bleeding, and probably lousy, on our bed.

Carefully I removed his bloody shirt, not sure what I'd find or where he'd been hit. But Pete—and I—were lucky. The ball was in the fleshy part of his arm just below the shoulder, and I thought I might manage to dig it out with a knitting needle.

Pete fainted halfway through, and I almost did the same. For a moment I closed my eyes, took a deep breath, then another, and hoped my hands would be steady enough to probe deeper.

"You all right, missus?" His partner watched me anxiously.

"Yes. Just hold him steady in case he wakes up."

I probed deeper, but the knitting needle proved useless. "Go in the house. Find me a spoon. A small one. And hurry!"

Fortunately, using both makeshift tools, I managed to get a hold of the piece of lead and pull it out. Blood welled into the wound, and I pressed a cloth against it, hard.

I'd been doing laundry when the men arrived, and

the wash water was still hot. "Pour me some water into that basin," I ordered. "And bring a handful of those rags."

When I'd washed and bandaged the wound, my legs gave way without warning, and I sat down on one of the stools and prayed I'd never again be called to dig into anyone's flesh, to see the sinister oozing of blood around shredded muscle, the skin torn apart as if it was only parchment.

"Take him home and let him sleep," I said. "And all of you try to stay out of trouble. I'm not sure I could handle this again."

"Yes'm. And thanks. You done as good a job as I ever saw." He lifted his friend as easily as if he were a child and strode off.

Haw found me, still sitting, my senses numb, my head whirling. "I came quick as I heard. Is it done? You all right?"

"Yes, but never again. I mean it."

He patted my hand. "I'm proud of you, Doctor Tabor. There's not many who could do it."

"There wasn't anybody else."

In a gesture that, for him, was oddly gentle, he dipped water from the wash pot and wiped my face and hands. I watched the water turn red with a stranger's blood and tried to think about supper. The very notion of food was nauseating.

"Supper's going to be late," I said. "You'd best tell them."

"Damn supper. You go take a rest. I don't want you taking sick."

It wasn't I who got sick but Maxcy who, by the time night came, was feverish and in bad pain.

"Mountain fever," Nat said.

"What is it? Is it dangerous?" I was rocking the boy in my lap, and the heat of his small body was so intense that I felt it through layers of clothes.

"Could be once it gets in the bowels."

Alarmed, I held Maxcy closer. "You mean it's . . . it's cholera?" The disease every man, woman, and child dreaded more than any other.

"Not that. But you got to control his bowels 'fore it goes too far."

The possibility of losing my only child left me witless. "How? I'm not a doctor, though everybody thinks so. How, Nat?"

Haw had been searching my chest of herbs and medicines, his love and fear for our son plainly on his face. Now he held up a withered, yellowish root. "Try this. It's what Ma always used on us kids for stomach complaint. She got it from the Injuns and swore by it. It worked on me."

"Just a little," Nat put in. "And some sweetening with it or he won't take it."

I gave Maxcy over to Haw and went to heat some water, praying we were doing right, that my little boy would come through, because if he didn't. . . . I shuddered. He had to! I'd see to it!

All the nights and days that followed, I nursed him, spoon-fed him the tea, bathed his face and hands in cold water in an attempt to bring down the fever. The miners came, one by one, out of kindness and their own love for the child they'd watched over, played with.

"He'll pull through. Don't you fret, ma'am."

"Why, lookee there! He's smilin'. Ain't you, boy?"

"Don't worry none about supper, Missus Tabor. You take good care of that boy."

And I did, never sleeping, alert to any whimper, change, or a whispered: "Mama. Hurt."

All I could think of was the hundreds, perhaps thousands, of children who'd died—on the prairie, in these forbidding mountains. I saw the graves that lined the trail, heard from far away the countless mothers weeping, the fathers swallowing their own bitter tears. But I did not weep. I had no time. Not then.

Perhaps it was the seventh day—I'd lost all sense of time—when, in spite of myself, I fell into a doze.

"Ma . . . Mama." It was such a little sound!

I snapped awake, and there he was, my son, sitting up on his cot as if nothing had happened, as if the past week had been only a hideous nightmare.

It was then that the tears came, but they were of joy, not sorrow. I took him in my lap, felt his cool cheeks, saw his smile through a haze.

Mountain fever. Worse by far than gold fever. I hoped I'd never see it again, but I was wrong.

It was after that, after I came to recognize the perils of life, the speed with which death can strike, that I began to take a few minutes each day to appreciate the beauty of the land around us. With the coming of autumn, the aspens on the highest mountains turned to gold, rivers of gold, more than was ever taken out from beneath the ground. There were moments when I stood transfixed, filling my eyes with the brilliance of a million small trees, their leaves dancing in the sunlight like candles, jewels, golden butterflies, so full of life, so unaware that time would fade and then destroy their beauty.

If there is a lesson in this, so be it. Time takes everything. I know. Haw—and that woman decked in diamonds and ermine, that woman who owes as much to me as to Haw Tabor—discovered the same truth.

With autumn came the first snow, a light one, that only increased the loveliness around us—the pine boughs etched in silver, the sky more blue than even in summer, the clouds that daily broke on the mountains, dazzling in bursts of sunshine.

There was snow, and there was danger. One of the old miners, a shifty-eyed fellow with a face like a fallen pudding, came to us with a warning.

"Come winter, there'll be snow slides. Yer missus and the kid might git buried alive. You, too." He spoke, and he spat, and I turned away from the disgusting mess.

Haw towered over the little man. "Snow slides?" We were newcomers to the dangers of the Rockies and had no idea of such a thing.

"Yeah. Anything can set one off. Rifle shot. Thunder. Best git yer family out while you can."

As always, Haw made his decision within a minute. "Pack up. I'll take you to Denver, then come back on my own."

And so we left, going once again over our old trail—up, down, muscles straining, our breath harsh in our mouths.

In Denver we found rooms above Vasquez's store and counted our money and the small amount of gold Haw had panned. All by myself, I'd made enough to pay off the mortgage on the Kansas farm, and Haw looked at me in amazement.

"By God," he said. "You made that just cooking?"

"And other things."

"I'll be damned."

"Not if I can help it."

Tom Jessup was a young man who'd tried his hand at prospecting but decided he preferred the routine of Kansas farm life. I entrusted him with the mortgage money and, with regret, gave him Petty. With everything but my small hoard of coins gone, I couldn't afford to feed my devoted dog.

Petty, at first, refused to leave, kept coming back to me like the constant companion he was. It was then that I tied a rope around his neck and, kneeling on the street, hugged him hard.

"You be good now and go with Mister Jessup. I won't forget you. Not ever. Go on."

All the way down the street he kept turning his head to look at me, and I felt I'd abandoned a member of the family for no reason except poverty. Slowly I climbed the stairs to our rooms, drying my eyes so Maxcy wouldn't see.

"I want Petty," he said as I entered.

"Petty's gone."

"Why?"

Why, indeed? "Because we couldn't keep him here."

"Why?"

"Because we can't."

"He could sleep with me."

"Yes," I said, laying a hand on the smooth, childish head. "I know."

His face crumpled. "Petty!"

That's what being poor is about. Having to tell a child his friend has been given away. I gritted my teeth. "Someday we'll get another Petty."

"No," he said. "Not ever."

Long before he came to the door, I heard Haw coming. He was swearing at the top of his lungs, and I suspected he'd stopped at one of the saloons before coming back from his claim.

I met him at the top of the stairs. "Mind your language in front of the boy! You've been drinking, too!"

"Hell and damnation!" He stomped snow and mud off his boots onto my clean floor. "That son-of-a-bitch! That Renquist, who warned us to leave, up and jumped my claim! Like a pair of fools we believed that snow slide story he told us. Hell, where we were the mountains ain't big enough! If I'm drunk, I've got a right. I damn' near killed him. Tossed him in the creek and left before I did worse."

I'd never seen him so angry. His eyes shot sparks, and his fists were clenched as if he'd like to take a punch at me or anyone else standing in his way.

I fought my own anger. All that work! All those

mountains scaled at peril for our own lives! All for nothing! "We'll find another, better claim. Maybe it's God's will."

"God's will, hell! There's got to be laws about that kind of thing."

But in those early days there were no laws about jumping claims, even about murder if there happened to be no witnesses. Many a body was found long after the deed, and no one around to take the blame, to stand trial.

I saw there was no calming Haw. Without another word, I took his coat, mopped up the floor, and put supper on the table—a pitiable meal, all I could afford.

"You expect me to eat this?" He slammed a hand on the rough wood, and the dishes rattled.

"It's what there is."

"Then you eat it." In one move he was out the door, lost in the darkness, the cold, the snow that whirled down from the mountains.

"Pappy's mad." Maxcy, who'd been playing on the floor, looked up, wide-eyed.

"He'll get over it."

"Why?"

I sighed, took him on my lap. Such a lovely little boy he was—well-behaved, curious, as much a part of me as if we were still joined. "There are people who aren't nice," I told him. "People who take what doesn't belong to them. Pappy doesn't like them."

He reached up and patted my cheek. "Pappy likes you. Me, too."

"Yes, baby. Pappy likes us. He's a good man."

Except that he'd gone out and was probably spending the last of our money on drunkenness. I sighed. Who could blame him? His claim—our claim—was gone.

Chapter Eleven

Our Christmas celebration that year was hardly festive. Haw went into the foothills and brought back a small tree, and in a package from home I found a flannel petticoat that I cut up and sewed into shirts and pants for Maxcy who was growing fast. For the men I'd knitted mittens, and for the Christmas feast I traded old Vasquez a lace collar for a piece of beef that turned out so tough I was sure it was mule meat.

Immediately after the New Year, I was taken ill. For most of that month, I lay in bed, weak, miserable, doing my best to keep an eye on Maxcy who, good boy that he was, kept me company much of the time.

Still, I was getting tired of looking at the room, its four, bleak walls. A part of me was longing for the cabin, for the sound of the creek rushing over its stones, and the sight of the hard blue sky. Cabin fever the old-timers called it, those prospectors, trappers, hunters who, during the long winters, were forced inside to pass the time as best they could. Call it what you will, I was almost glad when, early in February, Haw came in radiating excitement. The signs were easy to read—his burning eyes, his quick but awkward walk, head leading the way as if impatient at the slowness of his body.

I pushed myself up in the bed. "What's happened?"

"There's been a big strike west of South Park. A couple fellas just came in with the news. I talked it over with Nat and Sam, and we ought to leave as quick as we can. You up to traveling?"

Anything was better than being left behind in that room for which we were paying twenty-five dollars a month—money that might better be spent on food or put in the bank.

"I'll make it. When do we start?"

"I need two weeks to get an outfit together. And I'll have to sell the cow."

She'd been a good cow. Many a morning I'd milked her, rested my head against the warmth of her belly while she stood placidly, giving of herself to feed us and the men who stood waiting, tin cups in hand.

"If that's what you have to do, do it," I said.

He stood up. "Maybe this time we'll get lucky. But you can bet I'll record any claim I make. Nobody's stealing what I own out from under me again. And if I ever see that fat-faced Renquist, I'll. . . ."

"You'll do nothing. Go look for trouble, and you'll find it. God will take care of Renquist."

"Not soon enough."

"We don't know that. I'll start packing. And I'll be ready when you are."

And I was, though the men had to carry me down the stairs and lay me in the wagon where I stayed for two days, gathering strength. On the third day I got up, washed, pulled on my warm coat, and climbed out, determined to pull my weight.

Snow. Sleet. Ice. An impossible trail or no trail at all. Attempting to cook over a fire made of damp wood that smoked and gave out little heat. Around us the mountains deep in snow, the black shadows of the pines like sketches done with pen and ink, the wind howling, the sky gray, heavy with its burden. Each day the same as the last.

This time we weren't the only trail blazers. It looked like most of the male population of Denver was headed to the new strike. By wagon, mule, jack, on foot, and pushing hand carts they came, turning the snow to slush and then to mud, so the oxen and mules strained in their yokes and collars, and the untouched stillness of the mountains rang with shouts and curses, the cracking of whips, the creak of wagons and saddle leather.

Gold fever had become every man's impossible dream of wealth, of instant riches. With gold they would be freed from constant struggle, labor, poverty. But what struggles we, and they, went through can hardly be described.

Once again I was left behind while Haw and others went ahead to build a road through the trees where never before had there been anything more than a narrow trail for the deer, the Indians. Once again I sat by a smoldering fire and looked back on a life that had never prepared me for this loneliness, this exertion beyond physical strength. I was as bad as the rest—as that serpentine line of men winding toward riches. I was a woman caught up in a movement that would culminate in a blaze of glory and in the ultimate destruction of the man I'd loved and married.

Gold fever! As far away from Maine, abolition, and the horror of slavery as night is from day. Gold fever—a force as perilous as war or disease. And yet, and yet, if not for that, where would we be now, we men and women of Colorado? Perhaps back on the banks of the Kennebec, the Potomac, the Ohio, the Mississippi, secure in our houses, our safety, without recognizing who we were or what we were made of. What I know now, looking back, is that those mountains, gulches, storms, trials, and triumphs, those moments of despair, gave to me and to countless others a strength, a fortitude we never knew we had. I was forged there, for better or worse, while the forces against slavery gathered themselves into storm clouds as violent as any of those that battered the tops of the mountains, and meanwhile life went on in the East and the West, divided by geography and by purpose.

We reached South Park as the sun was setting, and the beauty of the place stopped my heart for one long moment.

"Oh, just look!" I said, and stretched out my hands as if I could capture the golden bowl where antelope and deer grazed unafraid of humans, where streams made a pattern of silver lace across the wide expanse, and the sky was banded crimson and saffron over the deepest blue of night.

Nat looked up at me and smiled. "That's something to see, all right."

"I don't think I'll ever forget this."

"Places like this one make all the troubles worthwhile."

I laughed. "Nat, you're becoming a philosopher."

But he was a simple man, plain-spoken. He shook his head. "No, ma'am. I jist appreciate what the good Lord made. And hope I don't live long enough to see what folks make out of it."

We'd seen our share of mining camps—the shanties, tents, crude houses, strewn garbage, the wreckage of streams that had once run clear, all the detritus of mankind left behind as soon as a new strike caused a stampede. No one, it seemed to me, cared for the land, only what could be gotten from it. No one recognized that a forest, felled, might never grow again. It was only the gold that mattered.

"Don't ruin it," I said. "Let's just look."

"Let's set up camp while we can still see," Haw said.

He never was one to appreciate nature. He was a doer, a builder, his surroundings of little or no interest. His visions were always of civilization and grandiose cities. For that, I suppose, he deserves credit, for he understood the necessity for law, order, power. But on that evening, with South Park in all its glory at our feet, I wondered, not for the first time, how it was that I'd married a stranger.

That was the night the burro came. Lured by the warmth of our fire, by the presence of people, he walked into our tent and stood, long ears at attention, and in his eyes all the wisdom of thousands of years of uncomplaining service.

At the first sound, Haw had grabbed his rifle and leaped up. Now, barefoot and looking slightly ridiculous, he said: "I'll be damned. Why'd he come in here of all places?"

"He's lonesome. And cold, poor thing." I got up, too, and went toward the shivering animal. Traced on his withers was the black cross of the true burro.

"I think he's a gift," I said.

"Who from? Who'd send us a burro?"

"God."

Haw snorted. "Don't go getting female notions. We've got enough problems."

What was it I'd thought about marrying a stranger, about this large, dark man who was looking at me as if I were some kind of female hysteric—a Victoria Woodhull, a believer in ghosts and spirits?

"Don't look a gift horse in the mouth," I retorted. "He's useful. Or will be, and, if you think about it, I'm not the one with the wild notions."

"What's that supposed to mean?" He was getting angry, his jaw thrust out.

"It means we're here freezing, our money gone, and

a child to care for. It means we could have stayed in Kansas and worked hard like everybody else, and had a roof over our heads. Maybe we'd have had more to show for ourselves than this . . . this tent, this snow, and a burro!"

"You can go back. I won't stop you."

"You'll stop me when you get hungry and when your clothes wear out!" Oh, God, I hated arguments! They tore at the fragility of self and of two lives bound together and left scars that never disappeared. "I'm sorry," I said. "It's just that I'm so tired."

"We all are." The fire in his eyes had died down. "So, what should we do with this fella?"

"He needs a rub-down, poor thing. I think I'll call him Jack."

"Very original."

There it was—that hint of sarcasm I was beginning to dread.

"Go back to sleep." I picked up a piece of sacking and began rubbing the wet hide. "I'll take care of him. He's mine."

In our journey up the Arkansas Valley that followed, little Jack proved his worth many times over, carrying Maxcy and me over flooded rivers and up the steepest mountains without complaint. At night he was always on guard just outside our tent, and, when we'd finally reach California Gulch, our destination, he appointed himself Maxcy's guardian, following him like a faithful dog.

Maxcy taught himself to climb up on Jack's back and rode proudly around the camp without reins or saddle, his laughter ringing out, and I had no fear that any harm would come to the boy as long as Jack was in charge.

It was Jack's loud bray that brought me running to the door of the cabin that was our living quarters, our small store, and the post office of which I was the unofficial mistress. In that cabin I also cooked and served meals to any prospector with enough money or gold to pay. Even if we didn't strike it rich, I knew that, with my contributions, we'd have enough saved to keep going for at least another year.

It was midday. I stood, shading my eyes with my hand, and watched a wagon and team make its slow way up the narrow trail that passed for a street. The driver was a small man, his face shadowed by a broad-brimmed black hat.

"Who on earth?" No miner had ever looked like this man who'd pulled up and was smiling at Maxcy.

As I approached, I saw he was a priest, neither young nor old, though his eyes behind round spectacles held all the knowledge of the world, both good and bad.

Seeing me, he removed his hat and leaped down lightly from the wagon seat. As I'd learn, all his movements were quick—as if he was on springs.

"Good morning. I'm Father Joseph Machebeuf from Denver, making what you might call my rounds."

"All the way here!" I exclaimed.

"God is everywhere. I come to remind people of that."

He was as quick of mind as he was of body, and I

laughed. "And I'm sure we all need reminding now and again. I'm Missus Tabor . . . postmistress, cook, laundress, and the mother of this young man. Have you eaten, Father?"

A smile creased his face from ear to ear. "I haven't. Is that coffee I smell? And bread?"

"Just baked. Maxcy and Jack will show you where to put up your team, won't you Maxcy?"

"You come with me." Maxcy kicked his heels into Jack's sides and moved ahead, plainly proud of his adult errand.

As I discovered, Father Machebeuf regularly toured all the mining camps that were, as he put it, "under his care". With him he brought the latest news—of recent strikes and the fact that Congress had made Colorado a territory—a Union one.

"And about time, too," Haw said. "Maybe this will help get us some laws out here that'll protect us miners and what we've worked for."

"The route to civilization is a long, slow one," the priest said with a smile. "Perhaps in another thousand years all our problems will be solved."

"Out here," I said, "we've almost forgotten about the fight against slavery. Our problems are different, as you know."

He sipped his coffee with the pleasure of a man who appreciated his food. "The fight will go on till slavery is abolished. One man cannot own another. That's God's law. We humans have only to make it ours as well."

"It'll take a war, Father," Haw said, repeating what

had been said around the table in Maine. "The South isn't going to give up what it has. They'll fight. We lived in Kansas and I can tell you we never knew when we'd have to fight back."

"I pray we'll be spared that, but then I never know if my prayers do any good at all."

His subtle humor was disarming. I'd never known a priest, and certainly not one like this man with his mobile face, his French accent, still so evident in spite of years in America.

Curious, I asked: "What do you do on these visits? Preach? Have prayer meetings? Does anybody come?"

He twinkled at me. "I say Mass. Hear confessions and pretend I don't recognize the sinners when I see them later. Whatever needs to be done, I do. You're not Catholic?"

I shook my head.

"But you believe in God."

"Of course. Whenever I take the time just to look around, I have to believe. None of us created these mountains. We don't have that kind of . . . of imagination. At least I don't."

His almost ugly face was radiant with what seemed to me to be a holy light. "God is God. Whatever religion you practice. And now, if you'll excuse me, I'll go about His business."

"Please come for supper. The others will be glad to hear your news."

As I expected, the talk at the supper table was all of politics, and Haw, as usual, was in the thick of it. "We'll never get anywhere . . . or get rich . . . without laws. A man can't work his fingers to the bone and then have it all taken away by some crooked bastard who wants something for nothing. And we need roads so we can come and go without risking our necks, so we can get enough supplies in to see us through. We can't wait for Washington to make up its mind, either. We've got to help ourselves."

I'd heard it all, even the rough language that I'd learned to ignore. Mining camps weren't high society, although I wondered what the priest must be thinking.

"Will you bless our meal, Father?" I asked.

The priest beamed at me, folded his hands, and began a prayer, and it did my heart good to see those hardened men bow their heads and give thanks.

But the next morning, after Mass which everyone, Catholic or not, attended, I was startled to find Father Machebeuf slumped over the tailgate of his wagon, his face flushed with what I knew only too well was fever.

"You're ill."

"It seems so." He got out before he fell into a faint.

I called to a nearby man for help, and together we got the priest into his wagon and laid him on his cot. As I would have expected, all was neat and in order, his religious robes folded into one trunk, a few ragged garments in another, and his pots and tin cup hanging from hooks close at hand.

I bent over and untied his boots that were nearly worn through. His socks were simply holes joined together heel and toe by the thinnest of threads.

"Missus Tabor. What happened?" He'd opened his eyes and was watching me, obviously bewildered.

"You have a fever. Lie still, and I promise you'll be better. I'll see to that. And you'll have a pair of socks to warm your feet," I added, hoping to make him smile.

A weak grimace was all he could manage, poor man, but I accepted the effort, covered him with a buffalo robe, and went to make the yellow-root tea that, along with a few drops of laudanum, had worked for Maxcy.

Machebeuf proved a good patient, though an apologetic one. "I'm making more work for you, my dear, and I'm sorry. But grateful, too."

"If I didn't work, what would I do?"

"You could try prayer."

"What I accomplish is prayer enough."

He gave a hoarse chuckle. "If offered to God, I agree."

"Don't try to convert me, Father."

Another chuckle. "I wouldn't dare, Missus Tabor. I haven't the strength, and, besides, I'm in your hands."

I laughed, too. He was a good man, kind, decent, devoted to his life, and there was a comfort in his presence. I was, in fact, sorry to see him off two weeks later, determined and still weak but wearing new socks with an extra pair in his trunk.

"Go safely, Father. Don't try to save everybody at once. And mind you keep warm."

"And may God bless you and yours. If you ever need me, for even the littlest thing, I hope you'll come find me."

Who knew? It could be that one day I'd seek him out, if only to talk, to share his gift of unstinted laughter. "I'll remember," I said, and watched till his wagon disappeared around a bend in the street.

Chapter Twelve

That fall, Haw, Maxcy, and I headed back to Denver. Haw, who'd gotten a taste for politics, had been chosen to represent the miners at a meeting of the newly formed Territory of Jefferson, at which it was hoped laws would be passed to punish claim-jumpers and establish order in the mining camps. It seemed to me that, once beyond the frontier of civilization, men reverted to beasts, shooting, robbing, in sore need of laws both civil and religious to restore their humanity.

We had almost four thousand dollars safely stowed in the wagon, much of which I'd earned myself. The rest was the gold Haw had taken out of the gulch. Was I proud? Too proud, perhaps, of my contribution? I suppose I was, but even now I can remember my pleasure as I counted the money I'd made with my own ingenuity, while Haw had been out politicking.

To be honest, I thought he'd wasted much of his time exploring the country, talking and socializing, leaving the store and most of the work to me, but I doubted I could ever change what he was. No woman ever changed the man she married, regardless of her strength of will, but I never had the sense to stop trying, even when it was too late.

"No more cheap rooms over Vasquez's store," Haw said as we came near to Denver. "And no need for you to work like a slave all winter. We've got enough to be comfortable for a change."

"But what will I do?" I asked, faced with six months of idleness.

"Get yourself some new clothes. Make friends. Do whatever women do to amuse themselves."

"Just because we have some money doesn't mean we have to spend it. Better put it in the bank. My clothes are good enough yet."

He let out a sigh of exasperation. "Gusta, for God's sake! I'm going to be meeting people. Important people who're running the territory. I can't be introducing the washwoman as my wife, now, can I?"

"I'm not good enough. Is that what you're saying?"

"Do you have to twist every word?" He was grinding his teeth. "What I meant was that I'd like a little help with all this. I'd like to see you dressed like you're somebody."

What he wanted was a falsehood. I was who I was regardless of what was on my back, but what he wanted was for me to reflect the glory of Horace Tabor, deserved or not.

I said: "I want to go home."

His jaw dropped. "Home? To Maine?"

"Yes."

He was quiet for a minute, probably weighing the pros and cons of being rid of me—the washwoman. "It's a good idea," he said after a minute. "Maxcy should know his grandparents, and you can take a rest. I'll come back for you as soon as these meetings are over. Now we're a territory, maybe I can get things done right. When d'you want to leave?"

"As soon as possible," I said around a lump in my throat that almost strangled me.

Maxcy watched as I packed a trunk for our trip East with a child's fascination.

"How far?" he asked. "How far to Maine?"

"A long ways. A month. Maybe two."

"How long's a month?"

"Thirty days."

"So many!"

"Yes," I said. "Many."

But I'd be working and have no time to count the days. Haw had given me a thousand dollars for the trip, but instead of purchasing two seats on the Leavenworth and Pikes Peak Express at the exorbitant price of one hundred and fifty dollars each, I'd found a wagon train headed East that was in desperate need of a cook. In exchange for my services, Maxcy and I were going to Kansas free.

"Only you, Gusta," Haw said with a laugh when I told him about my arrangements. "You could travel in style, but you won't."

"I'll have to after Kansas. But that money's better spent on other things."

"Like what?"

"I'll know when the time comes. But I'll still have the money."

The weather held good all across Kansas, that perfect, golden spell that comes after the first frost and before winter. "Indian Summer" they call it. A time for gathering, storing up, a respite from the searing heat, a blessing before the blizzards sweep down from the north. The grass, the short curled buffalo grass, had cured and crackled under the feet of the mules— six to a wagon—that took us East, and goldenrod, snake weed, the smallest of sunflowers, still bloomed along our trail.

I think I gasped as we came out onto the plains—in wonder at my failure to recall that limitless horizon, that perfect sky—and beside me Maxcy stared with the untarnished astonishment of the very young at the new, the strange, the unimagined, stared and then bounced with glee as we moved on, the sun at our backs, dust dancing in its long rays, and all around the beginning of shadows where the land rose up and shielded itself, gave shelter to windblown stands of trees painted with red and gold.

We left the train at a stage stop near Zeandale, where I borrowed a wagon and drove to the farm. There the stone house Haw had built stood, sturdy and well cared for. My house that I'd never lived in.

"This is where you were born," I said to Maxcy. "Right here nearly four years ago."

"Are we staying here?" he wanted to know, and I wondered what went on inside his head, if he'd sensed the acrimony between his parents but couldn't put his doubts into words.

"No, love. But it's ours. And I'm going to buy some more land as long as I'm here. It's a good investment."

"A what?"

"A way to save money. To put money to work."

The way I saw it, a child was never too young to learn thrift, and, if I had my way, Maxcy would grow up wise in the way of watching out for his money and himself. Haw doted on the boy, but his education was in my hands, and a good thing, too!

I did buy another one hundred and sixty acres before we left Zeandale for a visit with Hannah and John. Emily Tabor was no longer living with them, having married and moved away. We had a happy reunion, but it was soon spoiled by the talk of war and slavery. The antagonism between North and South had escalated to the point that war now seemed inevitable.

"The only question is when," John said. We were sitting on the porch after supper, enjoying the last of the day. "If Lincoln wins the election, you can be sure it'll be soon."

"Do you think he will?" Isolated as I'd been, I knew little about the political climate beyond the mountains.

John leaned back in his chair and puffed on his pipe, those eyes of his, that had always appeared to be seeing what others missed, fastened on the horizon. "I can only hope and pray for it."

"Will you fight?"

Hannah cast me a quick glance: "We've fought enough. Day and night it goes on, never ending. When John Brown was captured after Harper's Ferry, soldiers came back here looking for anybody who'd helped him. They tramped through the house, searched everywhere as if we were traitors . . . us! . . . and scared the children half to death. I'm sick of fighting. Sick of the whole business. Let the slaves help themselves!"

Hannah, bitter? It was a shocking comment, a preview of worse to come. "You don't mean that," I said.

"I do. I told John we should go out to Colorado like anybody with sense, but no. He'd rather stay and put his life on the line."

"Now, Hannah." He leaned over and laid a hand on her arm.

She twisted away. "Don't. I've said my say. I started out like the rest, believing it all, but I don't any more. All the killing, all the raids, all the fighting. I hate what you've done, and there's an end to it!"

After that we sat in silence for a long time, with me wondering if all marriages came to this—this head-to-head combat over money, ideals, politics. Was there no one in the world who was truly happy?

For no reason, I thought of Father Machebeuf, a happy man if ever I saw one. But, then, he wasn't married. He served no one, fought with no one unless, in his private moments, he argued with God.

"I hope you'll think seriously about coming to Colorado," I said. "Haw would love it, and so would I. It's hard being the only woman for a hundred miles."

"You poor dear!" Hannah's heart ruled, as always.

"And here I am going on about things that can't be helped. At least, not by me. Both of us need a good gossip's what."

John stood up. "That being the case, I'll take a walk. Stretch my legs. And leave you ladies to it."

"Be careful. Promise me." Her smile had disappeared, and I understood the source of her bitterness. Her world had gone out of control and she was frightened out of her wits.

"Isn't it ever going to end?" I asked.

She looked at me, stricken. "If and when it does, I hope it's not too late for us."

My whole family was at the train station when Maxcy and I arrived, and it seemed to me, standing there in the late autumn sunshine, that I'd never left, that the plains of Kansas, the mountain camps, were a dream, and I was still that young, frail Augusta, safe in the arms of my family.

My father swung Maxcy in his arms. My mother hugged me, and, when I felt her sturdy warmth, a shell I hadn't known I'd built around my heart cracked, broke, and left me crying and unable to stop.

"Look at you. Brown as an Indian. And your hands! Where are your gloves? What've you done to your hands?"

I looked down at my offending and gloveless hands and saw the result of four years' hard work—broken nails, calluses, the skin chapped and sunburned. How to explain? How say to her that I'd worked as hard or harder than any man and proud of it? That I hadn't a decent pair of gloves or even a whole petticoat to my name and that, in mining camps, such niceties didn't matter. I couldn't answer, and luckily mother's attention turned to Maxcy.

"Oh, look at this beautiful boy. Come here, love, and give your gramma a kiss."

"Where on earth did you get those clothes?" That was Becca, clutching her daughter Vesta's hand. The little girl had been named in memory of our sister, who'd died while I was in Kansas. "You look like you robbed the rag-bag."

"I'm glad to see you, too," I said through my tears. Obviously separation hadn't broken our habit of snipping at each other—or weakened our love.

With a blush, Vinnie stepped between us and introduced her soon-to-be husband, and then Ruthie, Lilly, Frank, and little Ed, all grown up, came for hugs of their own and refrained from mentioning my ragged bonnet, travel-stained and dowdy clothes.

"Enough!" My father shouted over the din. "Let the poor girl catch her breath!"

We rode home in two carriages with Maxcy sitting proudly on Mother's lap. It was good to be petted, well-fed, fussed over, measured for new dresses, the center of attention. Once again I became the fragile daughter, the one who was cosseted and waited on, and I made the most of it, lying late in bed in the morning, letting the familiar sounds and scents seep into consciousness like music heard once but never forgotten. There was the muffled blasting of granite from the quarry, a cow calling to her calf, a tree rattling bare branches in the winter wind, and overall the smells from the kitchen—a roast in the oven, bacon sizzling in the pan, the sweet-tart temptation of real applesauce. Luxury! I burrowed into the soft bed and gave myself up to it.

Everyone wanted to hear my stories of the mining camps, the gold that, so they'd heard, lay on the ground, waiting to be picked up. I suppose I glossed over the backbreaking work, the trials of blazing trails where no trails existed, the deepening rift between Haw and me. I'd not come to complain and wouldn't have, anyway. What went on in a marriage was private—between husband and wife—and, besides, there was Maxcy, proof of love, even if our original ardor had cooled.

Abraham Lincoln had been elected to office, and the friends and neighbors who came to greet me always wanted to know of the situation in the West and turned the conversation to the possibility of war.

"Secession" was the word on everyone's lips. In spite of comfort there were times when I wished I was back at the gulch, removed from constant talk of war, my problems simple in comparison with what the country was facing.

Lilly and Frank were my most eager listeners, and many nights we sat talking after the rest of the family had gone to bed.

"You make it sound wonderful," Lilly said. "So . . . so free." Her eyes looked past me into a place that didn't exist.

"Free depends on definition," I said. "Freedom has its problems, too."

"Still. I'd like to go and see for myself."

"Me, too," Frank said. "It sounds like a fella could make a go of things out there. The only job for me here is at the quarry, and I'm not much of a hand at that."

"If there's war, you'll have to go," I said with a pang.

He shook his head. "War isn't going to solve any problems at all, Gusta. Have you ever wondered what'll happen when all the fine talk, all the fighting, frees the slaves? The South's going to fall on its face, the slaves won't understand freedom, and it'll be us who have to pick up the pieces and solve the problems. We all sit around and preach morality, but war isn't the solution, and I don't want any part of it."

"You'd rather freeze in a Colorado blizzard, I take it."

He slapped his hands on his knees. "I'm not a coward, if that's what you mean."

"I know that. I'm just trying to think for you. Every life and place has its problems. Colorado's no different."

"I'm old enough to make up my own mind. And I won't fight for what I don't believe in." He got up and left the room.

I looked at Lilly. "What about you?"

She leaned her chin on her hands. "I really would like to go with you. Like Frank said, there's nothing here for me, either. Vinnie's got the only man worth having, and, if I'm going to be an old maid, at least I'd like to have had an adventure or two."

I laughed. Lilly wasn't the type to remain a spinster,

and the thought of having her with me was a happy one. How many times I'd wished for a woman to talk to, for laughter in the kitchen, for the simple fact of another who understood.

"What does Mother say?" I asked.

"She won't stop me. And Becca's not going to stop Peter, either."

"What's he got to do with it?"

"He wants to go with you, only Becca had a hissy fit and put her foot down."

Knowing Becca, I wasn't surprised. "I'll not interfere in that discussion."

Lilly laughed. "Nor anybody else, either. I can't believe she hasn't come crying to you."

"She will. She's just waiting for the right time."

"Pity you."

Pity me, indeed.

Becca caught me the next afternoon, plunging straight to the heart of the matter. "I suppose Peter's talked to you about going to Colorado."

I managed a look of surprise. "He's hardly said two words to me."

She hitched her shawl more firmly around her shoulders, like a knight adjusting armor before battle. "He will. He's got a bee in his bonnet about going West, and it's all your fault. Yours and Haw's. If you hadn't gone, none of this would have happened, and I want you to discourage him."

"How?"

"How should I know? Tell him how hard you work.

Show him those hands of yours. Tell him I'll be an old woman by the time he sends back for me, and he'll have wasted our lives. Tell him Vesta needs a father."

No woman ever changed a man with his mind made up. I knew that, but Becca obviously didn't. "I doubt he'll listen to me," I said. "And Haw won't discourage him, either. Not if his mind's made up."

She kicked at a chair, probably wishing it were I. "Then unmake it."

I sighed. Becca in a temper was always difficult. "Becca. . . ."

"Don't Becca me! Just do it!" she snapped, and with a swirl of her skirt left me standing there helpless.

"Where's that husband of yours?" Father's question startled me out of a happy daze. It was Christmas day, and we were sitting in the parlor after dinner, me in a new green wool dress and soft, kid slippers. The fact that I hadn't heard anything from Haw hurt more than I was willing to admit.

"He'll come when he's finished," I said. "You know how he's always been in the thick of politics. They need him in Colorado. He gets things done."

"He was quick enough to leave Kansas," Father said with a frown.

"You had to have been there." I shuddered at the remembrance of snakes under the bed, bushwhackers lurking just out of sight. "Just like you said, it was war . . . a sneaking kind of war. You couldn't always trust even your own neighbors. You didn't want to go to sleep at night for fear you'd be burned out. Colorado's different. Hard. But we don't worry about being killed in our bed."

"As long as she's happy," Mother put in. "You are happy, aren't you?"

I stared at her, annoyed. "Of course," I answered. "Haw's a good man."

Maxcy, who'd been playing with toy soldiers, looked up. "Is Pappy coming?" His face, his question, told me that he missed his father. But he was never a child who whined or complained. Even at his young age, he was a stoic, keeping his thoughts to himself.

"As soon as he can," I murmured. "Pappy's an important man with a job to do."

My answer seemed to satisfy them all, even Mother who had the knack of seeing into my mind, and Maxcy went back to his game, lining the soldiers up in rows. *At least he's too young to fight a real war,* I thought, understanding in a flash that it was sons who went off to fight while the mothers stayed home and prayed. It was men like Ed and Frank who risked themselves for whatever cause was being fought over, and there was a reason why Mother's glance rested so long, so sadly, on the faces of her sons. She was afraid, for them, not for herself. She was as frightened as Hannah had been about John, because war, declared or not, had no favorites.

On that Christmas day, the last peaceful Christmas the country would have for many years, the specter of war joined us in the parlor, hovered overhead, grinning hideously, and I wished for those high mountains that had so unexpectedly become home.

"Frank and Lilly have told me they'd like to come to Colorado," I said, then waited for objections that didn't come, for an explosion from Becca.

"Good experience," Father said. "Everyone should learn their own country, and the future's to the west the way I see it."

Mother looked from Lilly to me. "You'll take good care of her."

"Lilly is able to take care of herself," I said. "And of me, too."

Peter, who was sitting on the couch with Becca, cleared his throat. "I'd like to come along. Like Father said, our future is to the west, and I'd like to grow with it."

Becca's hands were clasped so tightly I thought the knuckles would burst through her skin. "You can't! I won't let you! What'll I say to everybody? That you've left me?"

Her husband slipped his arm around her shoulders, but his expression was determined. "You'll say nothing of the kind. I'm not deserting you, only insuring our future. You'll stay here till I come for you."

Becca's eyes were mutinous. "I won't!"

Peter looked at me. "You tell her."

Not for the world was I going to intervene. I shook my head. "This is up to you both. I'm going back because my life is there with Haw, but I can't decide for you."

It was Mother who had her say, who, in her quiet way, dominated all of us. She laid down her knitting, held up a small hand. "I raised you to take things in stride, Becca," she said. "And not to make private arguments public. You have every right to make your wants known, to demand respect, but that works two ways. You're Peter's wife and should respect his ideas. The world is changing, and that change is in the hands of men. Not"—she added with a smile—"that that's always a good thing, just the way it is. For you, you have to know when to let go, when to efface yourself. Now is that time, Becca."

She smiled harder, looked at all of us in turn, the light of the fire reflecting in her spectacles, a small woman with a backbone of Maine granite, and a heart soft as the wool that she held in her hands.

Becca sat as if turned to stone, her face white, her eyes gleaming with unshed tears, and I wanted to reach out to her, to say the words that would reassure, but no words came. Regardless of what I believed about the rights of women, it was a wife's duty to follow where she was led. In sickness and in health I had trekked across half the country and was the stronger for it.

Maxcy, who'd been listening, got up suddenly, crossed the room, and laid a hand on Becca's knee. "You come, too, Auntie," he piped. "You'd like it, and I'll take care of Vesta. I know what to do."

I saw the change come over my sister's face, watched as anger was replaced by that in her which refused, ever, to quit or take second place.

"You will, eh?" She took Maxcy's face in her hands. "You'll take care of Vesta and me? Do you promise?"

He nodded slowly.

"A champion," she said with a harsh laugh. "I have

a champion of my very own." She looked at Peter, and inwardly I flinched, knowing trouble was coming. "You heard him. Now you listen to me. All of you. I'm going, too, God help me. And you won't stop me, so don't even try."

Peter took her hand. "My dear," he said, "I wouldn't dream of trying."

Later that night, when I was putting Maxcy to bed, I said: "Well, now you have a responsibility. Make sure you can handle it."

He looked up at me, eyes serious. "Oh, I can," was all he said.

When Haw finally arrived in February, he was full of plans and bursting with the success he'd had in his Denver meetings. The fact that we were packed and ready to leave suited him perfectly.

"Every day lost is gold in some other fella's pocket. No sense wasting time."

In bed that night he said: "You happy about this? About Lilly and Frank and Becca and Peter?"

I was happy to be with him. I'd missed the intimacy, the warmth of another's body in my bed, his sometimes brusque passion.

"Yes," I said. "I just hope Becca isn't a problem. And I'm happy you're here. I missed you."

"The hell with her. She'll make out like the rest." He pulled me close.

No word of missing me. I shouldn't have expected any. But I did, and couldn't help wondering just how he'd spent his time in Denver with its hundred saloons and the bawdy houses Becca had warned me about. Was I jealous? No, not that. Simply unsure of myself, a little lost, saddened that life—and people—were never what one expected. But at least, if there had been another woman, he'd come back for me. That was something, wasn't it?

Chapter Thirteen

"War! It's war!" The cry was on everyone's lips. Fort Sumpter had been fired on, and the streets of St. Joseph, the lobby of our hotel, were filled with people unsure what to do next.

There were those who, headed west, sold their outfits and went back home to enlist, and there were others who simply milled in circles like trapped horses, unable to decide what course to follow. And there were also those who had already chosen sides, wild-eyed Missourians and bearded Kansas Abolitionists primed by years of hatred, who, at the first confirmation of war, took on their enemies with fists, knives, pistols, so that by going on about our business we were in constant danger of being felled by a stray bullet or caught up in a frenzied mob.

"Do we need to talk about what we're doing?" Haw asked over the breakfast table. "Or are we all agreed?"

Frank put down the newspaper he'd been reading. "You know what I think."

"I want to go home," I said.

Haw laughed. "Which one this time?"

"Colorado."

"Good, because that's where I'm headed. I spent enough years fighting the damned South. You see what it got me."

"A farm," I said.

"The hell with the farm! It'll still be there when the war's over. Let's get moving. Get our supplies while we can and get out."

At the mention of supplies, I began to wonder how difficult it would be to get them if the war went on for long. "I have an idea," I said, and waited till I had their attention. "We don't know how long the war's going to last. We can't be sure we'll be able to get what we need. Certainly not at the diggings." Haw was listening closely, so I went on. "I still have four hundred dollars left. We should buy all the supplies we can handle and take them along. We know we can make money from a store as well as by me cooking for the men, and, if we don't, we'll use the things ourselves. We'll always have to eat."

Haw whistled. "I take back everything I said about your penny-pinching. We'll do it even if we need two wagons. If my hunch is right, it'll be years before the war's over, but there's always money to be made in a war, and we'll make it. They might call it profiteering, but I call it smart."

By the time he'd finished, he clearly thought the idea was his own. I smiled to myself and let him think what he would.

Becca was horrified. "You let him take all the credit," she hissed. "You're smarter than he is."

"He can take the credit," I said. "I'll take the money and save it for hard times."

"How can you be sure they'll come?"

I pointed out the window at the mob in the street. "Seems to me they're already here."

The trip West was as miserable as our first, but at the worst moments, when the wind that blew night and day scattered our fire and blew our breakfast across the prairie, when Becca was about to drive me mad with complaints, there was Lilly to whom everything was new and different—her adventure come to reality. More than once, out collecting buffalo chips, I'd find her on her knees exclaiming over a stand of tiny white lilies or an early-flowering patch of buffalo bean, its pink blossoms much like sweet peas.

"They make little fruits," I told her. "I've eaten them, and they're good."

"How did you know they weren't poison?"

"The Indians ate them. Why shouldn't I?"

She wrinkled her forehead. "But . . . but they're Indians. Like that dreadful bunch that's been following us."

"Our stomachs are the same the last I heard."

She flipped a buffalo chip into her pail. There were less of them now, and we had to walk farther to find enough for our fire. "I never thought I'd be picking up cow pies and talking about Indians' digestion. It just goes to show you."

"That travel is broadening?" I asked with a smile.

"Something like that. Sometimes I feel like such a dolt next to you. I can't believe you're the same sister who was always sick in bed with a book."

"We do what we have to. I never imagined any of this, either . . . not the country, not the farm, not what it's like to climb a mountain. Certainly not what it's like to be married."

"Is it wonderful?" Lilly was like Vinnie in her view of romance.

"Sometimes."

"Not always?" Her voice rose and cracked.

I thought of our disagreements, the basic differences between Haw and me that, over time and due to circumstance, had become more pronounced, those very things that my father had worried about years before. I thought of giving birth alone except for Nat who often seemed less of a stranger than my own husband, who'd followed us from strike to strike and who was always there when needed. I thought of my doubts about leaving Haw in Denver where the saloons, the brothels were a constant lure. And then I remembered the pleasure of being in his arms, the safety of his strength.

"Like life," I said. "You take the good along with the bad and make the best of it. And you learn who and what you are along the way. What else is there?"

Becca trudged up out of a dry streambed with Vesta and Maxcy in tow. "I'll be damned," she said, cheerfully enough. "Here I am, blisters on my heels, picking up cow pies. And there's our husbands sitting around on their hands."

"My husband's going to be different," Lilly said. "If I ever find one."

"That's what we all said, and look where it got us. We're slaves, only nobody's fighting a war over us."

Lilly put down her pail and stretched out her arms as if she wanted to embrace the prairie. "But look where we are. Isn't all this wonderful?"

I thought there were hundreds of lonely miners who would be glad to take Lilly and her cheerful person as a wife. "You'll be fighting husbands off with a broomstick. Mark my words. Just wait till the first party and the fiddler tunes up and all the men want to dance with you. Now let's get back and start supper, or it'll be too dark to see. And keep an eye out for snakes."

As always, Becca had the last word. "Yes, indeed. Keep an eye out. No man will do it for you."

We had started setting a watch every night on that trip. The Indians were on the move and restless, possibly because so many soldiers were also moving around in the event the war came to Kansas. That night, after supper, I took my turn, settling down with Haw's big pistol in my lap.

Lilly's eyes opened wide. "It's nearly as big as you. Are you sure you can shoot it?"

I smiled grimly, remembering other nights alone and on watch. "I'm sure."

She sat down beside me, folding her skirts around her legs. "Mother would faint."

"Maine hasn't always been the way it is now. When Mother was little, there was a war going on, too. And if I know her, she'd take on the Confederate Army if any one of us was threatened."

"You think of things I wouldn't. I never saw Mother as anything but how she is at home."

"People become what life makes them." As I spoke, I wished I could become different from the way I was—shy around those I didn't know, unable to socialize like Haw wanted me to. I was always happiest working alone or in a small group of friends. Maybe my childhood and illness had turned me solitary, but who knows?

"You want Becca and me to stay up with you?" Lilly asked, sensing my introspection.

"Go to sleep. Keep an eye on the children. I'll be in when it's Frank's turn."

"For what it's worth, I want to be just like you when I grow up." Lilly giggled, bent over and kissed me, and then was gone.

I sat alone in the dark, troubled though I didn't know why, and I wasn't any closer to a solution when, at midnight, Frank came to take over.

"All quiet?"

"So far. But I'll bet those Indians we saw before aren't very far away. Keep awake. We can't afford to lose any of the stock."

Together we stood, listening to the silence. All that disturbed it was the wind, and, far off, a night bird making music in the dark.

Just before dawn we were awakened by the boom of Haw's Sharps. Lilly shrieked. Becca sat up so fast she banged her head. I reached for my pistol. "Stay here!

Keep Maxcy and Vesta. I'll see what's happening." My voice shook like my hands, but I told myself I wasn't afraid. I'd faced worse.

More shots cut through the night. I peered out the back of the wagon, saw the men silhouetted against the eastern sky. "Where are they?"

"All over the damn' place." Haw was whispering. "Get down out of there and stop making yourself a target."

Hastily I jumped to the ground and went to stand with the men.

"They were after the oxen," Haw said. "I saw at least two of the bastards. No telling how many are out there."

At that hour the prairie blended with the sky, its dips and hollows indistinguishable, each one a potential hiding place. However, the Indians who'd been following us were a poor lot, ragged women and children and old men wrapped in blankets, with not a weapon in sight.

Haw turned to Frank. "Get those oxen inside the camp. Pete and I'll cover you."

I was astonished to watch my brother slip away toward the rope corral as stealthily as any Indian, even more surprised when he returned, calmly driving the beasts in front of him.

"You must've scared the Indians away," I said.

"Bastards didn't want a fight. They just wanted to clean us out." Frank had, I noticed, quickly adopted the speech of the frontier.

"They're starving. You saw how they looked."

"Yeah, well, let 'em eat some other poor son-of-a-bitch's cattle." Haw cast a long look over the prairie. "It'll be light in half an hour. Let's pull out soon as we can. By tonight we'll be at Fort Kearney. We'll be able to sleep, and I'll make a report of the trouble."

"Are they gone?" Lilly peeked around the canvas flap.

"For now. We're pulling out."

She let out a breath. "Are they . . . will they come back?"

"They might," I said. "We'll have to keep our eyes open."

"Somebody better teach us how to shoot." Becca jumped down and came to stand beside us. "I don't care for being helpless."

Peter laughed. "The Pierce women aren't ever helpless. I should know. But I'll teach you myself first chance we get."

"Is it Injuns?" Maxcy stuck his head out, with little Vesta, wide-eyed, just behind him.

"It was, but they're gone," I said.

"For now," Haw muttered. "Damned thieving bastards."

"Hush in front of the children!" I warned.

He shot me a look. "He'll hear worse before he's grown."

That was true. The frontier and mining camps weren't known for their delicacy, and in my own way I was accustomed to the rough speech, the lack of civilized manners.

"Cold biscuits and milk for breakfast," I said. "Let's not waste any more time."

By sunup we were on the move, three wagons, oxen, mules, a milk cow. The three men and I were armed, but nothing disturbed us on the wide trail along the Platte, only the sound, the sight of migrating cranes high overhead in the blue air.

Beside me, Maxcy watched the birds with something of my own awe. "What are they?" His voice was hushed as if he'd frighten them.

"Cranes. On their way north."

"What for?"

"They make nests and lay their eggs, I guess."

He pondered that for a minute, then said: "Do the baby cranes fly?"

"Not right away. Just like sparrows, they have to grow up first."

"What's it like to fly?" His face, turned up, was lit with the small child's wonder.

Touched by the scene, by the haunting chorus that was growing fainter, I said: "Like magic. Like now."

He grabbed the rough wood seat with both hands and laughed in agreement. "Yes," he said. "Yes. Just like now."

It was April when we arrived in Denver, and May when, in spite of a blizzard that buried us all, we shoveled our way into California Gulch.

"Blizzard, my foot! This is a nor'easter! Best I ever saw!" Becca stopped shoveling, molded snow in her hands, and threw a snowball at her husband.

Her hair had come loose and was blowing around her face, and she was laughing. Her wildness was infectious. In another minute a battle was in full swing, with snowballs flying everywhere and all of us laughing with her.

We'd been forced to shovel our way into the gulch through four-foot drifts with a bitter wind blowing off almost invisible mountains—a back-breaking task as far removed from gaiety as possible. It took Becca, my indomitable sister, to free us from ourselves if only for a minute, to bring merriment to what had been hard and necessary labor.

"Can you believe this?" I said to Lilly, who was returning fire as fast as she could, a smile spread ear to ear.

"You mean Becca?"

"Who else?"

"She's sure different." Lilly grunted as she tossed a hard-packed ball of snow and ice, then cheered as it smacked into Becca's stomach.

"That's hardly the word I'd use." I ducked a flying missile, and tossed my own. "I couldn't have imagined her like this. Not ever."

"But you keep saying people change."

I had said it—many times—but in the last few weeks Becca—feisty, indomitable Becca—had become a force to be reckoned with, a woman who'd discovered strengths in herself that had laid dormant and, in the context of the East, useless. In the West, in the face of hardship, through the endless days of travel, she'd come into her own.

Now she drew herself up, eyes flashing. "Children, children!" she called. "Recess is over. Time to go back to work." Then she shrieked when Maxcy caught her with one last ball. "You'll pay!" she yelled. "Just wait, my little general."

Giggling, Maxcy and Vesta, who'd become his shadow, disappeared behind one of the wagons. "You have to catch me!" he yelled.

"Oh, I will! When you don't expect it. Snow in your bed, ice down your shirt. Frogs in your milk. Soon!" She bent down, picked up her shovel, and plowed ahead, and, if she was as tired as the rest of us, she gave no sign.

Haw gave me a quizzical look. "Do I know her?"

"It is hard to believe." My arms ached and my back was stiff. I felt I'd been digging for days and no end in sight. "I wish I was as tough as she is."

One corner of his mouth curled in a smile beneath his mustache that was frozen solid. "You're tough enough. You just don't know it."

His rare praise made me blush. I could feel the heat rise in my cheeks, but compliments always left me embarrassed. "Well," I said, "I got this far."

He peered ahead through the trees, the thousand acres of blinding white, and cocked his head. "Hear that?"

I straightened up, but all I heard was the whistle of the wind. "What?"

"Somebody's shouting."

I heard it then—voices from over the hill.

"They're digging out to meet us. Come on!" Haw bent, and his shovel flew. "We'll have a warm bed tonight or my name's not Haw Tabor!"

"You hear that, Peter?" Becca's voice rang out clear as a bell. "A warm bed and us in it. Dig faster! Dig faster!"

Peter, probably shocked by his bawdy wife, bent to work and didn't answer.

Oh, there was a welcome for us that night! The town had been snowed in for a month, and anyone who has spent a month in isolation can imagine what the sight of us did for those miners. There was a meal we women didn't cook, there was music, dancing, the warmth of a fire, the lights of a dozen lanterns hung from the rough beams of what was known as the Hotel DeBooth.

"A hotel," Becca said, looking at the cheerful but crude surroundings. "Well, damn my eyes."

"Watch your language. Mother would wash your mouth with lye soap."

"Mother isn't here," she said with a grin. "I am."

Her pleasure was, once again, contagious, and I grinned back, then pointed to Lilly who was being danced off her feet by every man in the gulch. "I wonder how long she'll be with us. The belle of the ball."

Becca patted her foot in time with the fiddling. "A while yet. She's got good sense."

"Not like us," I said with a twinkle.

"I'd say all us Pierces have it. And we'll have good luck in Colorado, too. I'm glad I came. And I'm sorry I was so hard to get along with back home."

I reached out and hugged her. "Me, too. Oh, Becca, I'm glad you came, too."

With my sisters around there would be no more

long, lonely winters, no more solitary labor with no one to talk to but myself, Maxcy, and the mountains that kept us isolated.

Becca hugged me back, and I saw what seemed to be tears in her blue eyes. "You poor little thing," she said. "To tell the truth, I never thought you'd survive. I was always scared when a letter came, thinking it was bad news. About you."

Thinking back over the last years, I had to agree that my survival was, indeed, a miracle. "To tell the truth, there were lots of times when I thought I'd just up and die. When I'd have paid my last cent for the sight of old Doctor Cobble and his black bag. But I guess I'm tougher than I look. Even Haw says so."

"Well, at least he knows that much." She nodded at Haw who was off in a corner, talking a blue streak to a bunch of miners. "Keeping up with him can't be easy."

"You don't like him," I said, startled. "Why ever not?"

She sniffed. "I don't know. Maybe because he's always wanting something. Always pushing. Never satisfied. And never giving a thought to anybody but himself. He gets on my nerves, but he's yours, and you're satisfied, so who am I to talk?"

"Yes, he's mine," I said, and wondered why I suddenly felt so lonely.

The next morning Maxcy came to me in tears. "I looked everywhere. Jack's gone. I wanted to teach Vesta to ride him, but he's gone."

I hadn't given a thought to our faithful little burro,

but my heart sank to my shoes at Maxcy's words. No one, in any camp, placed a value on animals, particularly in winter. They foraged for themselves or died. But how explain that to a child?

"We'll ask around," I said. "But he's probably gone off to find a family of his own."

"You mean wife?"

"Something like that."

"But I told him I was coming back."

For that I had no answer. "Come," was all I said.

Together we went out, squinting at the brilliance of sun on snow, making our slow way between drifts down the gulch toward that cabin that Nat shared with Hank Packard. Hank was out in front, shoveling a path, and he raised a hand in greeting.

"Mind you don't slip."

At that moment, a loud bray shattered the quiet.

"It's him! It's Jack!" Maxcy's cry was ragged, hope and fear combined.

"It sure is," Hank said. "I kept up my old mule, and Jack decided he wanted company. Reckon he missed you."

I let out a breath. "How can I thank you?"

He shook his head. "No need, missus. The kid's happy. That's enough."

How narrowly tragedy is averted. How precious the trust of a child. Silently, there in the snow-covered gulch, I thanked God.

No prospecting or serious mining was done in winter in the early years. Those who didn't head for Denver to spend their hard-earned gold, simply holed up in their cabins and waited for spring, which was usually long in coming.

But like spring everywhere, when it arrived, its beauty broke the heart. The creeks ran high and clear with snow melt, and all day, all night, frogs twanged and croaked on the banks, their music as welcome as the songs of nesting birds, the unaccustomed warmth of sun at mid-morning, as the scents of damp earth, rising sap, flowers blooming somewhere out of sight. Around us the world seemed to be breathing, to have expanded till it touched a sky so blue to look at it was blinding.

With spring, too, came more hopefuls who dragged themselves over the pass, the lure of gold lending them strength. Our little camp swarmed like an ant hill, and I was busy with store and boarders, thanking God for my sisters' help.

As always, Haw disappeared on the first fine day, searching for that elusive strike that would crown him king and taking Frank with him.

"Little boys playing Columbus," Becca said with a sniff. "And they're supposed to take care of us."

I attacked the pile of laundry the men had left me that morning, each piece worth fifty cents—in cash or its equivalent in gold. "We're not helpless."

She chuckled. "Lord, no. I even shot a branch off a tree last week. Maybe I should join a circus."

"Maybe you could help me finish this and get it hung out."

She wiped her hands on her apron, then turned and squinted up the muddy road. "Somebody's coming."

The riderless mule came at a trot, stirrups flapping, and at the sight my heart sank. Only a few days before, Hank Packard had set off for Denver, his gold in his saddlebags.

"Back soon as I've spent it," he had said with a wink. "It's been a hard winter. Now it's time to have me some fun."

I ran out into the road. Seeing me, the mule shied and came to a stop, its sides heaving. Along one flank was a raw wound, red against black hide. I walked up, stroked his sweaty neck, and grabbed what was left of a rein, feeling sick at heart. Hank had been a friend from the first. The thought of him, wounded or dead, robbed of his treasure, cast a pall on the bright morning, on the entire gulch where we, all of us, lived on the edge, balanced between life and death though we did our best to ignore it. The way over the mountains was filled with hazards, not the least of which were the outlaws, men without conscience or scruples, who lay in wait for those like Hank, saddlebags filled with gold.

"Something's happened to Hank," I said, stating the obvious. "We'll have to get somebody to go look for him."

"And, of course, Haw's not here to help." In an instant, Becca had reverted to her old self.

"Never mind. I know who will." I untied my apron and laid it aside. "Stir these clothes. I'm going to find Nat."

"The ever-faithful." Neither of my sisters had ever gotten over the fact that Nat had helped me birth Maxcy.

"Well, he is," I said. "First, though, I'll get the saddle off this old boy. He's had a rough time of it."

"That's a nasty wound."

I agreed, but didn't mention that it looked like a bullet had scoured the poor beast. "I'll see to that when I get back."

Nat's digging lay about a mile up a small side gulch that drained into the larger one, and I followed the narrow trail with caution, for the sides were steep and the stream was running high. A jay fluttered overhead, its *chack-chack* startling in the quiet, and I answered him: "It's just me. No cause for alarm."

"Just you?" Nat came around a bend, almost blundering into me.

"There's trouble." I relaxed as I spoke, knowing he'd take charge, which he did as soon as I'd told him.

"It's crazy to go alone," he muttered. "But he would do it. Couldn't stop him. You go on back. I'll get some of the boys and we'll see if we can't pick up his trail. And . . . I'm sorry, ma'am. He was a friend of yours, I know."

"You be careful," I said. "What would happen to me if something happened to you?"

A shadow crossed his face and was gone as quickly as it came. He grinned. "Nothin' will, ma'am. And you'd be fine like always."

Haw and Frank were still gone when the men returned with what was left of Hank Packard. He'd been shot and robbed. We never did learn who'd killed him. Disappearing in those mountains was easy to do, and what law existed was far away. We buried him in the small plot designated as a cemetery, not without difficulty, for the ground beneath the surface was still frozen, and I shuddered thinking of the bodies we'd had to keep frozen till the spring thaw. Hank, at least, had been spared that and was now at rest beside his fellows. Others, I knew, would follow.

Life hangs by a thread, and in those camps, in those high and perilous mountains, the thread was as thin, as fragile, as the finest spider's web.

Chapter Fourteen

Several months later, Haw asked if I'd ride with him to Denver, carrying our own gold. Although we had the only safe in the territory, Haw preferred keeping what belonged to us banked elsewhere, and more than once I'd saddled up, tied the bags of nuggets around my waist under my skirt, or hidden the dust under the saddle, and taken to the trail. No road agent would search or harm a woman, and our plan had always worked.

When I asked Becca if she'd keep Maxcy while I was gone, she was at first horrified and then angry, launching a diatribe against men, slave owners and slaves, and finally Haw.

"For God's sake, Gusta! You're a fool, letting him use you! I don't care if you have done it before. Things happen, as we know very well. Let him take Nat and Sam or some of the others. You stay here and mind your own. Has he lost his mind? Have you lost yours? Don't think I'll come looking for you, see you buried in that miserable place like Packard. If you won't tell that man he's no good, I will, and there's an end to it!"

I listened till she'd worn herself out before speaking, and controlling my temper as I did. "You won't tell Haw any such thing. You haven't the right to criticize. I've done this before and I want to go. It's a chance to do something else instead of cooking and washing, and I can take care of myself in case you hadn't noticed."

Becca's eyebrows shot up to her hair. "Something else, eh? Like falling off one of those cliffs? Being shot out of the saddle? How do you take care of a bullet in your own back?"

She was shouting so loudly I was afraid the whole camp could hear, and there was no reasoning with her. I turned away. "Never mind. I'll ask Lilly. She won't yell and call me a fool and embarrass us all."

Becca stamped her booted foot. For a moment I felt sorry for Peter who usually caught the brunt of her temper. "You should be embarrassed. *Yes, master. No, master. Whatever you say, master.* Honestly, you knew better when you were Vesta's age."

"When I was her age, I was in bed all the time," I objected. "This is lots better. And, for your information, I've never been a slave . . . to Haw or to anybody else. I do my own thinking. How do you suppose we survived out here the first few years? Because of me. Because I worked as hard as any three men, and liked doing it. That's how I am. That's how we were brought up. You pitch in and do what's needed, no whining, no complaints, and you know it as well as I do. So I don't want any more of your advice or scolding. If I need scolding, I'll do that myself, too!"

Astonishingly her face crumpled. "I didn't mean it. I'm sorry. I've just been so . . . so restless with Peter gone so much. Don't listen to me. I'll keep Maxcy, and you go on. Forget what I said . . . about anything."

Peter and Frank, with what has come to be called Yankee ingenuity, had put their heads together and gone into the lumber business, quite profitably as it turned out, but Becca was obviously unused to being without a husband for weeks at a time.

"She's jealous," Lilly informed me later. "You and Haw, going off on an adventure while she's stuck here by herself. She's got cabin fever, but don't worry. She'll be fine, and you'll make it all right."

Well, we very nearly didn't, and at the worst all I could think of was Maxcy, orphaned, crying for me and his pappy. It happened like this.

The trail over the Mosquito Range was steep and treacherous, blocked by snow in winter, slippery with mud and shale during the spring thaw and after a storm, and storms in those mountains are fearsome things, with always the danger of being struck by lightning. It's the lightning, the never knowing where or when it will strike, that has always terrified me.

That day the storm caught us halfway up the side of a mountain, a hen-drowning, boulder-rolling deluge that soaked us to the skin in a few seconds. I could barely make out Haw, riding ahead of me, hunched over in the saddle, but heard him call out: "Keep going!" It was a safer practice than taking shelter under a tree. So I urged forward my mule, that had turned skittish, and held on as best I could although I was shaking from cold and fright.

We were in the very heart of the storm. The thunder beat at my ears, a drumming that never stopped, and lightning struck where it would, splitting the trunks of the old trees as if they were twigs. Even through the rain, and the hail that was stinging my face and hands, I could smell the sulphur, the heat of flames quickly quenched.

On and on, and beneath me my mule as terrified as I was. He flinched just before every strike, his senses far keener than mine, but he kept moving, slipping on the trail that was now knee-deep in mud. Haw gave a shout and I saw that he'd turned off on a narrow ledge with an overhang that offered us some protection and, without urging, my mule followed.

"You all right?" Haw dismounted, and inched his way across the narrow shelf toward me.

"I'm alive." Though my teeth were chattering.

"Get down. Slowly. Don't worry about the mules. They aren't going anywhere."

I did as he said, slipping off as if I hadn't a bone left in my body, and he pulled me against him under the rock so that we were partially sheltered from the worst of it.

"Rotten luck," he said.

I didn't answer. I was too busy warming myself with the heat of his body. He always seemed to have a furnace hidden somewhere inside, a fact that had saved me on several occasions.

"Shouldn't last too much longer," he said. "Then we'll get over the top and maybe find some dry wood for a fire."

I peered out. "We'll never make it in that mud."

"Yeah, we will."

"How?"

"Let the mules drag us. Just make sure to keep out of the way of their hoofs."

Icy drops of rain dripped off his hat and down the back of my neck. I envisioned myself being dragged up to the crest, threatened by the kick of a mule, by the chance that it would fall, and I would fall with it down that perilous drop to the bottom. The thought that I might never make it—to the top, to Denver, back to camp where Maxcy was waiting, wiped out the last of my strength, and my tears came, hot on my frozen cheeks, evidence that I was still able to feel.

"Maxcy," I whispered.

"Maxcy's fine."

"That's not what I meant!" I squirmed around so that I was facing him.

He grunted, impatient. "Don't waste your energy on him. Save it for yourself."

Perhaps it was good advice, but no man has ever understood the love of a mother for her child—that ferocity to protect, that fury over any circumstance that threatens a child's well-being.

It was my love for Maxcy that lent me the strength to ascend the last hellish mile, that glued my hand to the stirrup so that, when I slipped and floundered, I was pulled along regardless. It was not love of self or love for Haw, but the thought of Maxcy, innocent, trusting, and, I admit, the sting of Becca's scorn that got me through. But I never told her about that day when we got home. I never wanted to admit that she could have been right. Besides, on our way back, we got word of a big strike near a place called Buckskin Joe, and in the excitement of moving again I hadn't time to reminisce.

For the next seven years we lived and prospered in Buckskin Joe. The population of the territory seemed to double with every new discovery, and I can still recite the names of towns and strikes by heart, names that were on everyone's lips: Malta, Central City, Fairplay, Blackhawk, Oro Number 2, Alma, Sow Belly Creek, Cache Creek—towns that blossomed, then went bust or reinvented themselves as Colorado Territory boomed.

As always, I kept a store and post office, boarded as many men as could pay for the meals Lilly and I dished out, and at Buckskin Joe, to everyone's surprise, I planted a vegetable garden that kept us in fresh vegetables for much of the summer.

I was weeding the plants when Maxcy brought me a month-old letter from Mother telling of Father's death. I sat down in the dirt and cried, for all of us, for myself who'd left youth and security to follow a dream.

In those years Haw was rarely at home. He'd been appointed supervisor for the building of a much-needed road over Weston Pass and superintendent of Park County schools, and in addition he was always on the search for the as-yet-undiscovered gold which he was certain was there waiting. Of actual mining, he did little, leaving me to sift through the buckets of black sand for what nuggets might be hidden there. How many nights did I curse the stuff! If only we'd known!

On the day I received news of Father's death I was alone with no one to share my grief. Bitterness is a strange emotion. It creeps up, builds upon small slights, slips of the tongue, and larger disagreements. It feeds on loneliness and exhaustion, and on the absence of love when love is what is needed.

Bitterly, then, I wept, wishing for Haw and recalling the times he'd failed me simply by his absence, and I didn't stop till a shadow fell across the garden, blocking out the sun.

"Are you hurt?" It was Nat Maxcy who knelt beside me, concern in his honest eyes.

I handed him the letter, unable to speak. He read it, then handed it back.

"Your father was a fine man. I knew him. I worked for him years past. You go on and grieve, ma'am, but think of the good things. And, remember, we come, and we go, and there ain't much we can do about that."

"Why'd I come here, Nat? I should've stayed home. I feel like I'm lost and don't know how to find the way."

He reached out and patted my hand. "You ain't lost. It's the rest of us who don't know what we're doin'. Out here, wearin' ourselves out for what mightn't be there in the first place. But when us men come in at night and sit at your table, it's like we're comin' home. You think about that. About the good you do for every last one of us and always have."

At his simple statement, I cried even harder—out of gratitude—but he didn't understand what his words had meant or how his kindness had shattered my hard-won reserve.

"Now I didn't mean to make you feel worse. Please, ma'am, stop your cryin'."

"You didn't," I said between sobs. "You're just so . . . so nice, and I'm not used to it. Go on now. I'll be fine in a few minutes."

He stood up, shoulders slumped, face filled with conflicting emotions. "I'll be over behind the store a while if you need me."

I thought maybe I'd always needed him, but didn't answer. As he'd said to me long before, it wouldn't have been right, would have opened a door neither one of us could go through and return. I put my face in my hands and let him go.

When I came in to the store a while later, Haw was there, just back from wherever he'd gone, Haw and a grubby little miner who smelled of liquor and worse.

"Take what you need, Leo," Haw was saying, paying no attention to what the prospector was stuffing into a sack.

Whether it was grief that made me lose my temper or hurt that Haw hadn't come to find me, I don't know, but lose my temper I did.

"Here, you!" I said to the man. "You put what you're taking on the counter so I can make a record, and you'll sign for it . . . if you can. You've been here three times, and haven't paid us yet, and don't think I didn't notice. This is the last grubstake you'll get, so remember that."

"Gusta. . . ." Haw was staring at me, his irritation plain.

"Don't you 'Gusta' me! Next thing, you'll give away the store, grubstaking any drunk who asks. And if *I* may ask, where've you been all week?"

"I had business, and you know it!" He was shouting now, as mad as I was.

"Business, business! Talk, talk! That's all you know how to do! You've a wife and a son in case you forgot. And a home that's empty most of the time. Empty when I need you most."

I threw the record book down on the counter, and the sound it made satisfied some deep urge in me—to be recognized, praised, petted, *seen,* instead of being the ever-dutiful and silent wife, what Becca had called the servant unseen, unheard.

"Enough!" I shouted. "Enough!" And then ran out the door.

Oh, of course, he came after me, all apologies and hugs, and I was so grateful he hadn't walked away from me, that I returned his affection. We women can be foolish at times—so sure we can't exist without a man, whether he be good or bad.

"Father's dead," I said after a minute.

That shocked him. "I'm sorry. I admired your father. A good man, and an honest one. If it wasn't for him, I'd not have found you. Come on, now. Dry your face and let's go back. You lie down a while."

I shook my head. "I'd rather do something. Anything. Finish my weeding." Work, as I'd discovered, was a blessing. It blotted out thought, took over the body with its own rhythms and necessities, eased hurts that otherwise would cause considerable pain.

"Whatever suits you. Just don't wear yourself out."

I was already exhausted, but gave him a smile. "Of course not." If there was sarcasm in my reply, he didn't notice.

It was only a few minutes later that a wagon and team came down the road, and with a cry I took off my apron and ran out to greet Father Machebeuf.

Over the years, the priest and I had become friends. I called upon him when I was in Denver, and saw him when he made what I called "his rounds" among the camps.

"You are, after all, a doctor," I'd said to him once.

He'd answered with a smile. "A doctor of souls. You, my dear, are the physician with your herbs and laudanum and good food."

That day it was my soul that needed cheering, my heart that weighed in my chest like a lump of lead.

"No smile for me?" he asked as he climbed down off the seat. "What is it? What has happened?"

I told him, adding at the last: "And I didn't know. I should have been there, but now it's too late."

"And so you blame yourself."

"Yes."

"We die when our time comes," he said, speaking slowly. "And we die alone, no matter who is with us.

You blame yourself for no reason. Your place is here with your husband and son, not there. Your life is your own, no matter that you feel otherwise."

"Why am I here?" I asked. "Sometimes I feel like I don't belong."

He gave one of those Gallic shrugs ingrained in him. "I can't answer that. Only God knows our purpose. We do what we do and hope we've done right. I'll say a prayer for your father and for you, too. You're a brave and admirable woman, Augusta, so take courage and stop feeling guilty for what you can't help."

"You make it sound simple," I said. "Nothing's simple, though. Nothing's easy."

"Why should it be?"

He took me aback with his plain truth. Here was a man who might have stayed in France and had a comfortable existence. Instead, every day, he faced life at its most dangerous, defying nature and his own frailty for a belief I found hard to accept but which, in him, I respected completely. With a sigh, I sat down on a flat boulder.

"I give in." I managed a smile. "Your logic, if that's what you call it, always defeats me."

"Logic is no more than truth if we can see it."

And what was my truth? I was Mrs. Haw Tabor, wife of a respected man, mother of Nathaniel Maxcy Tabor. Whoever Augusta Pierce Tabor was or could have been had vanished on the trail West. At not yet forty years old, I was cook, storekeeper, postmistress, doctor, mother-confessor to half the miners in Colorado, but what did that mean?

I said: "Sometimes I'm afraid. And then I lose my temper. Mister Tabor . . . he . . . gives everything away to any miner who comes. Grubstaking is like gambling, throwing good money after bad, and I worry the day will come when we've lost everything. That all this work will come to nothing."

"God looks out for us all," he said, a catchword I found irritating, even coming from him.

"I'd just as soon take care of myself, thank you."

He gave his rich chuckle. "And so you should. It's what I admire most about you. But remember that giving to those who need is charity. Try looking at your husband's grubstake gambling as good work. You'll feel better. And so, no doubt, will he with your silence."

Oh, he could take anything I said and lay out a path to follow! Simply by his presence, and with a few words, he was able to calm and comfort me.

"You win. Again," I said. "Now come see my vegetables."

Frenchman that he was and always would be, he couldn't resist a garden—or the thought that at supper my lettuce, beans, tiny onions would appear, cooked to what he called in French—*"perfection"*—on his plate.

He looked with astonishment at my neat rows, the glistening leaves, the vines and cabbages, then said: "My dear, you have a farmer's hand and an artist's eye. You've made beauty out of what is practical."

Such an idea had never occurred to me. "I have?"

"Absolutely." He paced the boundaries of the little plot. "You worry about belonging here, but let me tell you that we belong where we plant our gardens. Flowers, cabbages, orchards, it makes no difference."

"You see," I said. "Again you're making everything simple. Why is that?"

Once more that shrug that was so much a part of him and so charming. "At the root, everything is simple. We think too much and make complexity."

It was only after dinner that I realized the pall that had laid so heavily on me was gone. Machebeuf had that effect on people. He was, in his quiet, thoughtful way, a genius at giving comfort, a forgiving presence, and my much-treasured friend.

Chapter Fifteen

After a long and bitter fight between rival political parties and factions, Colorado was granted statehood in 1876. By then it was a far different place than the ant hill I'd seen for the first time fifteen years before. The war was long over. The slaves had been freed, Lincoln assassinated, Presidents had come and gone. My mother, bless her, had died two years after Father. Now half of my family, and Hannah and John and their brood, had moved to Colorado, along with wave after wave of immigrants in the form of hopeful prospectors, tourists, even tuberculars who had found the climate healthy.

Looking back, it seems that the entire world had changed, and changed again, while Haw and I sought our fortune, while I went about my chores isolated from war, from political debate and scheming, even from the Women's Suffrage Movement that was making itself and its demands heard in the West. Of course, I supported those indomitable women, but as Haw and I prospered, I gave little thought to their message as regarded myself. My life was bound by our stores, three of them—in Malta, Buckskin Joe, and Oro City—by Haw's comings and goings, by what I saw as my part in our success. And then, of course, there was Maxcy, almost twenty by the time life changed again, and as fine a young man as I could have wished. He was managing our store at Malta and doing well, and my pride in him was, in a way, pride in myself, for I'd had the raising of him since he was born.

For several years prior to 1877, there had been rumors that silver existed alongside the gold in vast quantities. Two men, Uncle Billy Stevens and Alvinus Wood, had been assaying samples, and quietly buying up abandoned or unsuccessful gold claims all over the area, but it wasn't till that year that they announced that the black sand we'd all found to be such a trial was really lead carbonate and contained enormous quantities of silver. The first silver strikes were made in the California Gulch near what was then called Slabtown—a motley cluster of tents, shacks, and saloons that justified the name, and the rush was on.

When Haw realized that the black sand we'd sifted through in our search for elusive gold nuggets had, in fact, been silver, he was beside himself. "We threw it away!" he shouted, tossing up his hands in disgust. "We damn' well tossed out a fortune!"

Since I'd spent months sifting that same black sand and cursing it, I felt the same as he. "But how could we have known?"

"We couldn't. Now we do. We're moving the stores

over to Slabtown. When this news gets out, there'll be a stampede, so let's get packing."

He was right. They came for the silver as they'd come for the gold, in wagons, on horseback, on foot. Slabtown doubled in size overnight, then doubled again and again.

No one who hasn't lived in a mining boom town can imagine the noise, the hammering as buildings were erected in the space of a day, the dust, the shouting and cursing in a dozen languages, saloons, gambling houses, and worse, open day and night, streets packed with wagons and drays, streets that turned from dust to mud in summer storms and to high-piled snow and slush in winter.

At 10,500 feet, Slabtown was home to clouds, frequent thunderstorms and blizzards, even when summer had arrived lower down. The crashing of thunder, the thinness of the air could steal a person's breath in a second. Living there I felt at times that I was, indeed, in the lap of the gods, but, as I very well knew, the gods were not always benevolent. They hurled their thunderbolts, toyed with us humans, and then sat back and laughed at the results.

By the time Slabtown was renamed and incorporated as Leadville, Haw had been elected the first mayor, and I had a house, a real one with wood floors and glass windows. I'd sent back to Maine for my grandmother's red velvet chair and her little painting of the Kennebec River and displayed them proudly in my lovely parlor. I even brought out my silver, tarnished from years of disuse, and polished it till it shone on the sideboard. I loved that house, loved living in the clouds, with the perpetually snow-covered face of Mount Massive towering over us. I loved the fact that I had women friends and family close by. Lilly had married several years before, and Becca and Peter had also moved to town where the lumber business was thriving.

It's a funny thing, but I've observed more than once that cattle and ranching didn't build the West. Mining did. The prospecting and discovery of gold, silver, copper, lead, coal—all the minerals needed for the industries that were rapidly changing the world. With mining came people whose wants and needs, even on the frontier, created business, not the least of which was the need for lumber to build railroads, houses, churches, schools, the corduroy roads that replaced the mountain trails, the enormous timbers that shored up the ceilings of mines that tunneled deeply underground. With wealth came the demands for the fripperies of civilization—jewels, caviar, oysters, fashionable bonnets and gowns, kid gloves and buckled shoes. With civilization came the need for places of worship that were something more than rude altars set up on packing crates, schools to educate both young and old, hotels, banks, depots, tearooms, and restaurants where the decent women of the town could go without comment.

My family and Haw, Maxcy, and I were prospering in the midst of the silver boom, and I was humming when I stepped out my front door one morning to check the weather.

"Augusta! I was just coming to call!"

Lottie Williams had been a schoolteacher in the gulch several years before. She was a determined, fierce little woman who used anything that came to hand to gain her recalcitrant students' interest, including a willow switch and an astonishingly loud voice. She was both well-educated and independent, an adventuress who'd found her calling in the roughest of camps where the children ran wild and unsupervised.

"I've come for your help!" she exclaimed in that glorious voice, in tone and timbre much like an oboe.

"Come inside. It's too cold to stand out here in the street," I said. "Besides, we could get run over at any second." As usual, Harrison Avenue was a solid wall of wagons and animals, the noise deafening.

"The march of civilization." Lottie removed her hat and gloves. "Makes me want to find a nice quiet mountain where nobody ever heard the words gold or silver, or even thought of putting up those stinking smelters! But there's things that need doing here, and I can use your help."

Lottie was a tireless organizer. Over a cup of tea served in my new parlor, she drafted me to help with a Christmas party for the miners' children.

"They're completely overlooked," she said. "They run wild, take care of themselves, if that's what you call it. And nobody makes them go to school, and, even if they do go, their pranks are enough to scare off most teachers. It's a disgrace. They're worse off than we women ever were, regardless of what the Suffragists say."

"How can I help?" I asked, knowing that Lottie already had a plan.

"Louise Updegraff, have you met her yet? No? Well,

she's the new teacher, and she came to me and suggested we have a party . . . food and toys for the children, especially the poor ones. We figure that way they'll at least get one good meal and one toy. If you and Mister Tabor will make a donation and ask anybody you know to do the same, it'll be a big help. We meet at the school on Saturday. Say you'll do it. Say you'll come."

"Did you doubt me?"

She sipped her tea and looked at me over the rim of the cup. "No. I remember how good you and Mister Tabor always were. Him grubstaking everybody, and you helping out any way you could. This town needs you. And I hear now that your husband's mayor we're going to have some decent sanitation for a change."

"He's working on all sorts of plans," I said. Some of those I didn't approve of, but we did need lighting, clean water, a fire department, especially in a town built of wood and canvas.

"We need men like him, and women like you. You're always so level-headed. So sure of yourself."

"Not really," I said, embarrassed.

"Yes, really." She put down her cup and stood. "I'd better be off. It'll probably snow before night. My nose says so."

"Your nose?"

"Snow has its own particular smell," she said with a smile. "One of my few talents is predicting the weather."

"You taught all those poor children to read and do their sums. That's a talent."

"More like a calling, I'd say."

What had my calling been? It seemed that I'd never

had time to ponder, had simply pitched in and done what was necessary to keep my family secure. Rarely, if ever, did I give away to introspection, and I didn't then. I gave Lottie a hug, saw her out, and went to the store to find Haw.

"A good idea," he said when I'd explained what I was doing. "Tell 'em we'll be happy to supply the food, too. Half those kids are hungry if I'm any judge."

"You're a kind man," I said, taking some cash from the drawer. "Forget all I said about giving things away. You meant well."

"Today I'm the mayor. One of these days I'll be more than that and looking for votes. I'll take 'em any way I can get 'em."

"Votes?" I couldn't imagine what he was talking about.

"I'm not going to stay mayor forever, Gusta. This state's in need of men who know what's what. Men who've lived here long enough to understand, not some patsy sent out here from the East who doesn't care about our problems."

"Oh," I said, putting the money into my purse, "that kind of votes." I was dumbfounded by his confidence in his plans.

He smoothed the mustache he was so proud of. "I'm thinking ahead. Not this year, but someday. For now, we take care of the kids."

To do him justice, he had a soft spot for children, had always wished we'd had a dozen. "We'll call it 'The Mayor's Christmas Party'," I said, and kissed him. "You just be sure you come to it."

"Wouldn't miss it for the world." He frowned as an idea struck him. "Where're you going to get these toys you're talking about?"

"Why . . . why from Denver, I guess."

"Better think again. It's November now. You won't get toys in here before the Fourth of July, if then. Anyhow, those kids need clothes more than play things."

"So what should we do?" I asked, hating the notion of giving up the party.

"Hell, go around and get donations of stuff. The kids won't care as long as they get something. Take what you need out of the store. Soap. Mittens. Candles. The parents'll be as grateful as the kids."

I burst into laughter. It was at times like these that Haw seemed the man I'd loved so long before. "Brilliant! And just so you know, you have my vote, Haw Tabor."

He laughed with me. "Your vote don't count."

In spite of the lack of toys, it was a splendid party. The ladies of the committee, including my sisters Lilly and Becca, had supplied the punch, Maxcy had gone up into the mountains and found a tree that the lumber men had missed, and we decorated it with paper chains and strung popcorn. True to his word, Haw attended as mayor—and had supplied us with many of the gifts, from pocket knives to clothespins, needles and thread as well as with a banquet fit for visiting dignitaries.

It was snowing by the time we began our walk home. Mount Massive had disappeared in clouds, and the air was bitter, but I was happy. "I have the feeling next year will be an exciting one," I said.

"About time, don't you think?"

"We've been happy, though, haven't we?"

He patted my hand that lay on his arm. "Sure. But one of these days. . . ." He let his sentence trail off, and I knew what he was thinking. So far the big strike had eluded him, the big strike that would make him the happiest man alive.

Winter up there always lasted well into what should have been spring, and it was April before the weather mellowed enough for much prospecting to be done. Haw was in his element, out staking claims of his own, pushing for decent streets and water and telephone lines, for anything and everything that would make the newly incorporated town fit to live in and get his name in the public eye.

His habit of grubstaking any down-and-out prospector who came in and begged for a hand-out had worsened, to my great annoyance. Supplies were hard to come by—still being hauled in by wagon, although Haw and others were up to their ears in plans for the arrival of the Denver and Río Grande Railroad in Leadville. But that April, our store shelves were getting bare, and I was worried.

"If you keep this up, we won't have anything left to sell," I told him.

"You mind your business, and let me take care of mine," he retorted. "I know what I'm doing."

"So do I. You're gambling with molasses and beans and salt and flour that we could sell, giving them away to every old fool who walks in and tells you a fairy tale."

"I get a third of any strike for my . . . gambling, as you call it. It saves me from tramping around myself. I've got other fish to fry as you know. And it keeps me at home where you say I belong."

That shut me up. He'd developed the habit of staying out late, sometimes all night, with his cronies and coming home the worse for drink—hardly behavior suitable for a politician as I'd told him more than once. Along with the silver strikes had come the gamblers, outlaws, and women who were always the first to arrive in a boom town, and my husband was busy enjoying the sordid company.

"At least make sure you write down what you give and get their names," I said at last. "The way it is, they could make a strike and you'd not even know it, not be able to tell one from the other."

He slammed a fist on the counter. "I'm not the fool you seem to think!"

"Neither am I! Though sometimes I think I'm a fool to put up with you."

There! I'd said it. As always, my tongue took off on its own, leaving me with regrets.

He took up his hat and coat. "I'm going out. Don't expect me for supper."

Maxcy came out from behind a row of shelves as the door slammed. Of course, he'd heard us, as he'd heard us so many times before.

"We're not going to starve," he said with a smile. "Or go broke, either. Don't worry about us."

"It's hard not to."

"Pappy takes chances. That's how he is. But everybody here is taking a chance if you think about it."

"Yes," I said bitterly. "Most of them in our store."

The words had just left my mouth when the door opened and Haw came back in, followed by two of the most disreputable men I'd ever seen. Of course, I knew them. Everybody knew them and laughed at their optimism, their methods. They'd been in a month before, begging for a hand-out, and for a bone for their scrawny dog. I'd fed the poor beast and looked the other way when Haw grubstaked them. Now here they were again, the dog at their heels, even skinnier than before.

It was too much! I turned and left them, saying only: "Make sure they sign the book this time. And give that poor dog something before it lies down on the floor and dies."

"It's dere, Mister Tabor," I heard August Riche say in his thick German accent. "Anudder veek. Give us anudder veek and ve'll all be rich."

"Or in the poor house!" I snapped as I closed the door behind me.

Well, I was wrong. August Riche and his partner, George Hook, struck a vein of solid silver ore on Fryer Hill less than a week later. They named their discovery the Little Pittsburgh, and with our one-third share Haw and I, overnight, were wealthy beyond any dreaming. And I was forced to admit that, for once, Haw's gamble had paid off.

"Now what do you say, eh, Missus Tabor?" Haw had me in his arms and held me high off the floor.

"Put me down!"

"Anything but that! What would you like? Diamonds for your little ears? A velvet gown? A trip to Europe? Hotels in Chicago and New York? The biggest mansion in Denver? Just name it. We're rich, damn it all! The world's ours!"

In that moment, what I wanted I knew I'd never have. Peace. Quiet. A life without worry or stress. A house with my family securely within. But Haw's visions weren't mine. Maybe they never had been. Maybe I'd labored in vain for twenty years.

"I can't think," I said.

"Then don't. I'll do it for both of us. By God, nobody's going to stop me now."

Stop him from what? I was afraid to ask for fear of the answer.

Those mischievous gods who lived on Mount Massive did their best in the months that followed. How they must have laughed at the sight of my husband, raking in riches and losing himself in the process.

"When will you have enough?" I asked him when he'd written a check for $40,000 and handed it over to that scum, Chicken Bill Lovell, for what appeared to be a worthless dig. "We don't need any more mines. We don't need more money. We can't use what we have. Put it away so it'll be there when we do need it."

I was beginning to sound like a parrot even to myself, or like poor Cassandra at the gates of Troy, her message unheeded. But, in truth, I was frightened, as frightened as Hannah and my mother had been at the possibility of war so many years before. Like me, they had sensed disaster but were helpless to stop it. In plain view, my husband was turning into a madman, deaf to any warning, blind to what I foresaw as trouble.

"Everybody knows Chicken Bill's a thief and a liar," I went on as Haw paid no attention to me. "You just handed over a fortune for something not worth ten cents. Everybody's saying he salted that mine. And with your own ore. I'm begging you, Haw, don't just throw our money away on any scheme that strikes you."

"It's my money, and there's plenty of it. I'll spend it any way I like."

That one sentence should have warned me, but I chose to ignore it. "Just . . . just be a little careful, would you?"

"Only if you'll stop carping and learn to enjoy yourself."

"I'm scared."

"Of what?"

"Everything. This all happened too fast."

He leaned back in his chair and lit a cigar, a good one I noticed, not the cheap varieties he'd had to smoke before he had a choice. "It's been twenty-one damn' years. In my mind, that's not fast enough. I want some god-damn' fun before I'm too old to enjoy it."

"All that drinking you've been doing will make you old before you know it."

No one had to tell me about those nights he didn't come home. Gossip and rumor spread quickly in that town. He hadn't touched me in months, and I wasn't sure I cared. What I'd felt that long ago day in South Park had come to pass. He was a stranger, and it wasn't in me to make love with a man I didn't know, a man who came home reeking of whiskey and cheap perfume.

"I'm sorry," I said when he glared at me. "What's happened to us? To you and me?"

"Damned if I know. You're supposed to be happy instead of following me around with a long face forecasting hard times. We've had our hard times. They're over and done. You can't handle success, Gusta, but you'd better learn."

"Is that a threat?"

He blew out a cloud of smoke. "It means I'd like some help. There's talk of me running for governor, and then for the Senate. It'd be nice if you'd appear to be my loving wife even if you're not. Who knows? We could be in the White House in a few years. How'd *that* sit with you?"

"You're crazy." The words popped out. Haw wasn't Presidential caliber, and I knew it even if he and his newly rich cronies didn't.

He leaped up like I'd shot him. "I'm not good enough, is that it? A farmer's son. A stonemason. Well, I'd do better at it than that weak-kneed cousin of yours, and there've been farmers before now who made President. I'll bet their wives supported them."

What did he think I'd been doing over the years? Had he even noticed? Worse, did he care? "My money," he'd said only a few minutes before, as if all I'd earned, all I'd paid for, counted for nothing.

"It's all such a mess. We can't even talk without fighting. Let's just sit down and start over. Please. Let's remember all our good times and who we are."

He leaned his elbows on the desk. "I'm the man you married. The man you believed in. Why can't you believe in me now that everything we wanted is in reach? You act like you're my keeper, for God's sake, but I don't need one. I need a wife."

I closed my eyes to hide the tears. "I'm a real wife," I whispered. "I've been real all along, all these years. I stuck, and you know it. I worked alongside you and never complained, and made the money that kept us going. I believe in us, but not in us acting above ourselves because we have a little money. Money's not everything."

Surprisingly he laughed. "It damn' well helps. Now blow your nose and go on to bed. I have a business meeting with Dave Moffat and Billy Bush."

A meeting that would, no doubt, end at one of the fancy houses patronized by Bush who we'd known for several years and who, in spite of my dislike, had become Haw's partner in various enterprises I tried to ignore. He was just the kind who'd enjoy leading a friend into debauchery, then sit back and smirk.

"I don't know what you see in that man," I said. "He's just another crook."

"I need a good manager for my businesses, and he's it. Leave me to be a judge of character. Leave me to do what I want."

"Fine," I said. "Go, do whatever. But if all this comes to nothing, don't come whining to me. I won't listen."

I got up, went to the door, turned, and saw him still hunched over the desk. He seemed suddenly old, his hair graying and receding, his neck sagging. Turning back, I dropped a kiss on his forehead—where the hair had long since vanished. Money couldn't buy youth or wisdom, no matter what he or anyone thought.

Everything happened fast after that. Chicken Bill's worthless mine, The Chrysolite, turned out to be one of the biggest silver producers in Leadville, and after that came The Matchless that out-produced them all, The Matchless that Haw believed would never play out, would keep him in wealth till he died. But who can know what lies under the ground? Who can say, with certainty, when a mine will play out, collapse, catch fire, be flooded? When a law will be passed that makes a thing worthless? And who but a fool stakes his life on a chance?

That fall, Haw was elected lieutenant governor of Colorado. And why not? He'd contributed hugely to the Republican Party, and it was hoping for a lot more. He employed hundreds of voters in his mines and knew most of the citizens by name. He had a finger in everyone's pie, political or not, and was involved in building his own bank and an opera house in Leadville, because, as he put it: "Folks need entertainment. They work hard. They should play hard. Have some fun."

Just as he was doing. Leadville wasn't so big that he could hide his sins from me or squelch the rumors that I heard everywhere. I heard, but said nothing and went about my own projects, appeared on Haw's arm when he needed to provide the appearance of a happily married man with his dignified wife. I drew the line at the celebration for his Light Cavalry—a group of citizens and friends that, supposedly, would act as an auxiliary police force in times of trouble. Haw, of course, was elected its commanding general and ordered an outfit befitting his rank—an outfit that even the newspapers found laughable.

"Look at you! Gussied up like some actor. Really, Haw, it's time you acted your age."

"I'm ageless!" He was preening in front of the mirror, attempting to fasten gold buttons over his paunch.

Poor, pathetic creature! I walked out of the room and left him to his own admiration. In those days I really tried to guard my tongue, for impressing him with sense or practicality was useless, and I'd grown tired of constant recrimination. I thought that, if he wanted to play general, it was better to let him, better to have him on horseback posturing than in the arms of one of his flings.

Was I, too, becoming ridiculous? I hoped not. I hoped I was behaving as I'd been brought up to behave, turning a blind eye to a man's failings, supporting him and marriage as best I could. If, indeed, there were those who thought I was a fool, they never told me. For that, I was grateful.

It was November. The Opera House, in all its splendor, was about to open to the public, and I was putting the final touches to my hair—still brown and thick, my one pride—when Haw came in.

"Good," he said. "You're dressed up. Everybody who's anybody will be there tonight." He handed me a small box.

"What's this?"

"I promised you diamond earrings. Put 'em on."

My fingers shook as I took out the jewels, held them up to the light. God only knew what they'd cost, but in that moment I didn't care. To be honest, I love jewelry as any woman does. I love the sparkle, the weight, the clarity of diamonds, the bold, earth-formed colors of rubies, emeralds, topazes.

I fastened them in my ears with care, moved my head so that they threw back pure light. "How'd you know I always wanted diamond earrings?"

"I didn't. They just remind me of you." It could have been a romantic moment, but he shattered the spell. "Not a woman in town has earrings like those. Everybody in the house'll see 'em. Can't hardly miss!"

I could have taken them off and thrown them at his feet. I could have said just what I thought, which was that I wasn't a stage prop to be used for his honor and glory, but I wanted to go to the Opera House, wanted to see what my husband had wrought, wanted, truth be told, a little lighthearted gaiety in my life. And I wanted the world to see me in my rightful place—at his side where I belonged.

"You might take a bath before we leave," was all I said.

"No time. Get your cloak and let's go."

Rich as we were, Haw had never changed his habits from the days when he'd labored in the mines. He wanted, I think, to appeal to the commoners as well as to the so-called aristocracy, and I never could convince him that cleanliness is next to godliness. Poor, deluded man!

If there were those who gasped when Haw, Maxcy, and I arrived at the Opera House, it was I who exclaimed over the beauty of the place, its perfection from the red plush chairs to the ornate ceiling and the gilding and mirrors that decorated our private box.

"It's a little jewel box!" I said, delighted. "And you made it so." Then, as always, I spoiled my praise. "How . . . how much did all this cost?"

Haw looked down at me, his irritation plain. "Enough."

We were led to our seats, champagne was poured into fluted glasses, toasts were drunk, and I sat dazed, unable to reconcile who I'd been with who I was supposed to be.

"Quite a show isn't it?" Billy Bush whispered in my ear in that unctuous way I never got used to.

"Quite," I agreed, hoping he'd leave.

"And just the beginning."

"Of what?"

"A new life. Politics. Power. He can do it, you know. And you ought to let him."

"Why?"

He gave me a wink. "Why not? Besides, it's the smart thing to do."

Then the lights dimmed, and the play began. It was an unmemorable performance, as I think back, up-staged, if that's what a vigilante lynching of three crooks can be called and which held a far more popular appeal than a second-class performance.

When it was over, when more champagne had been drunk, more hands shaken, more flattery spoken, Maxcy saw me home. Haw stayed behind to celebrate with his cronies.

"I'll see he gets home all right," Maxcy said. "Don't worry."

"He drinks too much. And I worry about you, too. Leadville's not safe for anybody these days in spite of Pappy's Cavalry."

He laughed. "I'll be fine, but you look tired. Why not go to bed?"

"I guess I will." What, after all, was there for me to do? The evening had come and gone, I'd appeared in my new jewels, my finery, and had then been discarded.

I stood on tiptoe and kissed Maxcy's cheek. A good son, an honest man. "Sometimes it seems Pappy's lost his mind. I need you to look out for him."

"I do the best I can but . . . but he's my father. There's things I can't say to him. I can't order him around. He wouldn't listen and it just wouldn't seem right."

Bewildered, he stood there in the doorway, and in his eyes I read not only confusion but shame for his father's behavior.

"You know how to act," I said. "You always did, since you were little. You don't have to worry about what anybody would think of you. And I don't expect you to do the impossible. Just make sure he's all right."

It had begun to snow and the wind was bitter. I

watched as he headed down the street. My son. The one good thing in an otherwise empty marriage.

From somewhere came shouts and pistol shots. The lynching, I gathered, had turned to celebration and drunkenness. Well, that was Leadville, Cloud City, Queen of the Silver Camps, beginning of the end.

Chapter Sixteen

Suddenly we were moving again—out of our house and into a suite in Billy Bush's Clarendon Hotel, the furniture chosen by Haw to reflect his importance. I gazed around at the massive pieces of ebony and mahogany, the lush Turkish carpets, a bed that could have slept four but which, I suspected, I would occupy alone—and missed the simplicity of the house next door.

"Why do we have to move?" I asked. A dozen men were straining under the weight of a desk that was stuck on the stairs. "What's wrong with our own place?"

"It's just a house, and it's too small. I need a decent place for business, and this is it. Get it through your head, Gusta, we're important people, and it's important how we live." Haw stood in the middle of the room, legs spread, king of all he surveyed.

"It seems to me you do most of what you call business in bars," I said. "You . . . I . . . don't need all this ghastly furniture. There's bars downstairs, and most of them have tables and chairs."

"Picking on my taste?" he asked belligerently.

"No. On your lack of it."

He slammed a big fist down on a table. "God damn it, Gusta, you're doing your best to be rid of me. You know that?"

"I'm trying to make you see sense. I don't want to be rid of you. We're married. We have Maxcy. We have what we hoped and worked for. We don't need fancy knick-knacks and carved settees to prove it. But we do need some kind of dignity." I was pleading now. His words had frightened me more than I'd admit.

"I suppose you think you're dignified? Still taking in boarders like we're dirt. Still the cook and the wash-woman."

Anger blurred my eyes and drove away fear. I flew at him, beat my fists against his chest, and screamed like a harpy, forgetting the men who were still struggling with the desk and doing their best to ignore us.

"And why am I those things, Haw? Because I was helping. Because I believed in you, in us, in our future. I damn' near killed myself for you, and where'd it get me? You want dignity? Well, it doesn't look like it to me. This place looks like a fancy house, and you look like . . . like. . . ." For a moment I couldn't think how to tell him, standing there in his dirty clothes, a diamond on his finger, although his hands were filthy. "You look like what you were. A dirt digger. How long's it been since you had a bath? You smell bad, and that's the truth, and I guess those fancy women of yours must get paid lots to put up with you."

He pushed me away, then grabbed me and shook me like a rag, but I kept on—a dam inside me had burst.

"You think I don't know about those women? I do, and so does everybody. There's an old saying, and I'll tell it to you, though God knows you won't understand it. 'You can't make a silk purse out of a sow's ear,' Haw, so don't tell me about dignity. Don't insult me, laugh at me, make fun of me. I don't deserve any of it."

Whether he shoved me away, or whether I was too weakened by anger to stay on my feet, I can't say, but I fell, lay on that lovely blue and rose and green carpet and waited for what would come next.

Nothing did. He marched across the room in that semi-drunken walk of his and sat down heavily in a chair. When he spoke, his voice was calm, clear, precise. "Do you want a divorce?"

The word hit me like a blow in the face. "A . . . a divorce?" I pushed up and saw him there—judge, jury, husband.

"That's what I said."

"No," I answered, horrified, sick at heart for my own shortcomings as well as his. "We're married. For better or worse. And . . . and you can't afford that kind of scandal. Not in politics."

"I can afford anything. It's your choice."

I shook my head. "Never. It's a sin. It makes all we've done a joke, a failure, and we'd be outcasts.

Both of us. And there's Maxcy. How would divorce affect him? You can't mean it. Please say you don't."

He shrugged, studied his hands, front and back, those big hands that had once touched me with tenderness, that had, I thought, given me strength. "Then shut up," he said.

It was as if he'd hit me again, even harder than the first time. He didn't want me, hadn't for a long time, and it was partly my fault. But groveling on the carpet at his feet wouldn't help, wasn't the least bit dignified, if dignity is what was called for.

I got up, straightened my clothes. "I've made my choice," I said. "I'll never divorce you. But I'm going away for a while. You can enjoy yourself as you like. I won't be here to watch or to help you destroy yourself."

I'd always longed to see Europe, a fascination that had its beginnings in my girlhood when I lay in bed and read anything that came to hand and then imagined myself in those magical, far-off cities—London, Paris, Vienna—ancient cities filled with music, art, magnificent churches, all the culture that was so lacking on the frontier. Without hesitation, I left Horace and went to Becca.

"I'm going to Europe and I'd like to take Vesta with me. It'd be good for us both."

Over the years I'd become fond of my niece who was now a charming young girl on the brink of womanhood and who, I thought, would benefit from a trip abroad.

"Running away?" Becca asked.

Only a week before Haw's involvement with Alice

Morgan, a dancer, had been the talk of the town, and, although I hadn't cried on my sister's shoulder, I'd been upset enough to mention my hurt.

Becca went on without waiting for my answer. "Face it. He's no good. And don't look so shocked. You must've figured that out years ago. Don't blame yourself, either. Nobody else does."

"I guess everybody's talking," I said. "Some days I'd like to bury my head in my pillow and not have to pretend it doesn't hurt."

"I'd like to kill him!" Her teeth were clenched, and she pounded her fists in her lap.

"Don't."

She laughed then. "Think of the scandal! Sister-in-law of Silver King stabs him with a fork for his indelicate behavior while scorned wife looks on."

At that I laughed, too, but her comment about running away rankled. Humiliated I might be, but no one ever called me a coward. "I'm not running away," I told her. "I'd just like to leave it all behind me for a while."

"And hope he grows up," she said. "How soon do you want to leave?"

Within a week Vesta and I were on our way East. Within a month we were sailing for Europe. Time, I hoped, would erase our words, heal our wounds, bring both Haw and me to our senses.

But I hoped in vain, for while I was gone my nemesis, the rock on which I broke, arrived in Leadville. Her name was Elizabeth McCourt Doe, who will always be remembered by the suitable but somehow ridiculous name of Baby Doe.

We were in London when Maxcy's letter reached me. I read it once, then again, and Vesta watched me across the table set for tea.

"Bad news, Auntie?"

"In a way. There's been a miners' strike. Leadville was put under martial law, and your uncle was in the thick of it."

"A strike?" She raised delicate eyebrows. "Why? What for?"

"Why are there always strikes? For better pay. Shorter hours. And the men wanted a hospital. Who can blame them? It's dangerous work for three dollars a day."

"It hardly seems worth going to work for that much."

"Exactly. We take out millions and expect the miners won't notice, but three dollars doesn't go far in Leadville if they've got a family to feed." I sighed, thinking of the children I'd seen stealing what fuel they could to warm their shacks, cook their food. "And Maxcy says Haw wouldn't give in. Wouldn't even raise their wages as much as fifty cents."

What had happened to him? I wondered. Surely he, of all the mine owners, understood the hardship, the danger, the back-breaking labor in a dark tunnel sometimes a hundred feet under ground. Where had his compassion, his early generosity, gone?

I folded the letter and put it in my pocket. "Drink

your tea. I'm going to see what I can do about a passage home."

"But . . . but, surely, it's all been settled by now," she said, plainly distressed at the thought of leaving. "Or will be by the time you get there."

"Yes. It's probably over, but I think your uncle needs looking after. What he did to the miners is going to cost him. I should've been there, instead of gadding about enjoying myself, but now I'm going home. I've been away long enough."

What I didn't tell her was that something Maxcy had written—or rather had *not* written—struck me. At the very end of the letter he'd scrawled as if in haste: *It's time you came home. Things are getting out of hand.*

What things I could only imagine, and the imagining was worse than knowing. I fretted all the way across the Atlantic, walked the deck, looked out on that immense ocean that I'd known only from the shore, and thought perhaps I'd done wrong by leaving, that maybe I could have done something to help the miners and their wives and children, talked some sense into Haw and kept things on an even keel. Of course, I couldn't have foreseen the strike, but still I wondered if I couldn't have averted the trouble somehow.

As far as Maxcy's reference to things out of control, I supposed he was referring to Haw's drinking. Or was he?

"Stop fretting, Auntie, or you'll make yourself sick. Then what?" Vesta took the deck chair beside me. "No matter what, we can't go any faster."

I laughed. She was a cheerful child and a good companion, much like her mother. "I know, I know. But it's my nature to fuss, and I've never been able to help it. I wish I could. My life might have been easier if I knew how to avoid responsibility and keep my mouth shut."

"You mean with Uncle Haw?"

"Yes." I pulled the rug over my lap, for the wind was cold. "He's a man who needs looking after, though he resents it and won't admit it."

She rolled her eyes. "Mother says all men need that."

"Some more than others," I said, but laughed as I thought of Becca. "All that money's gone to his head. It's like . . . like he thinks he's God."

"God," she observed shrewdly, "has common sense. I never noticed that uncle had much of it. He's always been running here and there, trying to do everything at once and getting nothing done at all."

Such an observant creature she was! "I have enough for us both," I said. "At least I thought I did till recently. But as I said, he resents it. And me," I added, then chastised myself for laying my burden on her young shoulders. "Oh, never mind me. Let's go in and dress for dinner and forget it all till we dock."

"We can try, anyhow." She leaned over and kissed my cheek. "Don't worry, Auntie, and do you think I should wear the green silk or the blue? And do you think that nice young man we met last night might ask me to dance?"

"The blue, I think," I said, admiring her youthful exuberance. "And I definitely think he'll ask you to dance."

But, as I knew, life didn't always turn out to be as we planned. I hoped, for her sake, that they would dance all night.

Great wealth, whatever its source, has advantages, and I certainly couldn't deny the fact that I was grateful for the use of David Moffat's private railroad car for the trip back to Denver. Mahogany-paneled, elegantly furnished and carpeted, lit by ornate gas lamps and crystal chandeliers, the comparison between it and the creaking wagon in which I'd crossed the country only twenty years before made me more than ever conscious of my new life.

"It's hard to believe that once none of this existed," I said to Vesta. "If I'd been told about it, I'd have laughed at the thought."

She was eating grapes out of a silver bowl. "It's nice being rich," she said. "I think I like it."

Of course, she did. So did I, with reservations. "The thing is that one can't or shouldn't show it off, shove the fact of money into the faces of those who haven't got it. We can't allow ourselves to forget common decency and good manners." I sighed, knowing Haw had forgotten both, and that I was returning to the same struggle that I'd left. "It's hard, Vesta. Don't think for a minute it isn't," I added, and dropped a stitch in the scarf I was knitting—I didn't know for whom, but I always liked to keep busy. Doing something with one's hands is soothing, even in the worst of times.

At my muffled curse, Vesta got up and turned on a lamp. "Glasses, Auntie," she said. "Where'd you leave your glasses?"

I'd probably mislaid them on purpose. Though they certainly helped me to see, glasses did nothing for my appearance. "I don't need them," I said.

"Why, Auntie, you're vain!" Her eyes twinkled as she spoke, and I forgave her the comment, accurate though it was.

"When you're not born a beauty, even the little things matter," I told her. "I've always tried to look presentable . . . and clean. A little pride doesn't hurt. It's when pride overtakes you that you need to worry."

"Here they are!" She held up my new *pince nez* that a doctor in New York had prescribed, "And *I* think you're pretty, by the way. You always look just right."

"I wish your uncle thought so," I said softly.

She fit the glasses carefully over my nose. "I thought we agreed he had no sense," she said, her face close to mine.

"He knows what he wants. Always has."

"And he wanted you."

"Then," I corrected her with a pang. "He wanted me then." It was the truth, and I knew it, as I knew he'd spoken the word divorce because he meant it.

When I walked into the lobby of the Clarendon Hotel and saw the little blue-eyed woman talking earnestly with Billy Bush, I knew, somehow, that I wasn't wanted at all.

Seeing me, Billy hurried across the room, an attempt at a smile on his face.

"Missus Tabor! Welcome back! We didn't expect you so soon!"

I'd have bet on that. "Thank you," I said stiffly. Billy always had that effect on me. "We made good time, and Maxcy met me. Where is my husband?"

He blinked. "Prob'ly in his office next door. Want me to go see?"

"I'll find him. Who was that woman you were talking to? An actress?"

His face went still for a minute, then he smiled again. "Oh. You mean Missus Doe. She's . . . she's . . . ah . . . engaged to Jake Sands. Came here from Central City a little while ago."

"Missus?" I asked.

"Well . . . ah . . . yes. Divorced, or so I understand. Can't tell you much more'n that, I'm afraid."

"That's enough," I said, and looked around for Maxcy, but he'd gone up with my luggage.

At her first glimpse of me the woman had disappeared in a swirl of a well-cut skirt and a glimpse of kid boots, and every male eye in the lobby had followed her exit.

Our suite was as I'd left it—cluttered, overfurnished, depressing after some of the houses I'd visited in Europe. I opened a window, then closed it immediately, for the high mountain air was tainted with the stink of industry, with the *clanging* of equipment, the *rumble* of heavily loaded ore cars.

"What have we done?" I murmured, more to myself than to Maxcy, who looked at me, perplexed.

"To whom?" he asked.

"To the mountains. We've stripped the trees, dirtied the rivers, made everything ugly. We ruined it all in a couple of years."

"It's called progress," he said with a smile. "But I know what you mean."

"And what did you mean in your letter about things out of control?" I asked. "You scared me."

He put his hands in his pockets and paced the length of the room. "You might as well hear it from me," he said after a while. "Pappy's been . . . well . . . he's making a worse fool of himself. If you read in the Denver papers about him having two wives, it's because of a woman. Willie Deville. She's been chasing him all over the country, and it's not doing his political campaign any good. I'm sorry to have to say any of this. I'm sorry to have to be a part."

"Don't be," I said. "None of it's your doing, and I guess nothing has changed."

Maxcy hesitated, then said: "Well, there's more. He bought a house in Denver. Looks like we'll be moving again. He won't listen to me, and I don't think he'll listen to you, either, any more than he listened to those miners who wanted a fifty-cent pay raise. I'm sorry for all of us."

"It's as if he has to make up for the whole rest of his life," I said. "And we can't help him do it. But surely he's not serious about this . . . this Willie woman."

Maxcy snorted. "Hardly. I mean, she's not exactly what a governor would want in his life. But, well, there's others."

"That woman in the lobby? That Missus Doe?"

His mouth twisted. "She came to town to marry Jake Sands, but it hasn't happened. Mostly she's been with Pappy. Billy introduced them."

Billy! How did I know that? "She's pretty," I said. "Not what you'd expect. Well dressed, too."

"They're all pretty!" He was pacing again, as if he was ashamed to look me in the eye. "And they're all just a bunch of fortune-hunters. Pappy falls for their praise, their acts, just like he's a child."

"And you?" I asked. "Don't the fortune-hunters come after you, too?"

He grinned. "I stay pretty close to home. You raised me right. I haven't lost my head or my heart, and, when I do, it'll be for a woman like you."

I gave a silent prayer of thanks for that son of mine, standing there as honest as his namesake, Nat Maxcy. Then I said: "I'd best go find him. Is he next door?"

"Might be. You want me to check?"

"No," I said. "I'll just change my dress and go myself. And hope for the best. I guess he won't be happy to see me."

"It's hard to say what makes him happy these days. Maybe nothing does. Maybe he got what he wanted and there's nothing more."

I wondered if Maxcy wasn't right. When you achieve all that you ever wanted, when you hold in your hands the dream you've chased for over forty years, what else is there?

A covered passageway connected the Clarendon Hotel to the Tabor Opera House. It was put in so patrons of both places could come and go without being exposed to Leadville's weather, or, as I often suspected, to make assignations invisible to anyone watching from the street.

I found Haw in his office deeply in conversation with Billy Bush. They broke off as I paused in the door.

"You're back," Haw said. "How was it?"

"Splendid!" I waited for Billy to leave, which he did so slowly that I was, as always, annoyed.

"That man!" I said as the door closed behind him.

"I need him."

"So you've said." A closer look at my husband told me that he'd aged, and that he was dyeing his hair.

"It won't help."

"What won't?"

"Hair dye. You're getting old, and so am I."

"Yes, and those glasses don't help you, either. Now you're back, are you going to start in on me night and day?"

I took the chair Billy had left. "No. Just commenting. I don't like the glasses any more than you do. Tell me about the strike. That's all I've heard about."

He reached for his cigars, chose one, lit it, then leaned back in his chair. "A bunch of upstarts agitating for more money. Can't give in to that sort of thing or they'll walk all over you. Yeah, it was tough for a while, but I showed 'em."

"That's what I heard." I'd seen the result on my way to the hotel, when several miners' wives, women I'd known and helped, cut me dead. "They don't look too happy about it."

"The hell with 'em! If they won't work, there's plenty who will. I reckon I made that clear."

"What about the families? The children?"

"Nobody worried about me as a kid. I turned out all right." He blew a cloud of smoke and grinned at me. "Whether you think so or not."

The change in him went deeper than hair dye and diamond cuff links. He was another person, a monster, and sitting there I was afraid—for him, for all of us. And for once I had no answer.

"It's good you're back," he said. "I bought us a house in Denver. Old Brown's place on Broadway and Seventeenth. I'll need it when the campaign heats up. And I'm leaving the furnishings to you this time. How's that suit you, Missus Tabor?"

Although Maxcy had warned me, my heart sank to my shoes. In Leadville I'd had a place, friends, family, work. In Denver, what would become of me?

"Is it big?"

"Twenty rooms. No more suffocating in a cracker box for me. You'll have plenty to do. And I want a party for the bigwigs when you've got it finished."

"When?"

"Soon as you can. No sense letting the place stand empty."

I couldn't help myself, though I knew my question would anger him. "Was it . . . very expensive?"

He thrust his face as close to mine as the width of the desk permitted. "Get it through your head. If I felt like it, I could buy the god-damn White House. I could move it here and set it up on Harrison Avenue. In fact"—he chuckled as a thought struck him—"I may buy it sooner than you think."

Chapter Seventeen

Such a scene I never saw! Wagons bulging with the furniture Haw insisted I take with me; carriages loaded with boxes and trunks; the coaches that were carrying Becca, Vesta, Lottie, and me to Denver. I didn't want Haw's excesses, but in a mansion of twenty rooms I planned to disperse and somehow hide that mahogany and mother-of-pearl desk, the massive sideboard, the silver stag mounted on a block of solid ebony—ghastly furnishings of a tasteless era. Haw wanted his own suite of rooms, and he could have his precious ostentation in them.

I had no say in what was packed or moved, but I'd done one thing and kept quiet. Before the movers arrived, I had gone through every drawer and taken the money that Haw was too careless to bank or to count—thousands of dollars just shoved away and forgotten and that surely would be stolen by the movers but which I intended to save for the day I was certain was coming. My purse, my carpetbag, overflowed with money and weighed me down with guilt and irritation. So much! So much!

Haw stayed behind in Leadville, making some excuse about business, to which I paid no attention, knowing only too well what he meant. With his conscience out of the way, he intended to do as he pleased, and surely as I knew my own name I knew his intentions toward Baby Doe. She was, after all, living in the Clarendon, which she could hardly have afforded on her own, and she was sporting jewelry that came, I suspected, from my husband, although, since I was no longer permitted to keep our books, I had no way of proving that.

With the silver strike on Fryer Hill and Haw's acquisition of The Matchless, our bookkeeping had been taken over by Lou Leonard, manager of the mines, although I protested.

"We're talking millions," Haw said. "I can't afford any mistakes."

"I've only made one mistake in twenty years," I reminded him. "And that was the fault of the post office. I can add and subtract no matter how many zeros there are."

"Leave it!" As always, he was annoyed when I brought up my past labors. "This is big business. Men's business, not those god-damned little record books you're so proud of."

Of course, it was big business. By that time, The Matchless, alone, was bringing in two thousand dollars a day—wealth beyond imagination, but on paper simply figures that I knew I could manage. But that, too, was being taken away, along with all the duties I'd performed and, most often, enjoyed. So, in a way, I was glad to be leaving for Denver where I could busy myself furnishing that big house that I loved from the first in spite of its empty rooms, the bare grounds that surrounded it.

I pitched in with a will, mustering the help of Becca and Vesta, several servants, and dear Lottie Williams whose organizational talents would, I knew, be needed. I had an ulterior motive as well, for Lottie had little money and was desperate for a decent place to live.

"Say you'll come," I'd pleaded with her. "I'll need all the help I can get, and there's all those bedrooms just sitting there empty. Besides, I don't want to live alone."

That was a weak excuse considering the places where I'd done just that, but Lottie hadn't noticed.

"If . . . if you're sure. If I can really help."

She had her pride, as did I. "You'll be my secretary."

Her eyes had widened. "Augusta, you don't need a secretary. You're the most efficient person I know. And I don't need charity, though I thank you for the offer."

"It's not charity," I had said. "Haw wants the house done up brown. He wants parties so he can make a splash. I can't do that all by myself. I really do need you. Together maybe we can show him. . . ." My voice trailed off. *Show him he needs me*, I was about to say, but that sounded as if I'd admitted defeat.

She had nodded then, a quick, decisive jerk of her head, and the feather on her bonnet had swayed with the motion. "Very well. I'll come. And I'll stay till you don't need me any more."

So the Brown mansion became a house filled with women, as Vinnie, widowed and lonely, came from Maine to stay, and one day Nat Maxcy showed up at the door, his face a study in concern.

"Why, Nat," I said, surprised yet glad to see him. "Come in. What're you doing in town?"

He hesitated, took off his hat, and stood there, as awkward as a boy. "I need a favor, ma'am, though I hate to ask you."

I dragged him in and shut the door. "Ask me anything. I owe you my life, and it's about time I repaid my debt."

His story came in fits and starts, a sad tale that touched me deeply, for I remembered the details, remembered how his sister, Euphrasia, had been married to a vile and abusive man, Bob Hoover, who'd been hanged for murder. After that I had lost track of her.

"She's got nobody. No place to stay, no money. I've lent her what I can, but, well, you know how I live, and it's no place for her. I wondered . . . could you have her here? Just till she gets on her feet? She's a milliner, and a good one, but in Fairplay nobody's interested in ladies' hats."

There were women worse off than I was, and well I knew it! "You bring her right to me, Nat Maxcy," I ordered. "And don't give it another thought. Have you eaten?"

His smile was one of relief. "No, ma'am. I just came

right here. And . . . and I sure thank you. You're a fine lady. Not like . . ."

He broke off, embarrassed, and I took his arm as if I hadn't noticed his slip. "Come on into the kitchen. There's a kettle of soup and the bread's just done."

"We all of us remember your bread," he said. "And what you could do with venison. And those vegetables. Remember them? How everybody said you couldn't do it, but you raised the biggest cabbages and the best beans we'd ever seen."

Oh, I remembered, even longed for those days when our only problems had been weather, food, staying healthy. "Sometimes I wish we were still back there," I said. "Before everything went mad."

He nodded sadly. "I know what you mean, ma'am. It's all a crying shame. It seems there's no place you can go and find quiet any more. I miss that more than anything."

"But we had it," I said. "And we can keep it alive in our minds even in the city. We can remember those cranes flying over the prairie. We were blessed, Nat, no matter what anyone says."

He took a big slice of bread and spread it with what looked like a half pound of butter. Then he looked up, a quizzical expression in his eyes, "I reckon that's the truth. We had the best of it, for sure."

A week later, Euphrasia came to stay—a tiny woman, scared of her own shadow, and who could blame her with the husband she'd had—but she fit right in, went to work selecting fabric and draperies, stitching away silently but with a will, and I was happy to have been able to do something good for Nat.

With me out of the way, Haw's pursuit of Baby Doe took on new life. Becca, who went back and forth between Denver and Leadville where Peter was still working, never failed to tell me the latest gossip, accompanied by a scolding.

"Instead of killing yourself making this palace for him to show off in, you should be up there fighting that woman off. Where's your pride?"

"Right where it's always been," I told her. "Think how it would look. Two women at each other's throat. It's better I ignore it. Other women do."

"The long-suffering wives."

"If that's how you want to put it."

I sounded prideful enough, but inside I felt I was bleeding—for both Haw and me. The threads of our life were pulled apart, the bond between us broken by the chance discovery of a vein of silver, and by the arrival of a small, blue-eyed temptress who knew what she wanted and how to get it.

Becca's heels tapped on the wooden floor like castanets. She could never sit still when making one of her speeches. "Wake up, Gusta! That woman's after him and won't stop till she has him. She got rid of one husband. Now she's after a rich old fool. They even say she had some man's baby while she was still married to Harvey Doe."

"She has a child?"

"Born dead. Better that way."

"Poor thing." To lose a child was, in my mind, enough to unbalance any woman.

Becca swept past my chair again. "You would say that! Your trouble is you let your feelings lead you, but you'd better start using your head before it's too late. Before you lose everything you've worked for."

"I won't . . . I can't make a scene," I said. "You spoke of pride. Well, my pride tells me not to lower myself, not to wash our dirty linen in public. As for what I was working for, I thought it was for Haw, Maxcy, and me. Now it seems I was wrong. All along, I was wrong."

The room spun around me, and I grasped the arms of the chair to steady myself. Nothing any more could be trusted, not even those things I'd known and loved. What I had believed had been simply what I had wished, a fairy tale and not reality.

"How can we know what's true?" I wailed, losing my battle with dignity.

Becca stopped her pacing and knelt beside me. "For God's sake, don't cry!"

"Answer my question!"

She caught my hand and turned it over in her own. "I can't."

"Have I lost my mind, then? Has Haw? That woman? I seem to be in a bad play and I don't know my part. Nobody's written it, don't you see?"

"I never thought you were helpless," she said, still holding my hand.

But I was. As I saw it, all I could do was pretend I

didn't care, go on as I always had. In those years, for a woman in my position, there was no other choice.

Haw arrived in early January and for a purpose. He wanted to begin his Senate campaign. A bit early, but he was too restless, too filled with ambition to move slowly or carefully.

"Here's a list. Invite 'em all," he said, handing me a piece of paper covered with his black scrawl. "Do it up big. Waiters, food, music, wine. And keep your old lady friends out of the spotlight."

"They're your friends, too," I reminded him. "Or have you forgotten?"

He stood there, legs apart, arrogant and cruel. "I'd just as soon forget," he said.

"And me with them, I suppose."

He sneered. "I wish you'd let me."

It was a stab to the heart, but, instead of breaking, I flew into a rage, forgetting dignity and all the manners I'd ever learned.

"Get out of this house! Go on back to that creature. Of course, I know about her. The whole world knows. I'll have a party, all right! I'll pull the place down and burn it, and tell the world why. You won't get to the Senate or the White House on my back, Haw Tabor. You've used me for years, but I'm through. Go see what good your little strumpet can do for you. And watch folks laugh at the old man."

For a moment he seemed shocked, as if he believed I'd do what I said, and I took advantage and went on. "Take a look at yourself. You're an old man, making a fool of yourself over a child who flatters you. How much do you have to pay to feel young again?"

His eyes bulged out. I thought he might have a stroke and wasn't sure I cared. Then he took two steps toward me, put his hands on my shoulders. "I could kill you for that."

"You've already killed what we had. Might as well kill me and get it over with."

He stared at me—the look of a child in a temper tantrum, a child denied what it wants and can't have—then his shoulders slumped. "Damn it, Gusta! You make me crazy. All I want is a little fun. All I want is my chance, but you make me say things, and they come out all wrong. I shouldn't have said it, and I'm sorry."

The fact that he'd apologized astonished me. Even more astonishing was the pity I suddenly felt for him. Even then, hurt, betrayed, treated as a nuisance, I loved him—for our past, for times he'd now chosen to overlook but which I never could.

"What do you want?" I asked, and waited, half afraid of his answer.

He ran a hand through his thinning hair. "I want a wife who's a wife and not my conscience. I want a woman who appreciates who I am. And I want that party."

"Very well."

Relief showed on his face. "You'll do it?"

"I'll do it for myself, Haw. Not for you. I'll do it for what we had together and for no other reason. No matter what you do, we're married, and I'll see to it that the whole state knows it."

"That'll do." He reached for his hat and coat.

"You're leaving?"

"I'm meeting Pitkin at the American House."

Lunch with the governor! Oh, he'd come a long way from that desolate Vermont farm, from my father's quarry, from that one-room shack on the treeless prairie.

I opened the heavy front door and let him out. Snow was falling. "Mind the steps!" I called after him, but he went on as if he hadn't heard, as if he was already hundreds of miles away.

It was an elegant reception, and everyone invited came. The newly elected Governor Pitkin, ex-Governor Routt and his wife. Attorney General Wright, state senators, generals, judges, all came to pay tribute to Haw and his millions and, possibly, to decide for themselves how things were between us.

I had a new dress—black silk piped in bright yellow—and wore the diamond earrings Haw had given me in Leadville and an ornate Spanish cross on a gold chain.

I stepped away from the mirror. The woman who looked back at me was not unhandsome. There was strength in her face, in the carriage of her head, a hint of steel in the blue-gray eyes. I nodded at my reflection. No one could ever call me cheap or common or accuse me of unnecessary frivolity. I was who I was, who I'd become, and my skin fit me very well. "You'll do, my dear," I said. "Now it's downstairs to see what's been forgot."

Maxcy caught me in the hall. "Help me with this tie, can you, please?"

I straightened the tangle he'd made, then stepped back to look at him, a man grown. Where had the years gone? "You look very handsome."

"And you look elegant."

"Me?"

He kissed my cheek. "Yes. You. Care to dance?"

In the drawing room the musicians were tuning up. "Not now," I said with a laugh. "I'd better make sure everything's ready. I've never done a party as ambitious as this."

"No. You've only fed about thirty hungry miners with nothing on hand but beans and flour. Compared to that, this is simple."

"I don't want to disgrace your father."

He took my arm. "You wouldn't disgrace the King of England . . . if there was one. As it is, you've done Pappy proud, and he doesn't deserve it."

"Not tonight," I said. "Let's not think about any of that tonight even though everybody will be wondering."

"Let 'em!"

Together we went down the stairs, all my apprehension gone. If anything made me proud, it was Maxcy.

"I wish I had ten sons like you."

He raised an eyebrow. "I'm afraid you'll have to make do with just me."

"You'll do fine. Now go check the wine room, and I'll go see what the cooks and caterers forgot."

In the light of hundreds of candles and crystal chandeliers, the dining room was a place of refined elegance.

Even Haw's portrait, which he'd had done in Leadville, looked as if it belonged on the wall, staring down at the long table. The caterers had done their job to perfection. Oysters gleamed on their shells atop chopped ice, and surrounding them were platters of wild Alaskan salmon, tiny quails in beds of delicate lettuces, cold beef, and Westphalian ham. Fruit jellies quivered in silver bowls, and later would come the plum puddings, sherbets, small, iced French pastries like so many delicate flowers.

Dominating the table was Euphrasia's masterpiece, a pyramid of fruit and flowers too beautiful to be touched or sampled, a creation by the little milliner whose clever hands and fertile imagination I gave thanks for every day. It was Euphrasia, with her eye for style and color, who'd helped me choose the velvet for the draperies that graced the tall windows, the satin that covered settees and chairs, the hangings and coverlets for the beds, and I thought that, if I'd done a good deed by taking her in, she'd more than repaid me.

"By God, Gusta! You've pulled it off!" Haw, glittering with diamond rings and studs, clattered down the stairs to stand beside me as I gazed at what could have been a painting.

"I did at that," I said, accepting the praise that was my due. "But Denver's gotten so sophisticated, anything I wanted someone could find. We couldn't have imagined this the first time we came, could we?"

He looked down at me, his face unreadable. "I don't want to talk about any of that. Not now."

"You might not, but I'm proud of all of it," I said.

"Of Denver, of Colorado, of what we've accomplished. Both of us. And if anybody asks, I'll tell them."

In spite of the bitterness between us, Haw and I stood in the receiving line, shaking hands, smiling, till I thought a smile would be plastered on my face in the morning. They came—all the new royalty of Colorado—to pay their respects, to dance attendance on the newest rising star, but they paid as much attention to me as to Haw which gave me a subtle satisfaction. Would he have stuck in that early, hard-scrabble world without me? I didn't think so. So I bowed and smiled, accepted compliments and congratulations, mindful of what we had, over the years, achieved.

The next day the *Denver Daily* ran a headline: SPLENDID SUCCESS OF THE RECEPTION GIVEN BY THE LIEUTENANT GOVERNOR.

"Guess I got 'em to sit up and take notice," Haw said, waving the paper at me.

For once we were sitting alone at the breakfast table, talking like any other husband and wife.

"It did go well," I said, overlooking his self-praise. "Everybody seemed to enjoy themselves."

"That's what money's for. By God, this is the life!" He slurped his coffee, slammed down the cup, and lit a cigar. "And don't say you didn't enjoy it."

"Of course, I did." Even though the preparations had nearly exhausted me.

He pushed back his chair. "Gotta get going."

"Where?"

"Back to Leadville. Got a problem with the mine."

He wouldn't look at me, and I knew he was lying, knew he'd come, used me, conquered, and was on his way back to that woman who'd bewitched him.

When I spoke, my voice trembled, but he didn't notice. "How long will you be away this time?"

"I'll let you know."

He went up the stairs singing off key. "I dream of Jeannie with the light brown hair. . . ."

It didn't take a genius to know he wasn't thinking of me.

Chapter Eighteen

It is possible to be lonely even in a house overflowing with relatives and friends. In the next years I was as alone as I'd ever been—a woman discarded, whose painful duty was that of appearing unruffled, untouched by rumors, gossip, the bitter truth. Haw came and went, using the house for his own interests as always, but for the most part living in the Windsor Hotel which he and Billy Bush were rebuilding and where Baby Doe now had an apartment of her own.

Oh, of course, I knew. I'd seen the woman for myself more than once. She took great care to hide her face under a veil, but she was unable to hide her person. Even if I hadn't been aware of all Haw's illicit activities, Becca kept me up to date.

"She was at the Fireman's Ball with him the other night. Oh, with that veil on her face like always, but it was her, dancing with Haw, throwing herself at him. Everybody's talking. This has to be stopped, Gusta. He's gone too far."

I shook my head wearily. One didn't stop a runaway freight train—only waited for the derailment. Besides, I'd done the only thing I could. I'd purchased a third interest in the hotel from Charles Hall, who'd signed the papers over to me with a twinkle.

"There now, Missus Tabor," he'd said. "What're your intentions?"

I'd answered with a smile of my own. "Why, I guess I'll go and oversee what's being done. As part owner, you understand."

"Quite right," he said, still twinkling. "I wish you luck."

Haw, when he found out, was livid. "What in hell do you think you're doing?" He was standing in the hall and shouting.

"It's an investment."

"Investment! What in hell do you know about investments?"

"More than you think," I said, keeping my temper.

"You just can't keep your nose out of my business. Can't get anything through your head. I'll buy you out. How much?"

"Not for sale, Haw," I told him. "Not to you at any price."

"God damn it! You go too far!" He paced the length of the hall, his boots thudding on the floor.

"I'll stop when you come to your senses," I said, following him. "You're destroying everything we had, all that we worked for. If you won't think about me, think about your political career. It's a scandal, Haw, and it'll break on your head. Nobody's going to vote for a man who flaunts his mistress in their faces. Can't you just come home? Can't things be like they were?"

Even as I spoke, I wondered why I wanted this wild-eyed, smelly stranger back, why I cared so much that I was reduced to pleading. Perhaps it was the intensity of my voice, or maybe that I'd caught up to him, stood looking up into his face, but, as I watched, his face changed into a furious mask, and, when he answered, spittle flew out of his mouth and clung to his mustache.

"Home? Home? My home's not here. Not today. Not any more. Get it through that thick head of yours and stop nagging me. I don't need your nagging. Never did. I don't know why I put up with you long as I did." Without waiting for a reply, he headed for the stairs in that awkward lope I'd once found charming.

"Where are you going?"

"I'm leaving. For good!"

In his room he began throwing coats, trousers, shirts, and collars every which way into a bag, and he kept shouting—terrible words I've tried to forget. Tried, but they come back at night to haunt me.

"Home! All you've ever been is a millstone around my neck. Never any fun, never any encouragement, just that long face and nasty tongue. Don't do this! Don't do that! Brush your teeth! Take a bath! Christ, I got where I am without a god-damn' bath or a stepmother nagging me. I left her, and I'm leaving you. You can sit here with your ministers, your old lady hen parties. Or you can go to hell."

He snapped the locks on his bags and stood glaring at me, his breath coming hard.

I was dizzy. My ears rang from his shouting, and my heart thumped so hard I thought I'd faint. What good love and marriage vows if they came to this impassible chasm? What good life?

I put out a hand, steadied myself against the door frame, and made one last attempt. "Don't. Please don't go."

His laughter was horrible. "Get out of my way."

I stepped aside, watched as he made his way down the stairs. "You'll ruin yourself!" I called after him. "You'll come to nothing. You and . . . and *her*. Wait and see."

Again that mad laughter echoed off the walls. "If I do, I'll have a hell of a good time before I go."

The door slammed. Around me the house was silent, as if it was holding its breath, as if all in it were cowering behind closed doors, afraid to come out, fearful of facing me in my abandonment. Somehow I got to my room, sat staring out at nothing, looking inward at the wasteland I'd become. A forty-seven-year-old woman whose entire life had been rendered meaningless and whose future held no promise at all.

It wasn't a week later that Billy Bush called upon me.

He stood in the hall, twisting his hat in his hands, as ill at ease as I'd ever seen him.

"Come into the parlor," I said, not liking him any better for his new attitude.

He sat down, still clutching his hat. "I. . . ."

I interrupted rudely: "If you're here to ask me to sell my shares in the Windsor, my answer is no. If you'd like a cup of tea or a lemonade, I'll ring."

He cleared his throat. "It's not the hotel."

"What then?"

"Haw wants a divorce."

His brutal manner, the ugly word, smacked me in the face, although God knew I'd heard that word before and feared this moment. I drew a deep breath. "Why didn't he come himself? Why send you of all people?"

"He's a busy man, Missus Tabor. You should know that by now. Besides, he figured you wouldn't see him."

I sat straight in my chair, praying for dignity and strength. "If he wants a divorce, he must ask me himself. There are matters to be straightened out that don't concern you."

Billy squirmed. "You don't understand."

"I understand quite well. Now you go back and tell my husband that divorce is out of the question."

"Look." He leaned toward me. "Look, why not just do it? The longer it's put off, the worse for you both. You file. You got reason enough. And Haw says he'll give you the house and two hundred and fifty thousand. Make it easy on yourself."

"I have never made anything easy on myself," I said, struggling for composure. "And I don't intend to start now. Of all people, my husband should know that. And that's a poor sum of money for all the years I labored for little or no wages. The years I spent as a devoted . . . *and faithful* . . . wife. Go tell him that, Billy, and let's end this charade."

I saw him out, then called for my carriage. It had been a long time since I'd visited Father Machebeuf, and that afternoon his warmth, his friendship, even his religion were what I needed.

A tall, austere priest answered my knock, and I stood for a moment confused, wondering who he was.

"Is Father Machebeuf here?" I asked, hesitant, for something in this priest's face told me he brooked no nonsense. "I'm Missus Tabor," I added, and with relief saw him smile.

"Jean-Baptiste Lamy, Archbishop of Santa Fé. Please come in, Missus Tabor. Joseph speaks of you, and your charity often." His smile vanished, replaced by a frown. "He's not been well. But I'm sure a visit from you would cheer him."

"Not well? How?"

"An accident. His wagon overturned on the way home from Blackhawk. His hip . . . broken. His spirit, also, I'm afraid."

I couldn't picture the cheerful Machebeuf in a depression. "He's always so joyous," I said. "Perhaps I should come another day."

Lamy put out a large, callused hand, a hand that had seen years of hard, unpriestly labor. "No. Come in, please. If you can take his mind off the fact that he'll never ride horseback again, maybe never walk without a crutch. . . ."

Immediately I forgot my own problems. "He'll find that very hard," I said. "I'll do what I can."

Lamy led me through the little brick house to the garden where Machebeuf sat like a shadow, his plump, pleasant face shrunken, his shoulders slumped.

Seeing me, he struggled to get up, but Lamy pressed him back into the chair. With another of those sudden, gentle smiles, he said: "Sit, Joseph. Missus Tabor's come to cheer you."

For a few minutes we exchanged polite conversation—on the new school and parochial building of which he was proud, and to which I'd contributed, on the weather, on the details of his accident, which I hardly wanted to hear—and then he leaned over and laid a hand on mine. "What is it, Augusta? What's made you unhappy?"

"It shows?"

"To me. Because you've always been a happy woman."

"Haw wants a divorce." There! I'd said it!

Sadly he shook his head. "Of course, I've heard . . . things. But then, I hear many rumors, most of which I pay no attention to. He wants this. But you?"

Without warning, I burst into tears, and my story came out between sobs. Oh, I hated it—the weakness of weeping, of laying my burden on the poor priest who sat listening, compassion in his eyes.

When I'd finished, when I could speak coherently, I said: "I'm sorry. I didn't come to make a scene, to worry you."

"You came because we're old friends," he said. "Because you needed to talk. I'm sorry, too, but not because you told me this. You hurt, and I can't help.

You've lost that light I admired so much. I can't condone divorce any more than you, but you aren't the one at fault."

"Maybe I am. I've said harsh things. I've made him feel . . . oh, I guess inferior. He says I nag. I guess I have nagged him. If only I'd kept quiet and just gone along. But I couldn't. I couldn't . . . can't . . . stand by and watch him ruin himself, destroy his family as if we're nothing. And for that woman! I don't know who Haw is any more, Father. I don't think he knows, either."

"He's a man who had nothing, and who now can buy anything in the world that he wants," Machebeuf said slowly. "I have always thought that excess is a form of insanity, sometimes temporary, sometimes not. Of course, he doesn't know himself. He was never prepared for these millions, not in his character, not truly in his own mind. He is like Doctor Faustus of legend who sold his soul for power, youth, and for a woman who, if I remember one version of the story, died insane."

"But that's a legend," I protested. "A story. It's not real life even . . . even if there's a similarity."

His chuckle was an echo from his past, but I welcomed his effort. "Legends are universal. The foibles of mankind are repeated in every generation. Ours isn't any different, though what will happen to your husband is hard to say. For you, my dear, don't destroy yourself over what you can't control. Hold on to your truth, your beliefs, and . . ."—he gave me a smile—"go and plant your garden."

The abrupt change caught me unawares. "My what?"

He leaned back in his chair and closed his eyes, and for a minute I thought he'd fallen asleep. Then he said: "You remember your garden in Buckskin Joe?"

Odd, how so many recalled that place. "Yes," I said.

"Make another. You told me you wanted to, but you haven't done it yet."

"Somehow it all seemed so hard. To no point."

"There's always a point to a garden. Think of it as creating life. If you do it, I'll ask Father Lamy to send you some seedlings. He grows the most astonishing peaches, you know. And cherries. And splendid flowers. It's a form of prayer for him, maybe for you, too. Try it."

Well, the house was in desperate need of landscaping—of trees, flowers, a decent lawn, and I'd neglected that, focused on the wrong things.

"I'll start today," I said. "I promise. You're a very wise man."

He opened his eyes, and I saw that he was tired and in pain. "A wise man would have been watching where he was going instead of driving off the edge of the road. But I'll come to see what you've done if you invite me."

I got up, bent down, kissed his weathered cheek. "Come any time, dear friend. No invitation needed."

WORK ON TABOR OPERA HOUSE BEGINS. LIEUTENANT-GOVERNOR TABOR SAYS IT WILL OUTSHINE ANY THEATER IN THE WORLD.

Without a word I handed the paper to Becca, whose face as she read reflected my own surprise.

When she'd come to the end, she folded the paper and stared at me. "He didn't tell you about this? Nothing at all?"

"He doesn't tell me anything any more. Just sends Billy to try to force me into divorcing him. When's it going to end? When will he come to his senses? It says right there in the paper that he's bought an entire mahogany forest in Honduras. What for? Why does he need one?"

"Seems to me he has more money than brains."

"He's trying to buy the Senate seat," I said bitterly. "But buying up land in places nobody's ever even seen won't help. He wants . . . oh, I don't know what he wants any more except to be rid of me."

Becca sniffed. "You'd be better off without him. At least Billy Bush wouldn't be knocking at the door every day. I really can't stand him, either, Gusta."

"You think I can? He has no manners to speak of, and he looks at me like I'm some . . . some misfit. Maybe I am," I added, swept by a wave of self-doubt.

Becca slapped the paper down on the table. "Nonsense! You're the only sane person in the affair. But before Haw throws all his money out the window, you should make sure you get some of it."

Sometimes it seemed that all we did in my house was to say the same things without coming any closer to a solution. Still, I asked: "How?"

Becca smiled, a wicked smile that narrowed her eyes. "Wait till the campaign heats up and he wants to show off his fancy woman. He'll come to heel then. You'll see."

I didn't want to see. I wanted my family back, intact, respectable, not ripped apart by Haw's inability to control either his appetites or his lust for power. "I saw *her* the other day," I said. "At the Windsor. She . . . she's beautiful. And I'm not. She's young. I'm not. I can't fight on those grounds."

"Hit him where it hurts. In his pocket," Becca insisted. "He won't miss a million or two. You should go see a lawyer. I'm thinking of it myself."

The idea was horrifying. "Why? You can't!"

"Well, I can. I'm pretty sure Peter's seeing someone. I come to Denver to pretend it's not true, but then I have to go running back and make sure. I can't live like this."

Although I'd wondered about the rift between her and Peter, she'd hidden her pain well. "Why didn't you tell me?"

"I didn't want to talk about it, and I don't now."

Was anyone happy in the world, or did everyone wear a mask like Becca and me, a mask that enabled us to pretend? "Is there . . . do you think there's something the matter with us?" I forced the question.

She looked up, eyes bright with tears. "Who knows? Maybe we were brought up wrong. Maybe all women are. But Lillie's happy enough. You and I, though, have always said what we think, and that's not how we're supposed to be. We're supposed to be mealy-mouthed little women and we're not." She ran her hands through her thick hair, making a tangle of curls that, I saw suddenly, were streaked with gray. "Never mind me," she said. "I'll be fine, but you need a lawyer."

I reached out and tried to straighten her hair while searching for the right words to express myself. "I can't make it all the more public," I said finally. "It's bad enough now."

"My dear," she said, pulling away from my hand, "when it's in the papers every day, you've got nothing to lose."

For a time, however, the papers ceased speculating on Haw and me and printed stories about the progress of the Tabor Grand Opera House, a five-story edifice that Eugene Field labeled "Modified Egyptian Moresque" to my delight and the hilarity of what can only be described as "Tabor watchers", Haw's toadies, cronies, political bedfellows, and Denver society in general.

At a cost of over a million dollars, carpets were being woven in Belgium, marble cut in Italy, cherry trees destroyed in Japan—all to prove the worth of Haw Tabor. And if the story that circulated was true, Haw's ignorance was also made public. It was common knowledge that, when he was shown a portrait of William Shakespeare that was to be hung in the entrance, he'd said: "Who the hell is that, and what did he ever do for Denver?" The miners, of course, loved it. Others, Becca included, sniffed in disdain, and once again Eugene Field attempted to bring the sacred Horace to earth with one of his scathing rhymes.

> The Opera House—a union grand
> Of capital and labor,
> Long will the structure stand
> A monument to Tabor.

Still, despite the joking, the veiled humor, I hoped all that long summer that Haw would ask me to attend the opening at his side just as I'd done in Leadville. How I waited for my invitation, scanning the mail each day, running to the door when the bell rang, expecting to see my husband there. But only Billy Bush came, as regularly as morning, always singing the same refrain.

"Give him what he wants, Missus Tabor. Let him get on with it. You ain't going to starve, and that's a fact."

"Tell my husband I expect to be invited to the grand opening," I said. "Say I would be grateful."

Billy snickered. "He won't care about your gratitude. Not unless you give him what he wants. Face facts. He ain't coming home again, and you know it as well as everybody else."

Summer drew to a close. In the mountains the aspens would be touched with gold. Mist would hang over creeks and rivers in the early mornings, while the sky echoed with the passage of migrating birds. All too quickly it was September, and no word had come from Haw. I'd been so sure that he wouldn't slight me that I'd ordered a new dress of royal blue velvet with a cape to match. They hung in my closet, a reminder of my own worthlessness.

Carved above the entrance to the Opera House were the Latin words: *Dies Faustus*—Day of Good Fortune. Whose? I wondered bitterly. Certainly not mine.

Two days before the grand opening, I sat down at my desk, picked up a pen, and humbled myself for the last time.

Dear Husband,

I am in town and would like very much to go to the Tabor Grand and witness the Glory that you are to receive. Believe me that none will be more proud of it than your broken-hearted wife.

Will you not take me there and by so doing stop the gossip that is busy with our affairs?

God knows that I am truly sorry for our estrangement and will humble myself in the dust at your feet if you will only return. Whatever I said to you was done in the heat of passion, and you know the awful condition I was in when it was said. Pity, I beseech you, and forgive me. And let us bury the past and commence anew. And my life shall be devoted to you forever.

Your loving
Wife

No answer came. I don't know why I expected one. On the night of the opening, I went to bed and pulled the covers over my ears as if to shut out the music, the laughter, the sound of applause. I lay there and did not sleep, filled with loathing for the trusting child I'd been—still was—and for the man who'd brought me to life only to abandon me.

Chapter Nineteen

At breakfast the next morning, everyone had questions for Maxcy who'd attended the opening with Louella Babcock, the sweet girl he planned to marry. Who was there? How was the performance? Was it true that Eugene Field had been so upset at a poem read about Haw that he'd had to be restrained from throwing a chair at the author? Had *she* been there—the woman, Baby Doe, who'd stolen from me the only man I'd ever loved?

Of course, she'd been there. Wild horses couldn't have kept her from applauding Haw's triumph, but she'd sat in the orchestra and not in the Tabor box that stood empty except for a thousand red roses. She'd sat, for once without her veil, wearing a dress encrusted with diamonds, the cost of which could only be guessed, and applauded long and loud when Horace had spoken his few words. Listening, breakfast turned to ashes in my mouth, although I forced myself to eat what was on my plate.

When Maxcy and I were alone, he came to me and kissed my cheek. "I'm sorry," he said. "It's not fair to you, none of it. You're the best mother, the best wife I know, and I hate to see you hurting."

"But what can I do?"

He sat down again and leaned his elbows on the table as if he was exhausted and had to prop himself up. "I can't tell you. Pappy's bound and determined, and he sure won't listen to me. He won't even talk about it because he knows how I feel. Maybe . . ."—he hesitated—"maybe you ought to see a lawyer. Just to protect yourself."

That word again! It ripped me open like a knife, exposing my wounds, my misery. "No!" My cry came from the heart and startled us both.

"I don't mean about the divorce. But it's a good idea to understand the law. Your rights. The way it is, Pappy could buy a divorce. Even buy testimony to hurt and discredit you." He looked at me, worry written on his face. "It could happen."

"To hurt me? You mean to accuse me of . . . ?" I couldn't say the word.

"It's possible." Maxcy picked up his cup, sipped the dregs of his coffee, put the cup down with a grimace.

You want to know how it feels to be helpless, to be reduced to nothing in an instant? I sat there, seeing my entire life made into a lie, my best intentions turned to grains of sand, manipulated by forces I couldn't control. When I could speak, I said: "Who should I see? Somebody who won't go running to your father."

"If you want, I'll talk to Amos Steck. He's not in

Pappy's pocket, at least not that I know. He's a good man."

Once, crossing a river in flood, I'd been swept out of our wagon into the current and had saved both baby Maxcy and me by grabbing onto a tree branch. A drowning woman—a mother—finds strength she never knew was there, takes hold of whatever hope she finds.

I pushed away from the table and stood up, though my legs shook under me. "Do it then," I told him. "Make me an appointment. And while you're at it, tell Billy Bush never to come here again. I won't receive him."

Amos Steck was a county judge who I'd met on several occasions and had liked. He was balding, gray-bearded, with the fine manners I always appreciated, and they were not lacking when he showed me into his office and seated me in a large armchair beside a desk buried in stacks of papers.

With a smile, he pushed some aside, the better to see me and said: "Like women's work, mine is never done. How may I help you?"

I looked down, saw my hands clutched together so tightly the seams of my gloves had split open. Everything was coming apart! But I was there on business, not to weep, or find comfort.

"You know my situation, of course," I began, and he nodded once but said nothing.

"What I want is legal counsel as to my rights. My husband is trying to buy me off for pennies as if I never existed. As if I'm like one of the slaves we fought to free. Between us, together, we earned what we have. I don't like injustice, sir, and I resent being treated as I have been. I hope we can bring my husband to his senses before we're both ruined."

Steck rubbed his hand over his beard and frowned, though his eyes were kind. "Unfortunately, bringing Haw to his senses is beyond my ability," he said after a minute. "I can't change a man who's set in his ways. All I can do is use the law to your advantage. I'll see that you get more than pennies, Missus Tabor, but can you tell me how much he's worth? Can you give me any idea of his holdings so I'll have an idea where to start?"

"I knew to the last cent when I kept our books," I said. "Now I can only guess."

He raised an eyebrow. "*You* kept the books?"

His skepticism irritated me. "You don't think a woman is capable? Well, I did. For over twenty years, and correctly, too, I'm proud to say, which is more than I can say for Haw."

He took the rebuff with a smile. "Make me a list. Be as thorough as you can. If nothing else, we can file for support, then watch to see what happens. He might not come to his senses, but he might be more inclined to listen to a court order, especially if it's about money."

I removed my gloves with care, hoping not to rip them further, then leaned across the desk. "If you'll give me paper and pen, I'll do it now."

"Now?" Goodness, the man seemed unable to accept the fact that, despite being female, I was competent!

"My marriage may be in trouble, but my mind, my memory is intact, Mister Steck." I softened my answer with a smile.

All that afternoon I worked on the list of our remembered holdings. The Matchless Mine headed them all, followed by The Chrysolite, The Henrietta, The Maid of Erin, The Waterloo, the mines in San Juan County, the banks scattered across the state, the opera houses, the Tabor business block, even the homestead in Kansas that remained in Haw's name only. The hundred and sixty acres I'd purchased years before I'd put in my own name and so didn't mention it.

They say the dying see their lives flash before them. That day I wrote my life and put a price on it—nine million dollars—and, if it had been possible, I'd have stricken it all from the record with one stroke of my pen. One cannot put a price on marriage, on what has been shared, on days of sorrow, moments of joy, on the memory of a flight of singing cranes high in the blue air. Love, as I found out, had no price at all.

We went to court with a request that I be given the house free and clear and in my name only, and that Haw pay me fifty thousand dollars a year for support, claiming that, to date, he'd given me nothing, forcing me to take in boarders to keep myself.

When Steck first showed me the document, I protested. "This isn't true. He's paid the bills, and I haven't taken any money from my boarders. Most of them can't afford it. I can't lie to the court."

He looked at me, annoyed. "Like horse trading, Missus Tabor, you always start high. You can come down, but you can't raise your price midstream. And when necessary you shade the truth."

Well, that made sense, and so we went to court. And lost. Colorado law made no provision for alimony or support, and Haw, in his new rôle as cheat and liar as well as good old boy to most of the lawmakers and politicians in Colorado, stood up and stated that his millions had been accumulated solely by him in mining ventures, without any help from me at all.

Hearing the truth twisted to suit his purposes, seeing the stern, emotionless men who held my life in their hands, enraged me, as did Steck's silence. If no one would fight for me, I'd fight for myself. So in that room filled with what could only be called my enemies, I stood up and spoke out—for myself, and for all the women I knew or had heard about who'd suffered at the hands of husbands and the double standard of the law.

"Gentlemen," I began, staring at each in turn, and particularly at Haw who attempted to avoid meeting my look, "our fortune, the one in question, was founded on a grubstake from a store in which my husband and I were equal contributors and partners, and in which we worked together. Therefore, I am entitled to half of what my husband now claims to be solely his. If the court cannot see this, then the law . . . or what you call the law . . . is a failure both of common sense and common justice. I am withdrawing my suit till I can find a way that it . . . and I . . . will be treated with the honesty and fairness I deserve."

Then I sat down, trembling.

"That wasn't wise, Missus Tabor," Steck whispered in my ear.

I turned on him, having watched Haw's triumphant, back-slapping exit. "Neither was your advice! Now I'm going home before I do something I'll really regret!"

At home everyone was waiting to celebrate, but one sight of my face sobered the gathering, and they clustered around me—Euphrasia, Lottie, Becca, and Vesta, and Vinnie who'd come to visit and decided to stay.

When I related the events of the courtroom, they petted and praised me till I began to feel that I had, indeed, won a victory for them as well as for myself.

"You told the truth." Becca was grinding her teeth in frustration. "You stood up for every woman alive."

"I'm proud of you." That was little Euphrasia, her voice its usual whisper.

Next came Lottie, trumpeting like a swan. "Women's day will come, ladies, and I hope I'm alive to witness it. As it is, we have our own Augusta Tabor to blaze the trail."

I waved them away, flustered by the attention. What I wanted was to be alone in my room, to let down my guard and mourn in privacy.

"All I did was speak my mind," I said. "There were enough lies being told, and not just by my husband. I expect any one of you would've done the same."

Vinnie plunked down on the parlor couch under

the unflattering portrait of me that had been done when I moved into the house. Plainly we were sisters, with the Pierce oval face and long noses, but in her eyes I read a great sorrow, perhaps due to early widowhood, or perhaps because her youthful romanticism had been wiped out and nothing came to replace it.

"Is this what life comes to?" she asked. "To nothing but lies and deceit? Bitterness? If that's all, I'm glad Arthur died when he did. I'm glad there's just me."

In spite of illness, disappointment, grief, there had always been a flame in me, a force that wouldn't quit, that pushed me on no matter the circumstances. I got up and went to sit beside her.

"Life's what you make it," I told her firmly. "It's up to you. To me. To everyone of us. 'As ye sow, so shall ye reap.' Remember that. And be happy with the little things that come your way."

Brave words! Did I believe them? I wasn't sure. And any belief I might have held to was wiped away a short while later.

I was in the garden, picking flowers for the table, when John, the coachman, came looking for me.

"A boy just give me this, Missus Tabor. He said I was to give it to you." He held out a grimy envelope.

"What boy?" I asked, hesitating.

"I dunno. He run off."

I took the paper, held it unopened a long while, fearing what I would read, sensing danger, but at last I sat on a bench and broke the seal.

The message, written in a fine, educated hand, was simple and stark:

I think you should know that your husband has obtained an illegal divorce in Durango. He has charged you with adultery, and has paid to keep the transaction a secret.

There was no signature.

I went to my room and vomited till there was nothing left, not even tears.

Chapter Twenty

Maxcy and Louella, married now, thank goodness, before Haw's accusation could taint their courtship, found me half conscious on the floor. Together they laid me on the bed, and Louella, dear girl that she was, wiped my face and hands with a wet cloth.

I struggled to sit up, the heat of ultimate betrayal giving me strength, but Louella pushed me down against the pillows.

"Hush," she said. "You've had a shock. Lie still a while."

"Shock!" I wanted to shout, but my throat and chest ached from the purging. "I'm betrayed," I managed to say. "By him who's worse than Judas. I wish I could die."

"I won't let you." Maxcy took my hand in his big, warm ones, and for a second I thought of his namesake, Nat, who was always kind, always there to comfort. "Everybody who knows you will know the truth," he went on. "You have real friends who love and respect you for what you are. All Pappy has is the men he's bought."

"Why wasn't I told? He owed me that at least." I clutched at Maxcy like one who was, indeed, dying.

"The whole mess is supposed to be a secret, and Billy swears he brought you a copy of the decree."

"Billy!" I wished I could spit. "I told you I wouldn't let him in the house. If he says different, he's another liar."

"Billy plays all sides against the middle," Maxcy said. "He's been on *her* side from the start. And now he and Pappy are butting heads."

"Well, at least there's that to be thankful for." I pushed myself up. "You know . . . you must know, both of you that I never . . ."—I swallowed, unable to say the hated word—"I've been a faithful wife. Whatever he's said, it's not true. It isn't!"

Louella patted my other hand. "Of course, we know. But . . . but there's worse. A rumor, but you'd better hear about it."

I closed my eyes, steeled myself, although I doubted there could be anything worse than being proclaimed an adulteress.

Maxcy cleared his throat. "I heard Pappy and Billy yelling at each other. Couldn't help it. They just about raised the roof. Pappy was accusing Billy of cheating him out of money, of messing up the Durango business, and then Billy said that Pappy had better back off or he'd tell about the marriage in Saint Louis. He didn't say anything else. Probably couldn't. It sounded like Pappy punched him. But Pappy was in Saint Louis a couple weeks ago, and she wasn't around, either, not that I looked for her. If they were married, they're keeping that a secret, too. I wasn't going to tell you this, but it's best you know the facts. Frankly, the whole thing makes me sick. Makes me sorry he's my father." He looked across me at Louella. "If I show any signs of turning out like him, I want you to shoot me."

Louella turned white. "I won't!"

Miserable as I was, I recognized the love between the two and intervened. "What your father's done has hurt all of us, but don't let it touch what you have. I love you both very much."

Louella's eyes filled with tears. She bent and kissed me, gently, on both cheeks. It was sweet, I thought, to have a daughter after so many years, a woman who in every way was a compliment to Maxcy.

"Thank you," she said. "I'm glad to have a mother like you. I'm proud!"

So, good things follow on the heels of horror. "I think I'll sleep. Or try to," I told them as exhaustion swept away my last strength.

Oddly enough, I did. I'd fought for a belief, for what seemed, now, like a dream, and fought well, but the decision had been made. There was no more for me to do except live it down, hold my head high. How wrong I was!

Although, as time proved, there had, indeed, been an illegal and secret divorce decree, the furor in my family was trifling when compared to what was happening in the rest of the country. In July, 1882 President

Garfield had been shot, and for the rest of the summer all eyes were on Washington, on the man who lay dying—slowly, to be sure—but there was no doubt that Chester Arthur would, at some point, become President of the United States.

For a time, the gossip, the scandal surrounding Haw, who I still thought of as my husband, and the woman, Baby Doe, took second place to what was happening in Washington, and I took advantage of that to make a trip back to Maine. I hadn't been well that year. How could I have been? I was broken, exhausted, sick of it all, needing the sight and sound of river and sea, the cool shade of the forest, the land that had nurtured me. I was still there in mid-September when word reached us of Garfield's death, and immediately I headed back to Colorado, knowing that the political climate, always unstable, was about to change once again, and with it my life.

My feelings were confirmed when President Arthur appointed Colorado Senator Teller head of the Department of the Interior, leaving a Senate seat vacant. Who would fill the spot? Why, Haw Tabor, or so he thought, but Governor Pitkin, who, after the scandal was no friend of Haw's, appointed another man to the position till the end of the year. In January the Colorado Legislature would then meet and appoint someone else—or two persons. One to fill out the seat for Teller's remaining thirty days, and another to serve for the usual six years.

The turmoil was like a match struck to dry kindling. The scandal erupted again, worse this time. In the papers Haw was being portrayed as a bigamist, an illiterate, a blundering boor. He was accused of having not one, not two, but four wives, his actions at the time of the miner's strike were recalled—to his detriment—but nothing seemed to faze him. Nothing except me and my silence.

As far as I was concerned, the papers weren't wrong, for I had doubts about the legality of the Durango divorce, but I hated hearing Haw's name damned without regard for the actual good he'd done for the state—the roads he'd built, the schools he'd supported, his early fight for law and order in the camps—all of which had contributed to the making of Colorado as it was now. I hated it that my part in those early times was also in question, for I knew the worth of what we'd achieved—together. Whatever else, we had been pioneers. We'd survived with hard work and decency, we'd taken care of the poor, fed the homeless, done what we could to right the wrongs of a new frontier.

When I thought back to those days, when I remembered the young Haw Tabor full of plans and adventure, the man who'd given me strength and a life I'd never have had, who'd fathered a child who we both loved, I could almost forgive him again, and that's the truth. He'd given me everything. In the light of that, who was I to deny him his chance at further greatness?

Since I had no answers, I kept my questions to myself, and, as Machebeuf had suggested, I worked in the garden all those brilliant fall days. If there was nothing I could do about events that shaped the larger world, I could, at least, shape the smaller one that was my own.

I was on my knees planting bulbs when Haw found me. His shadow lay long and dark across the newly turned earth, and I looked up surprised, half afraid.

"Who's the farmer now?" he said.

I climbed to my feet, stumbling on my skirt, and he put out a hand to steady me—a hand, I noticed, that was dirtier than mine. But all I said was: "What's happened?"

"I need your help."

"I'm sure you do. Bigamy's a difficult charge to fight."

He looked away, the small boy again, caught, guilty, but still demanding. "Don't you start," he said.

I laughed. "Why not? I'm the one whose good name's ruined. I'm the one you called an adulteress. And now you expect me to help. Who's going to listen to me?"

"Everybody," he said. "Even that god-damned Pitkin. I don't know how you did it, but this whole town loves you. You! And after all I've done. What I've spent."

Perhaps what he said was true, but he was changing the subject and that I wasn't going to permit. "Let's go inside," I said. "We can talk better there."

He planted his feet. "I'll say what I have to say out here with none of your old biddies around to butt in. I want a divorce. And I want it before the Legislature meets in January. I'm begging you. I want my chance at the Senate. I've waited for it long enough."

"You already have a divorce," I reminded him. "Isn't one enough?"

Two paces away, two back, his face twisted in frustration. "God damn it, Gusta! Quit tying everything I say in knots! For once, *for once,* give me what I want instead of acting high and mighty like I'm nothing. Do you know who in hell I am?"

I couldn't resist. "You're my husband. Whether you like it or not."

He kicked at my basket of bulbs, overturning it, and I watched the brown husks tumble out and lie exposed and helpless, the papery skins shriveling as I looked. Whether it was that or the sound of his breathing, harsh and irregular, that decided me, I've never been sure, but suddenly my whole body ached with a tenderness that almost tore me apart. We were like those bulbs, unable to bloom without someone to nurture them.

"Do you love her?" I whispered, and saw his face change in an instant.

"Yes."

One word. "Did you love me? Ever?"

He hesitated. Then: "Yes."

"When did you stop?"

Baffled, he shook his head. "I . . . don't know. I don't. But what's that got to do with it?"

"Everything," I said. "Because I love you. Because 'love is not love that alters when it alteration finds.'"

As always, literature stymied him. "What the hell are you talking about now?"

"Shakespeare. The man you said never did anything for Denver." Oh, why couldn't I stop taunting him? Why was my love always fractured? Why was I born flawed?

I stepped closer to him, stood in the darkness of his shadow. "Never mind. Because in spite of what you've done, I love you. I'll give you your chance, though it tear me apart." Brave words that nearly killed me.

He clenched his fists as if to control some emotion I couldn't read. "You mean it?"

The enormity of what was happening in that quiet place, with the sky blue overhead and the Front Range holding it up on massive shoulders, made me dizzy. I closed my eyes. "I'll go to Amos Steck in the morning."

He didn't answer. When I looked for him, he was gone. No thanks, no gentle parting, no reminiscences of a shared past, just gone as if he'd never been there at all.

I picked up the bulbs, finished my planting, and went into the house.

Chapter Twenty-One

On January 2, 1883, nearly twenty-six years to the day that I'd been married, Amos Steck and I arrived at the Denver District Court. It was snowing hard. The Front Range was hidden by clouds and the usual noise of the city was muted by the snow—a white shroud. I had been married in a blizzard, and now I was ending it in a similar storm, and the weight of the years, the snow that fell on my shoulders seemed too heavy to bear. I slipped on the icy steps and almost fell.

"Courage, Missus Tabor," Steck said, grasping my elbow. "It won't take long."

Courage? I had none. Only a belief that it was my duty to help Haw achieve what he wanted.

"If there's such a thing as a sacrificial lamb, then you're it!" Becca had said. "If he was mine, I'd see him in jail."

"My life is mine, though God knows I wish sometimes it wasn't," I'd answered. "But as it is, I'm not a wife, not a widow. I'm an obstacle, and he hates me for it. I don't want his hatred. I'm tired of it."

So I stood in the courtroom before Judge Harrington and divorced Haw Tabor on the grounds of desertion and non-support.

"Have you been coerced into this decision, Missus Tabor? I must ask this." The judge's question was unexpected but my answer came straight from my heart.

"Yes."

Beside me, Steck gasped. "Your Honor, Missus Tabor is obviously not herself as you might understand. What she means is that she's been persuaded to accept money and property in exchange for her consent to divorce. There's been no collusion except for that."

Judge Harrington was no fool. Undoubtedly he knew precisely what was happening and why, and suspected that, at the last, I'd changed my mind. But he did not question me further. Within seconds, he granted me the divorce I did not want.

What was left of me now? What had I done?

I stepped closer to the bench, looked up at Harrington, his expression stern but with what I thought was compassion in his eyes. "Your Honor," I began, and then the tears came, strangling me, as I attempted to say the truth in spite of Amos Steck, in spite of Haw and Baby Doe, the rock on which I'd shattered. "Your Honor, if you would please enter upon the record . . . this divorce was not willingly asked for. Dear God! Not willingly!" Again Steck attempted to silence me, but I shook him off. "Not this time. You've all heard me. Witnessed what I've said. I never wanted my marriage to come to this."

Harrington cleared his throat, then nodded. "I'm sorry it has, Missus Tabor. Believe that."

Someone—the clerk, I think—handed me the decree to sign. The words swam in front of me, a sea of black ink distorted by tears.

Who was I? I asked as I took the pen, holding it as if it was my enemy. "What . . . what is my name now?"

Steck answered. "Your name is Tabor, ma'am. It's yours to keep by right."

Right? I had no rights. Perhaps I'd never had any, and all that I'd believed was self-delusion. "It was good enough for me to take," I said. "It's good enough for me to keep. But I cannot thank you for what you've done. Not any of you here. I am not thankful, but it was all that was left for me to do."

Later, I remembered that all of them—the judge, the clerk, the sheriff, Haw's attorney, and Amos Steck had the grace to look ashamed of their part, perhaps embarrassed by my tears, or perhaps knowing that they, in collusion themselves, had set Haw Tabor free on a path of destruction.

Chapter Twenty-Two

Haw Tabor was appointed United States Senator from Colorado for the thirty-day term, the six-year seat going to Tom Bowen, but, according to Maxcy, his father was delighted. Thirty days was enough to get his foot into the door of Washington politics, to hobnob with the President, to impress his fellow Senators and Congressmen with his greatness. He and Maxcy were leaving for Washington in a private car and, as Maxcy told me, Baby Doe was to follow within days.

"He's going to marry her there," Maxcy said before he left. "Don't be upset, but that's his plan."

"Again?" My response was pure acid.

"He's found a priest who'll do it. He even has the invitations being printed."

What I knew about Catholicism I'd learned from Father Machebeuf, but I knew enough to question the fact because both Haw and the Catholic Baby were divorced. "How can that be? The Church doesn't sanction divorce."

Maxcy gave a wry smile. "I reckon even some priests are open to bribery. Either that, or the priest Pappy's found doesn't know what's been happening."

For the life of me, I couldn't see Machebeuf, or the stern-faced Lamy, or even the young priest who'd come to Leadville years before, accepting a bribe to perform what went against their faith. Stricken by a sudden, tragic thought, I said: "What if . . . what if this marriage isn't legal, either? What will happen to us, then?"

Maxcy shrugged. "You'll go on holding your head up like you have been. It's not like you ever did anything wrong, and, if I know Pappy, he'll just pay out more money to make it right."

"I nagged him." The old guilt tasted sharply in my mouth. "Maybe I just should have kept quiet. If I had. . . ."

He interrupted me. "I was there, too. I always thought you were Pappy's mother as well as mine, and he needed one. He doesn't think. He just plunges in. If he's over his head now, it's his own fault, and, if I could get out of going to Washington and watching the circus, I would. But like I said, you're out of it."

I could hardly avoid the gossip, the newspapers that devoted whole issues to the flamboyant Haw Tabor and his beautiful young bride-to-be. There were descriptions of Haw, glittering with diamonds—rings, cuff links, shirt studs, and a dreadful portrayal of the lace-embroidered, gold-buttoned nightshirt he'd flaunted in the hotel.

I imagined him in his glory, back-slapping political cronies, drunkenly toasting the President with champagne, loping through Senate chambers and the streets of Washington led by high spirits and political aspirations, with no idea at all how to comport himself.

As Maxcy had said, he was a child, and Baby Doe the furthest thing from a mother or a conscience that existed. Haw, making the most of his thirty-day tenure, gave a three-hour speech to the Senate, proposing the end of gold coinage. That done, he turned his attention to the wedding and to jewels for *her*— jewels that, so he boasted to anyone who would listen, had belonged to Isabella, Queen of Spain, and which I privately thought his emissaries had bought in a pawn shop, the property of some wealthy woman gone broke.

The queen's jewels were not for me, nor a wedding dress that had cost $7,500. When I read that, I remembered my own wedding dress, sewn so lovingly by my mother and worn with such pride and excitement. I remembered, too, how, when the dress was worn to threads, I'd used the remains to patch holes in Haw's trousers, taken the soft lining and cut diapers for Maxcy.

The new Mrs. Tabor would know none of the hardships I'd faced. She'd never labor in a drought-stricken cornfield, never bear children in a shack, alone and helpless, never strike out across a vast and empty land with only hope to ease her journey. All that she would face would be the sanctions of polite society, retribution for the scandal of which she was a major part. I knew she would never be received in Denver in spite of Haw's millions, and that gave me a subtle satisfaction, for what would she do with her life, her jewels, her costly clothes with no one to see or admire her?

As for me, I had a life that was satisfying, if not complete. I had boarders in the Broadway house, and I'd used the money from the divorce to invest—wisely—in real estate, apartment houses, and store property, acreage in the country that would only increase in value as Colorado boomed. I had friends who made sure my life wasn't the solitary one of a woman without a husband, and I had my civic duties that I took seriously—raising money for the new Unitarian Church, caring, as always, for the poor and for women without my advantages. And I had my garden into which I retreated when I needed to think or find peace, and which, in its abundance, gave me much pleasure.

I went there the day the next scandal hit the papers. Shortly after the wedding in Washington, a reporter had spoken with a clerk in Durango who'd revealed Haw's secret divorce, and the priest who'd performed the marriage ceremony spoke out in horror at the fact that he'd been tricked into performing an illegal marriage, made worse by the fact that, not only was Baby Doe a Catholic, but she'd never served divorce papers on her husband, Harvey Doe, who was still alive and residing in Oshkosh, Wisconsin. This made her, too, a bigamist, if that's what women with two concurrent husbands are called.

What did this mean? Was I still married, then? Could I go to the courts and ask to have my own decree nullified? And if I did that, would Haw return to me? Would I, in fact, even wish to have him living in the house that I'd made mine?

When I'd picked two baskets full of tomatoes, corn, healthy pole beans, I sat back on my heels, amazed at the bounty. There was more than enough for my own use, enough to feed several families several meals. And I thought then of Father Machebeuf, growing old as we all were, but still the kind and wise man I'd loved from the first. Without stopping to change clothes, I called for my carriage.

"See what you've done!" I said, when I dropped the laden baskets at his feet. "There's more food than fifty people can eat."

"But it's made you happy." He reached out, took a tomato in his gnarled hand, and bit into it.

"You, too, it appears."

"Delicious." He wiped the juice from his lips with a tattered handkerchief. "You have magic in your hands like Lamy. It's a gift."

I saw my hands, gloveless, browned from earth and sun, grown tough from years of work. "At least they're good for something," I said, sighing.

"I think you've taken this latest scandal too much to heart." He reached into the basket and pulled out a bean. "You're not at fault. Let things be. If you stir the fire, you'll only burn yourself. Or do you want Tabor back?"

Did I? "Sometimes. But he doesn't love or want me, so why should I bother?"

"Then leave him to his fate. Why interfere with God's plans?"

Always the skeptic, I said: "Plans? How do you know God has plans?"

"Because the legend always ends the same way, and, besides, I've watched the world for a long time. The guilty are punished, if not in this world, then in the next."

"I don't know if I believe in the next," I said, as I faced the fact that almost everything I'd believed had been proven false.

He gave one of his Gallic shrugs. "Then wait and see. But an immoral life, one full of excess, even cruelty, often comes to a sad end without interference. You can go to your lawyers, you can probably prove your case, but what will it get you? Only more trouble. Leave it, my dear. Be happy with the life you have. And . . ."—he added with a grin that wrinkled his old face—"keep bringing me your vegetables. They've brought back my appetite."

I laughed. "Your counsel is purely selfish, then?"

"But of course!" He crunched the bean between his teeth. "In old age I've become a slave to my stomach."

"Gluttony's sinful," I reminded him.

"But a lesser sin. For which I've forgiven myself."

I got up, retied the strings of the old hat I used to shade my face in the garden. "When I leave you, I'm always laughing. That's your gift, Father, and I thank you for it."

On my way home, I passed Baby Doe, taking the air in one of her splendid, enameled carriages. For a moment, our eyes met, held, and then she looked away as if the sight of me—my ridiculous straw hat perched on top of my head, my glasses slipped down on my nose, my dress, brown and unstylish—were an affront to her perfection. Or perhaps she was simply ashamed, for she blushed red. I saw it clearly before she passed out of sight.

So she, too, had a burden to bear, I thought, and perhaps hers was even heavier than mine. Guilt is not picky, can reside in even the most innocent. If I, at times, scolded myself for my behavior toward my husband, what did she feel—having stolen him, lived with him, lied for him and for herself, watched as I was cast off with no more compassion than an old and worn sock?

Machebeuf had spoken of a sad ending. The way I saw it, both Haw and his new wife were on their way to ruin, scattering coins, jewels, roses, crates of empty champagne bottles behind them. If that happened, it was possible that I, with my investments, might save them both.

Society's memory, even in the newly fledged city of Denver, is long. Although the scandal died down, no one called on the new Mrs. Tabor in her elegant suite at the Windsor, no one issued her or her besotted husband invitations to dinner parties, balls, not even afternoon tea. What was left her were evenings at the Tabor Opera House where she could display the queen's jewels that she wore beneath her velvet and ermine cloaks, bask in the admiration of those in the audience who were more interested in the performance going on in the Tabor box than that being given on stage. If it was a lonely life, it didn't show on her face or on Haw's, or perhaps she was a better actress than anyone assumed. But seen together they were the picture of wealth, good living, and, though I hated to admit it, marital happiness.

After a time, my own sorrow subsided, although it never entirely left me. It was as if my husband had died, and I had mourned, and then carried on, allowing life and work to ease the pain. There was always my garden, my friends, my boarders at the Broadway house, my work for the Ladies' Aid Society, the Women's Hospital, the Foundling home, the Unitarian Church. Vinnie had moved to Leadville and was living in my old house, and Becca and Vesta had gone back to Maine, leaving Peter behind. "There's been enough talk about this family," Becca had said. "I'm just going home and be damned to it all."

Although I missed them, I had Maxcy and Louella and, eventually, a new grand-daughter, Persis, to complete a life that was, if not eventful, at least busy and satisfying. While I'd neither expected nor wished it, I had become one of the leaders of Denver society, a part of the old guard, a pioneer who remembered the early years when nothing as civilized as society had existed. What I said, what I thought, was taken seriously and so, when Haw and Baby moved from the Windsor to an enormous house on Thirteenth Street—a house that had a hundred peacocks strutting in the yard— when word got around that no one would call, and that Baby was sitting alone in the opulent interior, I felt what I can only describe as pity—for her, for Haw, for a situation that had gone on long enough.

I thought that if I paid her a call, perhaps others, out of loyalty to me, would follow. Or perhaps not. But certainly my action would be noticed and discussed. And, I was sure, I would be thoroughly questioned by the ladies of the town as to the furnishings of the house, the jewels Baby wore, the cut of her dresses, many of which were copied by women who would not speak to her but who imitated her slavishly.

I dressed carefully for my visit in a dark green basque trimmed with jet and a flowing skirt, and I wore my diamonds—Haw's diamonds—for courage as much as for display. I was, after all, a woman of wealth and property despite what she and Haw had managed to take.

"Wait here. I won't be long," I said to John, the coachman, as we pulled up in front of the house.

He nodded, helped me out of the carriage, and then up the steps that led to the front door. Around us the peacocks were screeching.

"It's a terrible racket they make," he said. "How can they sleep nights with that goin' on?"

Maybe they don't. The thought came unwillingly. But to John I said: "Even birds have to sleep sometime."

A handsome woman came out the front door as we stood watching the birds. She was no one I knew, but her face, her bearing struck me, and I nodded and greeted her.

"Good afternoon."

She returned the greeting and smiled at me. "I hated to leave her in there by herself, but I see I didn't," she said. "It's good of you to come."

"I thought I should." I wondered at her familiarity, but passed it off.

"Too bad there's not more like us." Her face changed again as a strutting peacock approached. She shooed it off. "Nasty things, and bad luck besides."

"Superstition," I said, repressing a shiver.

"Maybe. Maybe not. But I wouldn't have them. There's enough trouble in this world without going looking for it."

Although the woman was obviously a lady, there was a freedom to her speech that I found disturbing. "I must say I agree," I said, and stepped past her.

While I waited for someone to answer the bell, I watched her go down the steps and walk away up the street. Who was she? No one from Denver, I was certain.

A male servant opened the door, took my card on a silver salver, and disappeared, giving me a chance to study the opulence of the entrance hall. Turkish carpets covered every inch of the floor. A Venetian glass mirror in a heavy gilt frame hung over a marble-topped table that had probably required ten men to move. A painting of the new Mrs. Tabor was hung prominently on one wall, and every surface was covered with vases filled with flowers, marble statues, costly knick-knacks, all the flotsam of the Victorian age, and all lit by enormous crystal chandeliers that twinkled and swayed overhead.

There was no peace in the place, nowhere one could

look and find unadorned simplicity, and the cost, of the entrance alone, stunned me. What was the point of spending all that money if no one came to applaud it? And what would I find inside?

The servant returned and led me into a parlor decorated in exactly the same fashion, with another, bolder portrait of the woman again hung in a prominent place. *She* sat upright on a curved, satin-covered settee, one hand playing with the pearls that hung nearly to her waist, her blue eyes wide and, I must say, frightened.

"Missus . . . Tabor," she said in a small voice, one at variance with the rouge on her cheeks and what I hated to admit was a figure in every way opposite to my own. Haw, I thought, had gotten what he deserved, a child ripe for picking, an ornament who would never, could never, dictate or serve as task-mistress.

"Won't you sit down?" Again that breathlessness that hinted at a bad case of nerves. And who could blame her?

I took a chair opposite, wondering, now that I was here, why I'd come. To solve the mystery of Haw's desertion—or to satisfy my own rigid code of proper behavior?

"Would you like tea? Or something stronger? I can ring."

I hadn't yet spoken, wasn't sure I could, but managed. "Thank you, but no. I came . . . because I thought I should. Because others might follow my example."

Her eyes widened more. "Oh." Then: "That's kind of you. I . . . I didn't expect you'd be so kind."

And didn't deserve it, actually. Still. . . . "We live in

the same city," I said. "And appearances count here just as they do everywhere. Though we can't like each other, we at least must behave in a civilized manner. And we should remember, after all, who my . . . your . . . husband is. His political career. His position in this state. Don't you agree?"

She gaped at me. That's the only word for the way her mouth dropped open. All she could do was nod so that her yellow curls trembled.

A child! He'd ruined us all for this speechless child!

"I'd do anything for him, you know," she said after a minute.

"Except give him up in the face of scandal." As always, my tongue ran away with me. "I'm sorry," I said after a moment. "I didn't come here to accuse or to throw stones. As I said, I hope I can make things easier for you."

"Mary's the only person who's come," she said. "Except you. Maybe the rest will follow."

"The woman who just left? She looked like someone I know, but I can't quite remember."

She smiled. "That was Mary Holliday. She's married to a dentist now, but I met her years ago. Her brothers had some mining claims in Leadville. She's been a good friend."

Everyone—in Leadville and elsewhere—knew of Doc Holliday and his associates, the Earps, and, of course, his liaison with Mary, a woman no better than she should be and known on the frontier as Big Nose Kate. It was just like Baby to have such a friend.

"Good heavens, child," I said, "he's more a killer

than a dentist. And now I hear he's back in Leadville, making trouble again."

She sat up straighter, frowning. "It's not like that. He's dying. Of consumption. Mary's on her way to try and save him from . . . well, from himself . . . the way she tells it. And you shouldn't believe what you've heard about her. She's been a good and loyal friend, when I had none, and she's as much a lady as . . . as you are yourself!"

So, loyalty exists even in women who stop at nothing! I found myself admiring her defense of her friend.

"I see," I said, though I wasn't sure what I meant. But I'd accomplished the purpose of my visit. Perhaps after this afternoon the new Mrs. Haw Tabor would no longer be outside the pale, waiting like some princess in a fairy tale for an audience that never happened. "And I wish you . . . and her well. Consumption isn't easy to deal with."

"No. But Mary's never backed away from a challenge, or ever stopped loving the man no matter what he did."

"I understand how that may be," I said, letting my sarcasm show.

She stood up then, and with a shock I realized she was with child. "Don't hate me," she said. "Maybe I deserve it, but, you see, I do love him. So much sometimes it hurts."

Had I ever loved like that? Odd, but I doubted it. Or maybe I was simply too old to recall how it felt to love with a passion. I put out my hand, and she took it in both of hers. "Hate is destructive," I said. "To all concerned. You must take care of yourself and not worry about what can't be helped."

She looked down at her swollen belly, then up at me. "I . . . thank you. More than I know how to say. You're a fine lady, and I'm proud you came. Haw will be, too. Maybe . . . maybe you can come again?" Those huge blue eyes were both hopeful and pleading.

"I don't think so," I told her. "I'm sure you understand why."

She bit her lip, downcast, then smiled with a mischievous radiance that shook even me. She was, in her way, irresistible, and my pity, in that moment, was all for Haw, trapped in a honey pot.

"I understand better than you think," she said.

Chapter Twenty-Three

In July of that year, Baby Doe Tabor gave birth to a little girl, and, as was to be expected, Haw celebrated with abandon, having one hundred gold medals made with the inscription:

Baby Tabor
July 13, 1884.

The child, christened Elizabeth Bonduell Lillie Tabor, had, it was reported, clothes, christening robes, and infant-size jewels costing over fifteen thousand dollars.

What could Haw possibly be thinking? Perhaps he was proud that, at his age, he'd fathered a child, or perhaps he was attempting to prove his respectability, making another futile attempt to buy himself a Senate seat. If it were that, he failed, as he failed to impress Denver's matrons who, in spite of my efforts, continued to snub Haw, his wife, his child.

I couldn't know the reasons for his flamboyant spending, but what I did know worried me, for how much money did Haw actually possess? Did even he have any idea? Even then, there were rumblings, not only about the price of silver and the government's purchase of it, but about the fact that a few of the mines were playing out. Silver and gold are, after all, finite, and once gone there can be no more.

Perhaps because of the way I'd been raised—to question, to think for myself—or because of my years spent managing what money Haw and I had—I'd followed the political and economic policies that applied, not only to gold and silver, but to the entire country. It seemed to me that the health of the nation depended on a solid but varied economic base, and that included the minting of both gold and silver coinage and the government silver purchases which kept the price stable.

Since Colorado was one of the biggest silver producers in the world, my own welfare, as well as the welfare of the miners, store owners, innkeepers, doctors, lawyers, milliners, and Haw Tabor himself depended on the price and the ongoing sale of silver both on the open market and to the Treasury. All through the decade, Denver was the center of the fighting that went on between the Western mine owners and the government—both the one in Washington and its unseen bosses on New York's Wall Street.

Yet, in the midst of unstable politics, it was hardly possible to ignore the ostentation of Haw Tabor and his wife, to avoid seeing the proud parents when they took their newborn to the Opera House, or when mother and child took the air in one of Baby's enameled carriages. Denver wasn't that big, and I wasn't bitter enough to snub the mother who seemed to adore her daughter, smothered though the child was in lace and embroidery.

It was a warm day in September when my carriage approached hers, and I called out to John: "Stop a moment!"

She and I spoke at once—"Missus Tabor. . . ."—then broke off, feeling foolish.

She laughed. "Guess we both are at that," she said, and held up the infant for me to see—a lovely baby blessed with her mother's looks.

I swallowed the remembrance of Maxcy in his rags of diapers and stitched-together trousers, and cooed at the precious child who gurgled and cooed back. And why not? She had all that any princess could want. She was warm, safe in her mother's arms, and surrounded by riches.

"Cherish her," I said.

The mother looked straight into my eyes. "I lost one. A little boy a long time ago. You better believe I cherish her."

The hint of sorrow, the fierce way her arms curled around her daughter, impressed me. "I do believe it," I said, then nodded to John who drove on without a word.

The decade passed swiftly. To my astonishment, I began to feel old, and the day came when, working in the garden, I found I couldn't get up off my knees.

"It's not fair!" I grumbled to the faithful Lottie

who'd remained with me as companion and listening post. "My head's not old. Not yet, anyhow."

"Time passes," she said, and I saw that she had aged, her hands knotty, her skin thin as tissue.

"What've I done with my life?" I asked, feeling in that moment as if I stood on the edge of a chasm I could not cross. "It's been all work, all scandal. What good have I ever done?"

She pulled her shawl closer around her shoulders as if she was cold, though the afternoon was warm. "My dear Augusta, if you've forgotten all the people you've helped . . . the poor, the homeless, the abused . . . if you've forgotten how you stood up to Haw Tabor in court all by yourself with no one on your side and spoke about equal justice for us all . . . then you *are* growing old. Think about it, and let me take my nap. That's what being old is. All you want is sleep."

When Lottie died a few weeks later, I was bereft and, for the first time, was alone in that empty, echoing house so full of memories.

That's the true problem of growing old. Friends die and leave you, and the past, with no one to speak about it, dies, too. Even Father Machebeuf had gone, but what he had done, for Denver and for all the little mining towns scattered throughout the mountains, would never be forgotten.

I was dressing for a solitary supper in the small parlor I preferred to the now empty dining room, when Maxcy and Louella came. They, too, had moved out of the Broadway house—not far, only to the Brown

Palace Hotel which Maxcy was managing, but their going had made me even more aware of my isolation.

I hurried down to greet them, a little flustered because of the hour and because of their solemn faces.

"What is it? What's happened?" Disaster, loss were always uppermost in my mind those days.

Maxcy hugged me. "Nothing's the matter. Sit down and have your supper. We shouldn't have come so late, but there was a problem in the hotel that needed attention."

"And whatever you've come to tell me couldn't wait till morning?" There I was again, the fussy old woman I'd always been.

"Oh, it could have." Louella perched on a chair and clasped her hands around her knees. "We just decided not to leave it any longer."

"Don't keep me dangling, then."

"We want you to move over to the hotel," Maxcy said. "There's no need for you to rattle around this place by yourself. Especially now Lottie's gone."

He looked like he was afraid he'd offended me, and I laughed. "I couldn't have said it better myself. How soon can I come, and can I bring Henry Ward Beecher?" Henry was the Mastiff I'd bought a few years before and he was my loyal and devoted shadow. His name, of course, was my joke, because to me, with his sad eyes and flapping jowls, he looked just like the famous preacher and libertine.

If I'd punched Maxcy, he couldn't have been more surprised. "Sure he can come. You'll just have to keep him out of sight or he might scare some of the customers. And you can come as soon as you're ready. Just decide what you want to bring. I'll take care of the rest."

There was precious little in that house that I wanted. Most of the furnishings reminded me of bad times and ruined hopes. It was, I thought regretfully, the garden that I'd miss—the scent of the soil, the dahlias with their many-colored petals, the six-foot stalks of corn that reminded me of long ago, the spruce trees I'd put in that were now fully grown, their fragrance that of the high mountains I'd loved.

With a sigh I said: "I'll give you a list in the morning. And now that that's settled, would you like coffee and dessert?"

Chapter Twenty-Four

Disaster came more quickly than anyone could have expected. Grover Cleveland was elected President for the second time in 1892. Although it had been kept quiet, the gold reserves had been dwindling to the point of near panic under President Harrison. There had been a steady run on the banks by people who, frightened by rumor, had begun exchanging their greenbacks for gold. But there was no more gold, at least not enough for the public.

In June, 1893, India, then the world's largest silver buyer, stopped coining silver, and within a month banks across the country began to close, twelve in Denver alone. Then Cleveland, in desperation, repealed the Sherman Silver Act which had provided for the purchase of silver by the United States Treasury and kept us all comfortable in so doing.

Although I hadn't known it, everything Haw owned was mortgaged. He'd spent and spent on borrowed money—for years as became apparent—sure of himself, his mines and insurance companies, and the now worthless mahogany forest. The only property he owned outright was The Matchless, idle now, for silver was, in effect, a commodity no one wanted. Within months he lost it all—the Opera House of which he'd been so proud, the Tabor Block of businesses, the yacht, idle in the harbor, the other mines, the railroad interests, the banks that could no longer afford to lend him money, that, in fact, had closed their doors. The Thirteenth Street house, furnishings, carriages, peacocks, and all, was the last to go, but it, too, had been mortgaged, built on a foundation of sand.

Overnight, as mines all over the state were closed, the city of Denver turned into a city of refugees as out-of-work miners fled the mountains in hope of finding jobs to feed themselves and their families. Tents sprang up, surrounding the city till, looking out, what I saw was the dusty, shabby trail town I'd seen for the first time more than thirty years before, except that those camped there then had been filled with hope and dreams of riches. All that anyone wanted now was a meal, a job, however poorly it paid. But there were no jobs, and the meals that were distributed were meager and often not enough to feed the growing homeless population. So it had come. The day I hoped would never come but for which I'd prepared. My investments, all of them, were secure, my money safe at hand.

Saying nothing to Maxcy, I dressed carefully and went in search of Haw Tabor, still my husband, deny it though he would. I found him on the sidewalk outside the Windsor, as disreputable in appearance as any one of the miners who clogged the street, his suit ragged, the cuffs and collar of his shirt grimy and in need of scrubbing.

When he saw me, he turned and began walking away in his old, awkward lope.

"Wait!" I caught up with him, stood blocking his escape. "Will you listen to me for a minute?"

He blinked red-rimmed eyes. "Not if you've come to gloat like the rest of 'em."

"I've come to lend you money."

His mouth twisted under a graying mustache. "Christ, Gusta, your damned pennies can't help me now."

I gasped at his arrogance, but kept on. "I can write you a check for two hundred and fifty thousand. Maybe a little more. Yes, *that* money, but I kept it, and it's hardly pennies."

For one moment I saw what appeared to be a grudging respect in his eyes, then he threw back his head and laughed—so loudly that people passing stopped and stared, before hurrying on, probably eager to spread the word that Haw and I were laughing while around us the world crumbled.

I tapped my foot. "Do you want it or not?"

He composed himself, wiping a hand across his face. "So your penny-pinching paid off, and you've got the last laugh. Well, no, I don't want it. It'd be gone in a minute. It's a drop in the bucket compared to what I owe." Those bloodshot eyes focused on me. "I've still got The Eclipse down in the San Juans.

Gold. Not silver. I'm headed down there in a couple days, and then we'll see about Tabor's luck.

"You and who?"

"Me and nobody."

Worried, I leaned toward him, hoping he'd pay attention to me. "You're too old for pick and shovel work. For goodness sake, Haw, take care of yourself. You've got a family to think of."

"Well," he said, "I ain't dead yet, and, as far as Baby's concerned, she's already got offers from fellas with dough."

I was so shocked that, for a moment, I was dizzy. Was the man actually considering letting the woman he'd ruined himself for sell herself? "You can't mean . . . ?" I stopped, not knowing how to go on.

"Naw. She slams the door in their faces. She loves me. But they've offered, damn them. In times like this you find out who your friends are . . . or aren't."

"You have me."

"Yes," he said. "Why?"

"Because I loved you once. Maybe still do." God knew, it was the truth!

He looked away. Talk of love obviously embarrassed him. When he answered, his voice was harsh. "Damn it, Gusta, let go. I'll make out. I always do. And keep your money. You sure as hell earned it, no matter what I said back in court. Now go on home. The streets aren't safe for women alone these days."

That was as close to an apology as I would ever get. I never spoke to him again.

* * *

I went to Baby next. It was the thought of those two little girls—Rosemary Echo Silver Dollar Tabor had been born in 1889—that took me to the little house where the four of them were living in poverty. It was a sorry place—no peacocks there, only a weed-filled yard, a door in need of a coat of paint, cracked and filthy windows. Inside, one of the children was crying, a heart-breaking cry because it spoke of fear and desperation. I knocked.

"Who is it?" Baby's voice was shrill.

"Augusta Tabor."

The door opened a crack, and she peeked out, blue eyes hard and wary. "I'm not receiving today."

"Don't speak to me in that tone," I said sharply.

Her face crumpled. "Please. . . ."

I cut her off. "Let me in. I've come to help."

"How?" She stood back, and I went in, appalled at her appearance, at the disorder of the small room where the two girls sat side-by-side on a couch with its stuffing coming out, silenced by my visit, tears drying on their faces.

Obviously Baby's talents didn't extend to housekeeping. Dirty dishes lay on a rickety table, and the girls' dresses were soiled and wrinkled, as if they'd come out of a rag-bag. Baby herself had a stain down the front of a cheap cotton frock.

"You see?" she said.

"I see you're falling apart, and this isn't the time. Get yourself together. Your family needs you. And you must have managed to save at least some of your clothes."

Her laugh verged on hysteria. "Sure. But who needs velvet and lace in here? They don't know what hit them." She gestured at her daughters. "And I can't explain. They want their ponies, their nurse, their dolls. They want strawberries and cream when we're lucky to get a loaf of bread. And you tell me to pull myself together. That's funny. It really is!"

Legends repeat—but not if I could help it. I stripped off my gloves, untied my hat, and hung it on a lopsided coat tree.

"We'll start with the dishes," I said, and to the girls who hadn't moved: "Who wants to help me?"

Elizabeth stood. "I will. Silver might break something."

Silver wailed. "I won't! I won't, either! I want to go home."

Poor little elf, with her wide eyes and unblemished skin, her mother had been right. How could tragedy be explained to children who'd never been denied the slightest wish?

I knelt in front of her. "Don't cry. Of course, you won't break anything. But I think your mother wants some help sweeping the floor." God knew, it needed sweeping. To Baby I said: "They need security. And love. And Haw needs a home more than ever. Don't fail him."

"I'm here, aren't I, for whatever good that does. Haw begged fifteen thousand from Winfield Scott to work The Eclipse. That must've been some scene. Scott didn't even know who he was at first. Thought Haw was a beggar off the street." Her mouth twisted.

"Everything's changed. Everything's all wrong. It wasn't supposed to be like this!"

Stiffly I stood up. "Pull yourself together. What matters now is self-respect. A little pride. Your children."

She snorted. "Look where pride got me."

I handed her the broom that had been leaning in the corner. "You'll be worse off without it. Now, stop feeling sorry and get this place cleaned up."

She held the broom as if she wasn't sure which end to use. "Why're you doing this? Why do you care what happens?"

Why? Dear God, wasn't it plain enough? "I think you know the answer."

She looked down at the stain on her bosom, the filth on the floor, and her lips trembled as if she was holding back a sob. When she spoke, it was in the smallest of whispers. "I'm . . . I'm sorry. If it wasn't for me. . . ."

I supposed she was sorry—for all of it—but I wasn't in the mood for apologies, tears, confessions. "It's all of our faults, not just yours. Now let's get to work!" Taking Elizabeth by the hand, I went into the kitchen.

When I left several hours later, I gave Baby all the money I had in my purse. "For the children. Make sure they're not hungry. Get them their strawberries."

She grasped it tightly. "I'll pay you back. When The Eclipse pays off. It will, you know. Haw's always been lucky."

But as even the best gambler knows, winning streaks always come to an end.

* * *

Time, which in the 1880s had moved so swiftly, seemed to falter and slow as the depression held on. Always now, Denver's streets were filled with hollow-eyed hungry men and women in search of work, their hardship due not to their own shortcomings but to the greed and folly of those in power. I ached for them all. I ached for Haw whose Eclipse mine had yielded only a spill of rock tailings. While Baby and the girls remained in the West Denver shack, Haw returned to Leadville where, so Maxcy told me, he was hauling slag at a salary of three dollars a day—the same wage he'd refused to raise during the miners' strike years before. What regrets he had as he wheeled his barrow from smelter to slag heap would have been enough to burden any man, but it was his age that finally broke him. Ill, penniless, he came back to Denver and joined the rest on the streets.

I'd been ill myself, a return of my old weakness, but I gathered my strength and went to Maxcy. "You have to help him," I said. "No matter what, you can't have your father begging on the street, and he won't take anything from me. I tried."

"I already have. After that scene in the hotel with Winfield Scott, I had to do something." Maxcy's eyes, tired but kind, met mine. "Stop worrying. They won't starve as long as I've got money. God knows Pappy's been through enough, but he's not a quitter. I give him that. He's still hoping that silver will make a comeback and he'll be able to reopen The Matchless."

"Will it?"

Like everyone else, I'd paid close attention to William Jennings Bryan and his silver crusade. Bryan's speech at the Democratic Convention had stirred all the old fervor, rekindled hopes that had gone dry. *You shall not press down upon the brow of labor this crown of thorns. You shall not crucify mankind upon a cross of gold!* Strong words, but were words enough to win him the Presidency?

"Who knows?" Maxcy rearranged the papers on his desk as if contemplating a chess move. "I sort of doubt it. It's always the East and big money against us out here, and I can't see an end to that. But Bryan's turned Pappy into a Democrat. Given him something to work for."

"Better a Democrat than he loses all hope. But he's sixty-five years old and sick. What will happen to him . . . to all of us . . . if Bryan loses?"

"Then 'the play is played out.' Maybe it already is. But I'll take care of Pappy . . . and the children, so put your mind at rest. And take care of yourself. You've been coughing a lot."

I had, though I'd been trying to ignore the pain in my lungs as simply a symptom of worry. Long divorced, I was still bound. Cast off, repudiated, I was, in my heart, still Haw's wife and responsible for him.

As for regrets, I had plenty of my own. *If only. . . . If only my warnings, the acid way I'd spoken them, hadn't been ignored. If only I'd been more—what? Feminine? Less concerned with security and more concerned with the happiness we'd once had? If only I'd shown my belief, given encouragement!* I had won a battle but lost a war, although I'd been fighting, not a war, but destiny. We all make our own. Nothing I could have done would have changed Haw Tabor and the path he chose, though it was upon my sacrifices that he'd built his kingdom.

"What good have I done?" I'd asked Lottie, and now asked myself in the dark hours when I couldn't sleep. Haw had been my life. Without him I was useless, a dried husk, an old woman with only memories.

Forced to answer, looking upon the wreckage, I responded.

"None." And felt my strength crumble.

Chapter Twenty-Five

So now I am here, packed off, bundled up like the old woman I've become, too ill to spend a winter in Denver, and with nothing to do but sit, think, stifle regret. Maxcy and Louella write often. Haw has been given a job as postmaster—a token in recognition of the fact that he had donated the land where the post office stands. At least he's got his dignity back. At least he's not dependent on hand-outs. Removed from it all, my life appears like a dream. Scenes play out behind my closed eyes when I least expect them, and I watch, wait breathless, as if I can make them turn out differently.

A week ago, several of us here at the hotel made an excursion. I had a longing to see the ocean again, and we went off through fields of flowers, groves of oranges, the fruit ripe and glowing among the leaves like Japanese lanterns. Machebeuf would have beamed his happy smile at the sight. I did, remembering the feel of just-picked fruit, sun-warmed, filling my hands.

But it was the Pacific, the immensity of water, the curve of beach stretching miles north and south, the fact that, beyond the horizon lay not Spain on the other side of the Atlantic but the Orient, that shook me so that I sat on a crumbling wall and stared off with a hunger that rose out of my bones. In the curve of every wave was perfection, seen once, never repeated. They came and they came, those waves, without pause or guidance, the force that formed them the breath of the earth itself.

Who was I? Who were any of us faced with the sea, with those mountains that had carved themselves into memory. We live our puny lives in struggle and desperation, grateful for the pause before the next surge brings us to our knees—till the last, when humbled, we admit to failure.

But had we failed? I asked myself, the wind off a sun-streaked sea strong in my face. Like so many, Haw and I had conquered a new country, fought for survival, and won. Was it our humanity that had forced us into our final rôles, or something else, a destiny we could not control, a legend rewoven, retold over centuries? Perhaps Machebeuf had been right, and there is, no matter what we believe, an ongoing struggle between good and evil, a battle raging unrecognized around us. How plainly I saw it then! That Haw and I had been a part of history, of the movement West, and yet it was our own, smaller story that mattered— Haw's inability to deal with the wealth and power he craved, his insatiable greed, his lust for a woman who was herself unable to cope, the rigid code that had ruled me and in the end betrayed me.

Overhead a gull hovered, his crying swept away on the wind, and I thought I was back on the plains, hearing the cranes singing in the midst of their journey. I was standing on a mountain top, reaching out to other, farther summits, my heart crying out in wonder. I was holding baby Maxcy, and Haw was looking at us both with love in his eyes, a love that could not be denied existence.

What I believe is that failure is simply a word, a sound without meaning compared to the magnificence of the earth, the struggle of mankind, those precious moments of unity with another that we, in our aloneness, call love.

Augusta Pierce Tabor died in Pasadena, California, January 30, 1895.

Epilogue

"Hang onto The Matchless, Baby."

Those were the last words my darling Horace ever spoke. He believed, you see—in me and in the mine, and so I've hung on, year after year. I've worked that shaft by myself till my hands bled, my feet turned to open sores. I've begged, borrowed, manipulated, stolen the money to keep on, and I'm proud of what I've done.

I've hung on, though I lost everyone I loved, even my sweet girls whose faces I see every night in my dreams. Elizabeth was first to go. She hated Leadville, hated the mine, our poverty, and me.

"I won't do this! You hear me? I won't work down there and you can't make me. You're crazy, digging in a played-out hole. I'm going back to Grandma Mc-Court, and you won't stop me."

"After all I've done!"

She was packing what few clothes she had into a battered carpetbag, and what she said next broke a heart that I thought had already been shattered. "What've you done except ruin everybody's life?" Then, in a voice so bitter it felt like salt on a wound: "Including your own."

I didn't answer. I let her go. My strength was for The Matchless and a promise given.

Silver Dollar's gone now, too. Dead in a Chicago tenement.

What I have left are dreams—and the spirits who talk to me in the long nights when the snow falls, the wind blows through the cracks. They lead me into the mine, into tunnels filled with gold, and I can hear my own laughter echoing through the dark. It's there—all the gold and silver in the world—if I could only remember how to find that glittering room when I wake. If only the devils didn't come when the spirits have gone. They squat in the corners, grinning at me like dragons, breathing cold fire, threatening me with death and damnation.

Oh—I'm used to them. They're company, and I'm alone. And hungry. My food is all gone. It's snowed for days. The door is snowed shut. The real fire has burned out.

Is this death, then, this purple shadow that hovers near the ceiling? Are these grotesque devils all who mourn for me?

When I'm gone, who will take care of The Matchless? When I'm gone, who will remember?

* * *

Baby Doe Tabor was found frozen to death in her shack next to The Matchless in March, 1935—thirty-six years after the death of Haw Tabor in Denver in 1899.

Author's Note

Although *The Silver Queen* is based on the true story of Augusta and Horace Tabor and Baby Doe, I have taken some fictional license, as those familiar with their history may recognize.

The Leadville miners' strike occurred in 1881, not in 1879, and Augusta at the time was not in Europe but in Leadville, very much on the side of the miners. In later years she did, however, make several trips to Europe, accompanied by her niece Vesta.

Likewise, I have, in places, changed the order of events that led up to the scandal and the Tabor divorce—again for the purpose of making the novel come alive—and William Jennings Bryan's famous "cross of gold" speech was given during his Presidential campaign, a year after Augusta's death.

I have used several quotations from Augusta's memoirs. There are three versions of her reminiscences. One version, "Cabin Life in Colorado," dated 1884, is now part of the Bancroft Collection. Another is in France, the property of the Laforgue family. Persis Tabor married Paul Alain Laforgue. A third version can be found in Betty Moynihan's excellent *Augusta Tabor: A Pioneering Woman*.

Acknowledgments

Writing about those who made history, particularly those long dead, is a slow and often labyrinthine process. I owe enormous thanks to David Wright of Universal Systems, Inc., Buena Vista, Colorado, whose four-hour video, "Leadville's Story of Baby Doe Tabor," aroused my curiosity, not only about the legendary Baby Doe, but about Augusta Pierce, Horace Tabor's first—and perhaps only—legal wife. David graciously shared all of his research material on Augusta, which proved invaluable.

Likewise, Mary Billings McVicar, owner of Doc Holliday's of Leadville, patiently answered my interminable questions and opened a window on the past with photographs and clippings from her vast collection as well as with her personal knowledge. Like me, she feels that Augusta Tabor was a true but greatly misunderstood heroine.

Bruce Kirkham, Research Assistant at the Kennebec Historical Society in Augusta, Maine, answered my questions about the Pierce family and 19th-century Maine.

Lastly, but not least, I thank my husband, Glenn Boyer, for his immense knowledge of Western history, his pertinent insights and advice on the Tabors, on Colorado, and on the Border War in Kansas.

About the Author

Born and raised near Pittsburgh, Pennsylvania, JANE CANDIA COLEMAN majored in creative writing at the University of Pittsburgh but stopped writing after graduation in 1960 because she knew she "hadn't lived enough, thought enough, to write anything of interest." Her life changed dramatically when she abandoned the East for the West in 1986, and her creativity came truly into its own. *The Voices of Doves* (1988) was written soon after she moved to Tucson. It was followed by a book of poetry, *No Roof but Sky* (1990), and by a truly remarkable short story collection that amply repays reading and re-reading, *Stories from Mesa Country* (1991). Her short story "Lou" in *Louis L'Amour Western Magazine* (3/94), won the Spur Award from the Western Writers of America as did her later short story, "Are You Coming Back, Phin Montana?" in *Louis L'Amour Magazine* (1/96). She has also won three Western Heritage Awards from the National Cowboy Hall of Fame. *Doc Holliday's*

Woman (1995) was her first novel and one of vivid and extraordinary power. The highly acclaimed *Moving On: Stories of the West* contains her two Spur award-winning stories. It was followed in 1998 with the novel *I, Pearl Hart*, and then her novel *The O'Keefe Empire*. Other story collections include *Borderlands* and *Country Music*. It can be said that a story by Jane Candia Coleman embodies the essence of what is finest in the Western story, intimations of hope, vulnerability, and courage, while she plummets to the depths of her characters, conjuring moods and imagery with the consummate artistry of an accomplished poet.

Betrayed by the girl he loved, disgraced before his commander, wounded in battle and left for dead, John Murray thought he'd hit his lowest point. But the sweet touch of a lover he'd never thought to see again taught him that no matter how far a man falls, with the right woman at his side, he can always stand tall.

Fallen
by
Cindy Holby

Aberdeen, Scotland, 1773

A fine mist fell. John Murray could not help shivering in his shirtsleeves as he stepped out into the damp gray gloom of early morning. A shudder moved down his spine as his eyes fell upon the post planted in the middle of the courtyard at Castlehill. The ground around it was trampled, torn, and filled with the muck from the mix of rain and free-flowing blood. Ewan Ferguson's blood. No comfort for him there; his blood would soon join it.

Was she watching? His blue eyes scanned the ranks of his peers, all standing at attention in the despicable weather, all surely cursing his name because they were given orders to rise early this miserable morning and watch his punishment.

Where was she? Surely they would force her to watch since it was her fault he was here in the first place. Surely they had made her watch her brother's lashing, as it was his fault that two men now lay dead.

There. He saw her. She stood next to the general with her chin held high and her shoulders squared as if she had just handed down the sentence herself. In some strange, turned about way, she had. Luckily for her, the general was magnanimous in his show of mercy. She was a woman, after all, and nothing more than an instrument in the treachery of her clansmen.

Her hair was plastered down against her head instead of the usual mass of springy curls that framed her face like sunlight. This morning it seemed darker than its reddish blonde, whether from the rain, or the doom and gloom that hung over the courtyard, he could not tell. Her dress was stained dark with blood and the neckline gaped open, torn by him in his haste the afternoon they were together. Of course she would have had no way to mend it, so it hung open, teasing him, tormenting him, just as she did the first time he met her. She had gotten into his head that day, damn her. She had no choice but to live with the state of her dress since her hands were tied before her. Even though the distance between them was great, he could feel her deep brown eyes upon him. That gave him a measure of satisfaction. A small measure, but it was something to hang on to.

If only they would lash her also. Did she not deserve it? Was she not as guilty as her brothers and her father in the planning and the plotting and the betrayal?

John looked at her. Isobel. Izzy. It was her fault. He trusted her with his life, with his soul, with his heart and she had betrayed him.

Fallen

Coming next month.

JANE CANDIA COLEMAN

Allie Earp always said the West was no place for sissies. And that held especially true for a woman married to one of the wild Earp brothers. She had no fear of cussing a blue streak if someone crossed her, patching up a bullet wound, or defending her home against rustlers. Every day was a new adventure—from the rough streets of Deadwood to the infamous OK Corral in Tombstone. But through it all one thing remained constant: her deep and abiding love for one of the most formidable lawmen of the West.

Tumbleweed

ISBN 13: 978-0-8439-6104-1

PAMELA CLARE

MacKinnon's Rangers: They were a band of brothers, their loyalty to one another forged by hardship and battle, the bond between these Highland warriors, rugged colonials, and fierce Native Americans stronger even than blood ties.

UNTAMED

Though forced to fight for the hated British, Morgan MacKinnon would no more betray the men he leads than slit his own throat—not even when he was captured by the French and threatened with an agonizing death by fire at the hands of their Abenaki allies. Only the look of innocent longing in the eyes of a convent-bred French lass could make him question his vow to escape and return to the Rangers. And soon the sweet passion he awoke in Amalie had him cursing the war that forced him to choose between upholding his honor and pledging himself to the woman he loves.

ISBN 13: 978-0-8439-5489-0

LAURA DREWRY

Author of *The Devil's Daughter*

"The best of Americana, with the right hint of devilishness." —*Romantic Times BOOKreviews*

HELL HATH NO FURY...

Deacon knew Rhea wouldn't exactly be happy to see him again. But he didn't think she'd shoot him. Right in the shoulder, no less. He'd experienced worse pain in his life, though. Besides, now Rhea would have to let him stay until she could nurse him back to health. Oh, the hardship.

LIKE A WOMAN SCORNED

His convalescence would give Deacon a chance to convince Rhea he'd turned over a new leaf, that he was no longer the son-of-a-devil who up and left her all those years ago in a puff of sulfurous smoke. Now he's a man who knows what he wants. And no matter what kind of trouble Rhea has gotten into while he was away, what he wants more than anything is to win her heart.

DANCING WITH THE DEVIL

ISBN 13: 978-0-8439-6049-5

Bobbi SMITH

New York Times bestselling author

WANTED: The Texan

Even the most successful bounty hunter has to settle down sometime, so when a run-in with a pair of killers leaves him wounded, Josh Grady decides to make a fresh start at the Rocking R Ranch. Compared to his last job, wrangling cattle and repairing fences seem downright relaxing. But that's before he meets the boss's daughter from back East. Emmie Ryan's highfalutin manners make him testier than a rattlesnake, but he's convinced that her oh-so-proper exterior conceals the wild nature of a true Texan. All Josh needs to do is help her to forget that she's a lady…and remember that she's a woman.

"Nobody does a Western better than Bobbi Smith."
—*Romantic Times BOOKreviews*

ISBN 13: 978-0-8439-5851-5

✁ □ YES!

Sign me up for the Historical Romance Book Club and send my FREE BOOKS! If I choose to stay in the club, I will pay only $8.50* each month, a savings of $6.48!

NAME: _____

ADDRESS: _____

TELEPHONE: _____

EMAIL: _____

□ I want to pay by credit card.

□ **VISA**   □ **MasterCard**   □ **DISCOVER**

ACCOUNT #: _____

EXPIRATION DATE: _____

SIGNATURE: _____

Mail this page along with $2.00 shipping and handling to:
Historical Romance Book Club
PO Box 6640
Wayne, PA 19087
Or fax (must include credit card information) to:
610-995-9274
You can also sign up online at **www.dorchesterpub.com**.
*Plus $2.00 for shipping. Offer open to residents of the U.S. and Canada only.
Canadian residents please call 1-800-481-9191 for pricing information.
If under 18, a parent or guardian must sign. Terms, prices and conditions subject to change. Subscription subject to acceptance. Dorchester Publishing reserves the right to reject any order or cancel any subscription.